TELLERS

www.tellersnovel.com

Also by Rick Moss

Ebocloud
(www.ebocloud.com)

TELLERS

a novel

Rick Moss

AERODYNE
PRESS

Tellers
Copyright © 2016 by Rick Moss

tellersnovel.com

For information and ordering:
Aerodyne Press
PO Box 150546
Brooklyn, NY 11215
info@aerodynepress.com

ISBN: 978-0-9831666-2-7

For Catherine

TELLERS

Their stories:

TWO DAYS AND NINE HOURS PRIOR

Panera Bread, Fredericksburg, Virginia

Mr. Leonard takes deliberate steps like he's measuring the distance back to the car, his boot soles rocking forward to their silver tips — *tuh-click ... tuh-click*. He arrives and eases his long frame into the passenger seat. He snaps four tissues from the dispenser on the dash.

"You got to do that?" Cappy covers his phone. "Drip, drip every time you come back from damn bathroom. Why you got to dry hands in my car? Wipe your damn hands in bathroom like everybody."

Mr. Leonard swings his door closed, lowers his window two-thirds down, and drops the damp wad out onto the asphalt. "Restaurant bathrooms are crawling with microbiotics, man. What's the point in washing your hands and then making contact with some infected fucking towel knob just to re-get a bunch of microbes?"

"What you think? Think no germs out here? You wipe your ass out here, too?"

Mr. Leonard unrolls the sleeve of his linen shirt and buttons the cuff. "Yeah, of course the car's cleaner. It's the whole concept. I don't touch things in there once my hands get sanitary."

"You spend lotta time in there, no doubt." Cappy mimes the act of pushing up sleeves on his sleeveless tee. He dangles a limp wrist and twitches his fingernails at Mr. Leonard's face. "You got no problem checking yourself out all damn day. Combing hair, checking yourself out."

Mr. Leonard flips his visor down to display the vanity mirror. He smooths the platinum hair back from his temple with one palm, then the other, back and forth six times, wrapping the even strands around his skull as tight as a silver bowl. He secures a three-inch ponytail with three rapid flips of an elastic band.

He nods at Cappy's phone by the gear shift. "Get that picture?"

Cappy pokes the home button, then puts the phone to sleep. "Don't need picture to tell me not him. I told you, didn't I? Not him."

Mr. Leonard pivots so he has a view of the hog-tied figure curled on the back seat. "That's his face, man. He shaved is all, and a little trim maybe."

"We seen Reitman three damn times, asshole. That not him."

"Different lighting. Pretty sure we got him." He reaches back and pulls up on the gag until the man's lower cheek separates with a snick from the seat where the blood has congealed. He lets the head flop back.

"Either way, you up shit creek. He damage goods. Better hope he come to."

Mr. Leonard turns back and resettles himself. He snatches another tissue and wipes between his fingers. "So where's my Classic Salad?"

"Fuck I know? Go in and ask. Under my name."

Mr. Leonard makes a "cuh" sound. "I'm not calling out your queer name. You go."

Cappy grips the wheel, his sinews taught up to the shoulders. He rubs his knuckles together, rotating his rings this way and that. "They text when ready. Food here suck anyway. Sick of damn Panera. Food got no taste." Three rings of various designs adorn his left hand and two on his right, his bare fingers etched with tattoos approximating the rings to come.

"If you can find a good place with vegetarian on the road down here, you just let me know," says Mr. Leonard.

"And for sure you paying me for detailing my leather. Fucking mess back there."

Mr. Leonard cants his head until he gets a crack. "See, you're saying taste but you're thinking greasy meat. People like you got animal desires when it comes to what you eat. I'm not putting that foul animal waste into me. I've got respect for myself. I don't put grease on my person either."

Cappy scratches behind his ear. "Gel, asshole, not grease."

"T'yeah, well, now that's a distinction only a queer person would know about."

"And fuck you, respect for yourself. What you got to respect about? I rather die of greasy meat than live with no taste." A car pulls in a few spaces down. He raises his window.

Mr. Leonard leans out his window and cranes his neck toward the front entrance. He sits back. "I hate coming down South. Why do they think that dickless Reichman came this way anyway? It's easy to see there's nothing worth doing down here for his type of hipster asswipe. Nothing to do and nothing but backwards people."

"Not Reichman — Reitman. His name is Whit Reitman, and don't matter why. He come this way is all that matter. Maybe he got old girlfriend down here. Maybe he just freak out go nuts. Maybe he just fucking with your idiot head is why."

"Heh. I think if he's fucking with anybody it's our esteemed Senator Jasper. A geek like Reitman, he's probably three steps ahead of Jasper and whatever hayseeds he's got working on this. Ask me, I'm thinking Reitman never left town. He probably just checked into some hotel out in the Meadowlands or even Brooklyn maybe."

Cappy shifts in his seat to face him. "That Senator not dumb and his people not dumb. They know Whit Reitman, he rented his car and come this way. You don't need try and think. Thinking what got you in that mess back there. Soon, they text me exactly where Reitman is. We be on him like fly on shit."

Mr. Leonard nods. "OK. Little Cappy boy's gonna get a text. I guess we'll see."

Cappy twists the fat gold ring on his index finger with his thumb so the tiger faces down. "That right. We see." He clacks it a few times against the shift nob and then turns it back.

Mr. Leonard looks at him dead on now. "Hey, but so what's your real name, man? You must have a Chinese damn name. Especially if we're out on a run or something and I'm like, 'Hey Cappy' in front of people, people think I'm all sweet on you or something calling you that. It's a queer damn name."

"Cappy, that my name." He turns forward.

Mr. Leonard snickers. "Well, yeah, but it's a bullshit name. You're like just-off-the-boat Chinese. What's your real damn name?"

"Fuck you." Cappy stabs his index finger in Mr. Leonard's face. "I'm not Chinese. Cambodian. Cappy is all you need to know. I call you Mr. Leonard. I don't give you shit about your shit name."

"Cambodian my ass. That's just an excuse for a queer's name. Won't hear me calling you Cappy anymore. Who started calling you that, anyway?"

"My father said Cappy is all."

"So it's a nickname."

Cappy watches the family exit their car to his left. "My father, he used to say coffee like cappy. He say, 'Go get me cappy,' was like one only damn English thing he know to say. He like coffee in morning with his Viceroys. So he give me a dollar fifty and I go get at the Korean grocer. Every day. At the Korean grocer that's what I say. 'I want cappy.'"

Mr. Leonard smiles with one side of his mouth. "Ha, coffee. Pretty funny."

"So my father, he got caught in a rooming house fire. The crowd they stomp him to fucking pulp in a fire."

Mr. Leonard looks interested. "Whoa. Trampled to death. No shit."

"Yeah, trampled to death. I got out. But I got no family. I living on the street, so I sweep up for the Koreans and get some food. They say, 'Hey, that Cappy kid here?' And Cappy, that all they need to know and it all you need to know. You wanna call it queer name, Mr. shit-name Leonard? See if I give rat ass. It good enough for you."

The back seat occupant issues some dry throat noise. Mr. Leonard reaches back and flicks the man's jaw a couple of times. He gets no response.

They sit for a bit.

"I'll call you Fong or Wong or some shit. Ain't calling you that queer's name."

Cappy pivots toward him. "You go right head." He puts his finger in his face again. "First time you call me one those Chinese names, I cut you. You go try. I open your cheek up."

Cappy's phone chimes. Mr. Leonard smiles full on. He looks down at the screen. "OK, don't fucking get excited. There's my salad."

"Just try it with me, mother fucker. You see."

THREE WEEKS AND TWENTY-ONE HOURS AFTER

The Colony, Greenport, New York

Sam is paused outside the swinging doors that lead into the Multi-purpose Room. The voices inside are faint but the rancorous tone is unmistakable. He blows out a breath and reaches toward the double doors.

Far behind him, the outer door creaks. Its hollow, metallic slam echoes to him down the corridor.

He turns and mops his eyes with the sleeve of his t-shirt.

Kesi appears around the corner, stepping into an area illuminated by an overhead bulb. "Hey." Her bare scalp and shoulders are glossy with sweat.

Sam clears his throat and pulls his bangs back behind an ear. "Hey. You hear the fence rattle out there? Did you check out front by the gate?"

Kesi flaps the bottom of her tee a couple of times for some relief. "Actually, no. I was out back by the root field. Stefan left a can of gas out there. You OK?"

Sam puts his head down, releasing the blond locks back over his eyes. He huffs again. "I keep hearing shit out there. It's stupid. I know it's nothing but I keep ... anyway, yeah."

Kesi nods toward the entry. "Claudia on Whit's ass again?"

He scratches behind his ear. "Kesi, will you ... ? I don't know if I want to do this with everybody."

"It'll be fine, just —"

"I can't stand hearing him."

"Right. Well you know that Whit's not doing the storytelling tonight, so maybe you won't have to."

"What's this all proving?" He shoves his hands into the pockets of his cut-offs.

She puts a hand on his shoulder and turns him toward the swinging doors. "What it's proving is we're not going to let Whit Reitman fuck up our lives. Come on. It'll be OK."

The gymnasium-scale room is dim, lit solely by a candle flame at the far end where the group congregates. Sam and Kesi saunter into the space catching the lethargic evening breeze drifting in through the factory windows to their left.

Claudia's delivery is amplified by the acoustics. "It's about dignity, Whit." She stands before a gathering of five Colony residents, her graying curls gone frizzy in the candlelight. Everyone else has settled on throw rugs piled two and three deep over the polished concrete floor.

"Some of us are of the opinion it would be hypocritical to ask you to leave, Whit, before we get started on this. I'm not among them." Claudia gestures with a legal pad she has flipped open to her starting point. "I don't think we should include you in this process, but I admit fighting about it would be counter-productive. And if I were you ... I don't know, like I said, it's about dignity. I couldn't stay."

Whit reclines to Claudia's right and a full length back, arms crossed behind his head. "Funny, you know, for me dignity has never been a motivating factor."

Sam breaks from Kesi and shuffles the length of the room, head down. He snatches up two rugs from an open spot beside Whit and circles behind him, passing Stefan and his twins, the toddlers lying belly down, head to head, engaged in a staring game.

Portia, sitting straight, hands resting on her Buddha-worthy belly, watches Sam's progress. As he steps near, she raises the candle from the floor in front of her. "Would you bring this to your mom, Sammy?" She relieves Sam of his rugs and arranges them beside her.

Everyone watches Sam as he carries the candle forward, hand cupped around the flame.

Claudia reaches for the candle, but Sam passes her by. He grabs a stool by the back wall and carries it back to her.

The light sputters to near extinction as Sam pours a puddle of wax on the stool's metal seat. He secures the candle, waits for the flame to restore itself, and goes to his listening spot.

"Thank you sweetie," says Claudia.

Kesi drops down cross-legged in front of Whit. "Dignity or otherwise," she says, without turning to him, "I'd say everyone's best not knowing what motivates you."

Stefan laughs. "Oh Shjesus, yes, we should not go there." At this, Stefan's toddlers spring up and flop onto his knees in mock hysterics.

"You know," says Kesi, laying her palms flat on the floor in front of her, "It may seem like ages, but Whit and I haven't even been here a full month. You guys never accepted us into the collective, not formally, so if you want us to go before you start with the storytelling, that's your —"

"No way. Is ridiculous." Stefan has managed to get both kids sitting still by allowing them to twist his beard into sausages. "Kesi, you are invitee. That is word, yes? Invitee? And now after this horrible thing that you and us, we all went through, you are now family. For Whit, well not so much. He was simply not given an invitation. That says the difference for me. He just was nagging along."

"Tagging, dear. Yes," says Portia, her voice high and honey-sweet, "but we did all agree that Whit should do the storytelling with us and that's because he shared in the tragedy too."

"For me, Portia my dear," says Stefan, "I think there is crazy huge difference between sharing of tragedy and making tragedy to happen out of stupid disregarding of people. But yes ... we vote yes."

Squeej enters through the kitchen door behind Claudia, mopping the pot-washing sweat off his forehead. "What we voting on, bro?" he says.

Whit splutters like a nag and rubs at his beard scruff.

"Andre called it the luxury of blame," says Portia. "He said, you can't afford it. When you're all devastated, you have to put that blame away in a drawer and just tell your stories. If dear Brother Andre were here, he'd say now is the time to dive into our own selves and pull out the stories. That's what we need to do now. And Whit is included."

"Yes, but with this things Whit has done," says Stefan, "are we not responsible to find the justice, Portia?"

She smiles. "Stefan, baby, when have you ever in your life seen people get satisfaction out of justice? Was there justice for you in Croatia? Is there justice for people of my shape and color in the streets of America?"

"True that, a fool believes in justice." Squeej runs his bandana up and down the length of his fully inked arm. "Look, I know, coming from the religiousness of whence I come, forgiveness might be easier for me, being it's a learned thing. And I know it's not fair asking that you all go there yet, but let's not make this family smaller now, yo."

"Yes, this is about our Colony family," says Portia. "Being able to share our ideals and love ... well, living here is a precious thing. We need to heal, and healing comes from understanding, and I don't see asking Whit to leave helping anything. One night soon, it'll be time for Whit's story and that will help us understand why he did what he did, right baby?" She keeps her eyes on Whit as she strokes the back of Sam's hand.

Whit's eyes are closed, thumbs twiddling on his chest. "Oh, I have no doubt it will bring a more complete understanding of me, and with it more nuanced feelings of repugnance."

Sam's head slouches nearly to his lap. "OK, but Andre's whole thing, though, assumes we've got stories to tell."

He sits out the silence before tilting his head up toward Portia.

Portia pulls him to her and presses her cheek against his scalp. Her braids cascade down, the bottom beads clicking together. "You've got yours, baby, don't you start thinking otherwise."

Squeej slides in on Sam's other side. He stretches forward, rips the sandal off Sam's foot, and slaps him on the thigh. Sam stays buried, his head nuzzled in Portia's breast, but manages to backhand Squeej across his arm.

"Alright, then," says Claudia. "I know the stories aren't exactly flowing yet, so I brought Andre's notebook."

She holds the legal pad out at arm's length and swings it in an arc the way teachers do. The pages are curled at the bottom edges. Two dried coffee rings are embossed into a drawing rendered in emphatic black marker. In the sketch, a wall cuts through rows of tenements like a cleaver through a side of ribs. The barrier rises well above the homes, stretching into the distance and bisecting the city.

Claudia flips to a page filled, lines and margins, with dense scrawl. "Andre wrote this a few years ago, but I thought it would give us a feel for what he meant by telling our own stories. There are three in here, and the beginning of a fourth. This is my favorite by far."

Andre's Story

The soldier returned from the war to the city he imagined was home.

Outside the station, he shouldered his duffle and started up the broad avenue, indifferent to the screaming signs and lurid come-ons.

He walked without purpose but, after a while, like a cat seeking shelter, turned from the noise, working his way into the unlit neighborhoods.

He became aware of familiar sounds. He heard the scraping of wind-blown litter along the pavement and the hollow ring of rolling cans. From the homes, he heard the whimpering of tired children and couples trading hurtful insults. And the smells seemed familiar as well — souring garbage, street urine, and smoky cooking oil.

But he chose not to let memory have its way with him. He turned one way, then the other as his feet led him.

At a point, midway along a treeless block, four small, black birds cut down in front of him and collected on a window ledge. They drew his attention to a defaced row house — the stone stairs and landing had been removed. Walking on, he realized all the homes along the street were in this condition. In many cases, the stoops had been replaced with crude wooden stairs, but most had nothing, leaving a sudden drop from the front door to the broken pavement.

He hoped to ask someone about the cause of the damage. Few people were about, and his worn fatigues and untied boots gave him the appearance of a vagrant. One young woman crossed the street away from him, hurrying along through the dank chill.

In the heart of one neighborhood he came upon two full city blocks that had been razed. Here, more black birds hopped between piles of brick rubble and lengths of splintered lumber. He could find no clues as to what once stood there.

Deep in the night, he rounded a corner and felt the bitter breeze subside. About twenty yards in, the cross street was blocked by a wall. Rising to at least twice the height of the tenements, it stood against the dirty orange night sky, blanketing the block in soulless shadow.

Arm extended, he walked into the darkness until he reached the wall. It felt smooth and smelled of poured concrete. He followed the wall to the left, dragging his palm along the surface, but found the structure featureless.

To the far left, the barrier met the corner of a row home, leaving barely a finger's width of space between. He reversed his course along the wall until he reached the house on the opposite side. There too, the wall abutted the home.

He turned to leave but froze at the hint of movement in the darkness. A silhouette danced before him. It was half his size, as if shrunk in right proportions. The figure skipped from foot to foot and whipped its arms in derisive gestures.

In the next instant, the phantom was gone.

He backed away, attentive to his surroundings, but the vision did not return.

He rounded the block to his left and continued on his way, tracking the wall as it cut through each side street.

As a dismal dawn emerged, a middle-aged man in oil-stained overalls approached him on the sidewalk. He carried a lunch sack and toolbox.

"Friend," the soldier asked the mechanic as he came near, "where does this wall end?"

The mechanic stopped and looked him over. "There is no end. It wraps around all four sides of the city center."

"But why did they build it? It blocks the way."

"That's not how they see it," said the mechanic. "They tell us it's here to protect us."

"But no, that's ludicrous. It keeps us out."

"Yes, of course. We're not fools. They built the wall because they feel threatened by us."

The soldier leaned against a street sign, turning to look down the shortened block. "And friend," he asked, "why are the stoops gone? What sense is there in tearing them out?"

"That's where we would hang out and talk, you see," said the mechanic. "In the evenings, we traded stories with neighbors and played music."

"But what sense is there in taking that away?"

"When people gather, they make plans, soldier. They dream of what could be and of change that threatens the powerful."

"And friend," he asked, "those blocks reduced to rubble — what stood there?"

"That was the marketplace where the artists brought their work. It's where the cheese makers and butchers sold their goods and the farmers brought their produce."

"But why did they tear it down?"

"Again, soldier, it was a place to gather, to meet a neighbor and debate the policies of the city. The city pulled the market down."

The soldier rubbed his forehead.

"Where are you headed?" said the mechanic.

The soldier looked forward along the street and then back from where he had come.

The mechanic shook his head. "They send you boys off to war. You give your young lives to protect their wealth. Even the ones who come back, you've given the best of yourselves. And now, this is the welcome you get — a wall to keep you out."

He relieved the soldier of his pack. "Come on. You'll stay in my son's room. He's not coming home."

The soldier stayed with him, and the weeks passed. The mechanic took him along on his rounds. They descended underground, passing beneath the wall, under the City Center. They repaired boilers and generators in dark, restrictive spaces. They got disabled machines humming again, restoring power to outed streetlights and sending heat into the airy, bright apartments and offices high above the dark passageways in which they crept.

The soldier found the work strenuous and unfulfilling. With his hands occupied, his thoughts wandered to the wall and the tenements trapped beyond it. He pictured the families secluded in their apartments, bitter with isolation. He imagined them turning on each other in frustration. At times, these images led to memories of the war and he would have to break from his task to catch his breath.

When he slept, though, his resistance to the memories weakened.

There were nights when his dreams brought back the pounding of shell fire, the cackling of rampaging men, and the wordless submission of the murdered. His screams woke the mechanic who would sit up in his bed and weep for his lost son.

One evening on their walk home, they came upon the scene of a killing. A man, a former soldier as well, stood on the gravel scar where a stoop had been. On the ground beside him lay the body of his lover, the blood still bubbling from wounds in her chest. The killer, wild-eyed, held his knife out to them on an open palm.

Later that night, back in the apartment, the memories for the first time overpowered the soldier while he was awake. He collapsed in the kitchen, shaking from the violence of his visions. The mechanic sat with him most of the night.

"You know," said the mechanic once he could see that the episode had subsided, "dreams are stories. And as long as memory is the storyteller, it has the upper hand."

"I know," the soldier said, "but I don't know how to stop them."

"There is a way, but it's not easy. You must find a way to become the storyteller. You must wrench the power back from your memories."

"But it's so painful. And the memories only come back in the nightmares when I'm at their mercy."

After some thought, the mechanic said, "Memories always seek out a place. They cling to a classroom or a corner market or a bedroom. To gain mastery over them, find those places."

"I don't understand. Those awful things all happened far away. You want me to go back?"

"No, the memories have followed you here to the city. To become the storyteller, find the place where memory has found a home. It's not how you begin, it's where."

The soldier was confused, but at least he had a reason for hope and a chance to get started.

He sought the places where his memories might have taken

refuge. After work, he parted ways with the mechanic and walked the streets. Often he would come upon a place and feel that he had made a discovery. It might be the late, angled sunlight hitting a wall or the scamper of feet in an alleyway. Fiery shocks of recognition would pull the breath from his lungs. And yet nothing of value came to him in these moments, only the suspicion that his memory was torturing him.

Then one cold night, as he worked his way back to the mechanic's apartment, he entered the two-block scene of devastation he had learned about his first night. The sting of smoke from a trash fire stirred a memory. He felt his legs weaken and the need to turn from the place. But he was surprised by the sound of laughter. Rounding a mound of rubble, he discovered five young men gathered by a barrel fire. They stopped their talk at the sight of the soldier, but he nodded for them to carry on.

"That's right," said the smallest of them, "I saw her clear as I'm seeing you. She was naked up top, sitting at her bedroom mirror, doing up her hair. It was early morning, still dark. I was in my room, right across the airshaft, not ten feet away."

"And you did what? Hid in the dark?" said one of his friends.

"I'd want her to see me, if it was me," said another with red hair.

"Well, it wasn't you. And she did see me, later. She saw plenty of me," said the small storyteller.

As the soldier listened, his heart lifted. He knew he had found the place he was seeking. The mechanic was only partly right. He need not find the place where the memories rooted. He knew then that he could draw the memories back to him if he were in a place like this, where stories could be told.

In the weeks that followed, the mechanic joined the soldier as he made his appeal to neighbors. They went from building to building, climbing the littered stairways, knocking on apartment doors. They asked for old tools and spare materials and volunteers to help build a new gathering place on the site of the old market.

They found progress slow at first, but each week, as word spread of his project, the explanation became easier and the donations more generous. He soon had an abundance of volunteers, some of them veteran soldiers.

They began by clearing the lot. It was a tremendous undertaking without the use of machinery, but they had plenty of hands and the cooling fall weather made the work go easier. On some days, it seemed that the entire neighborhood had turned out to help. Many were skilled tradesmen and helped direct the others. Some who weren't gathering and sorting the material prepared meals for the workers.

As the clearing work neared completion, the soldier became anxious. The new building would not take shape in his mind. The thought of restricting people's movement within the walls of a building felt wrong. Late into the night he struggled with his drawings, and by morning they lay crumpled at his feet.

One late afternoon at the work site, he confessed his frustration to the mechanic. "It's the walls. Every room I draw looks like a prison."

The mechanic smiled. He led the soldier to a corner of the lot where the bricks and cinder blocks had been stacked to a great height. They clambered to the top, their arrival launching a small flock of black birds.

"At times like this, you must be patient, my friend," said the mechanic waving his hands over the activity below. "The plan will reveal itself to you."

They sat and watched. On one side of the lot, the cooks prepared dinner on folding tables. The workers broke from their tasks for the day and milled about and chatted. They pulled up crates and blocks to sit on, forming loose circles. A few musicians gathered near the center of the site and improvised. Some of the workers turned their seats in the direction of the music. Some circles widened as more people joined in. Others tightened as their discussions intensified.

Dinner was announced and lines formed at the tables. As people returned to their seats, the circles shifted to make room for the cooks and servers. More musicians arrived and the tempo picked up. A young woman rose from her seat and danced, threading her way through the groupings to the musicians in the center of the lot.

As people finished their meals, others joined her. Some in the discussion circles moved off to the periphery of the site where they could continue their conversations. Other circles broke, then reformed into larger assemblies around the dancing.

After a time, the mechanic climbed down and joined the activity, but the soldier remained on his perch, mesmerized. *I haven't failed*, he thought. *The fact is, there is no single design that would work. The needs of the space change moment to moment, and the design renews itself moment to moment.*

That night, he sketched a plan for a broad, open plaza. The pavement of reclaimed bricks would slope at gentle inclines, directing the rainwater toward three curving pools defining the outer boundaries of the lot. He included stepping stones so people could cross the ankle-deep water and children could sit and splash. Garden plots would hug the curves adjacent to each pool, two planted with vegetables and herbs, the third with flowers and ornamental grasses.

He avoided walls entirely, using posts where necessary to support a canopy — a shelter from the sun and rain that would sweep in a gentle arc over roughly half the area. He worked out plans to reuse much of the fallen lumber for construction of the canopy, portable seating, and storage bins.

The construction went slowly as most volunteers could work on the project only in their spare hours. From time to time, they halted the work to scrounge more materials. Finally, two and a half years after they began, the meeting place was completed. It was early June and the first plants were rising in the garden beds. On opening day, they celebrated from morning until late afternoon with food and music, dancing and games. They reserved the inaugural round of storytelling for the evening, and the soldier was asked to be the first.

He worked his way through the revelers, carrying his seat to the position left open for him. Some were still eating and most of the children were involved in play, but when he sat, a hush overtook the plaza. He waited in silence as the celebration became an audience, shifting into concentric circles around him.

He closed his eyes and began with the worst of it, plunging into his most hideous memories. His first words took great effort, but he pushed on. As the story began to flow, he reopened his eyes.

He saw before him, as he had on his first night back in the city, a small, horrid figure, so dark that it seemed to absorb the light around it.

The phantom shook like the shadow of a wind-rattled tree. It seemed to shout, hands cupped around its mouth, but no sound reached him.

The soldier was unnerved, and yet the presence of his neighbors gave him the courage to continue.

The shadow demon threw itself into the air and spun, arms lashing about. It made obscene gyrations and doubled over in mock hysteria.

The soldier spoke on, holding nothing back. He could see the terrors of his past reflected in the eyes of his neighbors. The dark creature twitched as if stung by each new detail of the story — or perhaps excited by them. It beat at its groin and tore its hair. It fell to the patio, flopping in spasms at his feet.

Claudia lowers the legal pad and lifts her eyes.

Stefan's fingers stop on his beard in mid-stroke. "No. No, shit?" He straightens and looks around at the others. "You say it ends in that way?"

She holds up the final page. There are three paragraphs at the end obscured by scribbles. "Seems he struggled with a resolution."

Whit, still outstretched on his back, scratches at an armpit. His T-shirt reads, ENTROPIC, SAY IT LOUD, SAY IT PROUD.

"Andre and his demons," he says. "Ironic, don't you think, that demons mess with him even when he's trying to write himself out of their grip?"

"As usual, Whit, you do not understand nothing," says Stefan. "The story he tells, it heals the soldier. Is plain to see, no?"

Whit grimaces his way to a sitting position and turns to Stefan. "Or maybe the soldier's just off-loading his psychic horrors onto his neighbors. Maybe he's infecting them with torturous visions and not ridding himself of anything. Andre seems doubtful at the end if this catharsis-by-way-of-storytelling crap will work."

"Hey now, some respect," says Squeej. "I'm with Stefan. The soldier's still got some dark shit to deal with, no doubt, but ... you know, he's gaining master-hood over them demons."

Sam stands, eyes down. He turns for the exist but then shifts back toward Claudia. "You know, Mom, you should have read Andre's one about the family — the one that told what happened in that house. Maybe I'll use that for my story since I don't have one."

Portia sighs.

Claudia pulls the pad to her chest. "Oh no sweetie. You really should try to —"

"It's just ... I've got nothing about me I want to write about so —"

"Hey, Sam, look." Whit has rolled over to his side. "If talking about the past is too shit-awful, man, think about the future. Tell us a story about where you'll be in ten years."

Kesi turns and gives Whit the full measure of her glare.

"What?" he says to her. "I've had some coursework in these things, you know."

Sam looks at Whit for the first time all night. "Yeah, OK. Maybe."

Squeej raises his hand.

"Yes?" says Claudia.

"Andre's story made me think that real lies is, like, realize."

She closes her eyes and pinches her tear ducts. "Would someone care to help Squeej?"

"Yo, y'know," says Squeej, "like sometimes, you realize, like, it be real lies."

"You OK, dude?" says Stefan. "You sound like you are having stroke."

"Yeah, no, you get me, like, Andre with that wall and all and then the no walls, it's like sometimes he makes you realize the real lies being perpetrated, is all."

Stefan covers his face with his palms. "OK, man. Please stop."

Claudia nods to Kesi. "How about if you go tomorrow night, hon? Didn't you say you had something?"

"Whoa." Kesi's eyes stretch wide. "I'm not ready. Let Whit go."

"I could," Whit says, "but come on, Kes. You're going to tell us how you met Carlton, right? When he saved you from the ravages of the road?"

"No, that's not my story." She stands and circles wide around him on her way to the exit. "And it didn't happen like that. And, by the way, fuck you."

TWO DAYS AND SIX HOURS PRIOR

I-81 Northbound, Near Troutville, Virginia

"See, now that's just the kind of meaningless talk that gets people no-where," Carlton says, baritone edging into raspiness. "Doubly true? Just no sense in that."

"Sorry?"

"You're saying it's doubly true people won't pick you up 'cause of how you look, which I don't really know what that means anyway about your looks."

For the first time since settling in the passenger seat, Kesi turns to him. "What I mean to say is normally people won't stop for you out on 81. And if you're of color," she says, "that would be doubly true."

He nods, his face sober, eyes fixed on the empty interstate lanes before him. There's a hunch to his shoulders as with men his size used to ducking through doorways. His hair is military short and razored at the edges, and that fussiness extends down through pencil-thin sideburns and a goatee honed to a point. A snake tattoo twines around his considerable forearm accompanied by the inscription, I DON'T MIND DYIN.

"OK, well I'd put that color thing aside 'cause it's not like you're off-putting or something." There's a concentrated effort in his voice. "But being true, that's a total ... whatcha call —"

The cab is hushed, belying the size of the engine, leaving only the repetitive snicking of the monster tires on the road seams as the pickup scales a slow-curving incline through the mountain pass.

He turns to her for help.

She shrugs.

"You know, things that's just one or the other thing. Things that can only be one thing."

"An absolute?"

"Yeah, being true is an absolute."

"OK."

He looks pained. "Well no, it ain't OK."

She twists and locates her pack on the floor behind her seat. His eyes catch hers as she turns back.

"Look," she says, "it's just a figure of speech. It's just to get a point across. There are half-truths, whole truths, and then there are things that are doubly true."

"Half truth. See, no damn business using that, either." He's more animated now, popping the wheel with the heel of his hand. "And people go on saying it and never thinking what's coming off their lips."

She leans forward and squints at the blue road sign emerging around the curve near the top of the ridge.

"It's important for things to have meaning," he says, eyebrows down. "Sometimes that's all you get."

"So you always mean what you say?"

He nods. "People say shit just because they think it's expected. 'That guy's a genius,' they'll say maybe 'cause he smoked a great damn barbecue or something. You hear me calling somebody a genius, you know I mean it. Pro'bly won't because I'll pro'bly never meet one."

He checks his side views and drums the wheel with his fingers. "What you say your name was?"

A taxicab-yellow Range Rover overtakes them in the right lane. The late afternoon August sun blinks off the chrome above the driver's window, blinding Kesi. She reopens her eyes on a girl of maybe ten staring at her from the back seat. "I didn't say."

"OK, well that's up to you. I'm just givin' you a ride is all."

"It's Kesi ... K-E-S-I ... not Casey, like Casey Jones ... Kesi."

"Fine. There ya go."

He glances at his side view again and punches the pickup into the passing lane. Out his window are terraced walls of rusty stone where the interstate is chiseled out of the mountain.

The cliff walls end, clearing their view of knobby-topped mountains, receding like waves into dusky blues and grays toward the horizon.

"What's yours?" she asks.

"Carlton."

"Carlton. That's a good name. Carl for short?"

"Nope. Carlton."

"Mine's from the Swahili. Do you want to know what it means?"

"No consequence, the meaning of names. Names is just names, unless you give it to yourself. You the one come up with Kesi?

"No."

"There ..." he nods at the blue sign as it passes. "The Troutville rest stop's coming up. Not much of a place. Sure you don't want me to take you further? Maybe you should get to Lexington or Harrisonburg for the night."

"Sorry, what?"

They round the top of the ridge and begin the descent. He tugs on his earring, eyes straight ahead. "I could take you on further is all."

"I thought you said you were only going as far as the rest stop. Harrisonburg must be another two hours off."

"Hour and a half, not even."

She opens her mouth to speak but winds up faking a cough.

"I'm just giving you a ride. I didn't have no partic'lar plans. I'm not a creep or nothin'," he says.

Kesi shifts in her seat and gives him a solid look. "OK, so what you're saying is you were just cruising around looking for people to pick up."

"No, I come looking for you, specifically."

"What?"

"Back in Roanoke, yeah. I was at the Salt Lick getting coffee just after you was there. And Phaedra — you know, who likely she was your server — she says, 'A girl ...' Actually, she says, 'A bald, sweet-looking, African American girl' was in here and was askin' around for a ride. She says somebody lookin' like a meth cooker who she knows I happen to know, he took you up to 81 to hitch. I thought that didn't sound like a safe situation, knowing Timmy McGarry, which if it was Timmy, he's actually too damn strung out and incapable to be a cooker, so I come looking for you."

She clears her throat. "Yes, it was Tim something."

"And like I said, I got nothin' partic'lar going on. I got no work this week."

TWO DAYS AND FIVE HOURS PRIOR

Route 1, North Raleigh, Virginia

"I say text. It not a damn email. It text."

"Just watch the road, Cappy boy. This damn Droid of yours makes no sense. On my phone, it doesn't matter if it's email or text or damn Zulu drums, it's on the home screen. This phone's fucked."

"Was on home screen before you go screw it up. Give here."

Mr. Leonard bats Cappy's hand back.

The tires cry out as Cappy swings left to avoid a car that fails to move with the green light. He downshifts and accelerates through the intersection, rocking them back.

Mr. Leonard thumb-swipes slowly. "Bitchin' vehicle, Cappy, I'll give you that. Not sure you're man enough for it, to be honest with you."

He whips them back to the center lane. With nothing ahead until the next light, he speed shifts up to fifth. "Dodge Challenger R/T got 372 horsepower. It got 400-pound feet V8. Damn good car, made in America."

"It was at that, just like me."

Cappy is stiff-arming the wheel, hand at 1 o'clock. He taps two of his rings together — one two-two, one two-two. He looks twice at Mr. Leonard, still swiping at a measured pace.

"You slow as shit. You still find no text? It easy, shit-a-brain. Press button twice. Move left, move again. Then click green message thing. Then scroll, find text from 'J.' Then click 'J.' Then scroll to read fucking Jasper. Then read fucking text. How fucking easy it got be?"

"Like I said, it's a fucked up, useless, probably Cambodian or some shit phone."

"You the one useless. You a' albino racist pig fuck, plus you useless."

"Hey, watch that. 'J' like for Jasper? Are you saying Senator damn Jasper sends you texts? I don't see that happening."

"No, shit-a-brains. You think Jasper a moron? Somebody work for Jasper, he said he will send text. It some lap dog VoG idiot. Senator Jasper? Give me break. Just find text so we know where cock-sucker Whit Reitman is. I have enough full up of these Southern fucks down here. Soon I get this done, get back home. Damn sure had enough you too, that damn sure. You as stupid as VoG idiot who sending damn text."

He puts the phone down on his lap. "I'm not a Vogger, man. And you better watch your ass addressing me in the way you're doing."

"I no need watch my ass. My ass fine. Just read damn text. Where that cocksucker Reitman?"

"And I'm not albino. I got a pigmentary deficiency in my hair, not my skin. I can tan as good as the next guy. Me not wanting to expose my skin to cancer-causing elements has got nothing to do with my pigmentation ability."

"You a pasty, mother fucker pig fuck and I counting seconds till I done with you. What text say?"

Mr. Leonard begins to lift the phone but drops his hand. "And you better work on improving your demeanor. We get in a situation and your demeanor is going to get us fucked. I'm starting to see your demeanor as a big problem."

Cappy shakes his head. He maintains the speed of the car until thirty yards shy of the red light, then downshifts into third and then second, leaning heavy on the brake.

Mr. Leonard holds the phone up again. "OK, it says, 'Car found in ditch off 460 2 miles west of bedford. We r close by. Scouting possibles.'"

Mr. Leonard turns the phone toward Cappy. "You believe this numb nuts? 'Scouting possibles.' Who the hell's he supposed to be? I'm telling you man, these lame-ass Voggers are gonna mess with our shit."

"Yeah. Where that? He say 460. Look that up. Voggers is shit-a-brains."

"You got Google Maps on here?" Mr. Leonard is swiping again. "Yeah, you got that right, Cappy boy. Loggers are shit-a-brains — good ol' God-fearing, Cracker Barrel-eating, made-in-America, shit-a-brains."

THREE WEEKS, ONE DAY,
AND TWENTY-ONE HOURS AFTER

The Colony, Greenport, New York

Whit alone is active. Everyone else in the group is sprawled and content with stasis after a day of outdoor labor. So far, Whit has swapped a low stool for a taller one from the kitchen — claiming the need for a "higher station" — returned to the original seat in deference to its more "rationally positioned foot rungs," only to shove that too aside, condemning the convention of seating.

At Whit's request, Sam rises, crosses the room, and kills the overhead fluorescents. Sam nearly makes it back to his lounging spot before Whit changes his mind.

"No, dark won't work," says Whit, starting into a pacing pattern. "I'll miss your looks of wonderment and adoration. Who's missing?"

"Portia," says Stefan. "The sweetheart, she is watching our twins, who I am thinking their minds are too impressionable to hear what it is I am expecting someone like you has to tell."

"Wise ... and ironic because my story is actually about impressionable minds, or more like what's indelible versus what's more squidgy and fungible."

Whit comes to a halt, transferring his jitters into a stiff-legged, toe-to-heel bounce. He cranes his head toward the ceiling and stretches his jaw to its max, cranks it from side to side and claps it twice like a ventriloquist's dummy.

"Yes, minds are malleable." He slaps his hip pockets in syncopation. "That's thanks to brain cell regeneration. You may have heard that neurons don't come back once they're gone. That, in fact, is a myth perpetrated by old stoners looking for excuses. There was a study done on adult monkeys showing that, while there's loss throughout life, neurons are being continually added to the cerebral cortex, which may or may not prove that old monkeys are less goofy than old stoners. Hard to say unless they include stoners in the data sampling —"

"Why don't you just get started?" says Kesi.

"Sure." He shakes out his arms and resumes his pacing. "I'll just let you have it and we'll assess the brain damage later."

Whit's Story

I used to work in corporate, although we're talking cushy Silicon Alley corporate. It was cushy because, being unnervingly gifted, self-delusional young geekoids, the world owed us foosball lounges and flex hours and vegan lunch service. The loft ceilings were high, our scraggly-ass dogs roamed at will, and the espresso hissed out hour after hour as we burrowed into code like hunger-crazed weasels. We were always together and got tight with each other since we were pretty much captive to the cushiness.

Not that it matters so much what we were coding, but it was inter-relational protocols for social platforms. Investors back then were fire-hosing cash at social. The land grab was on and we'd staked out our little fiefdom. Besides my computer science masters, I'd gotten my PhuD in cognitive neuroscience, so I got hired to be the resident expert in human being-ness. As you know, most propeller heads aren't good at the human being thing, so management thought the answer was to create a senior job position for that, and I was it.

They asked me to write my own job description. It read: "To quantify in neat rows of code what it means to be human." Business model-wise, the code we wrote was supposed to make your average socially clueless Millennials think they were acting more human and more connected to other humans. More pointedly, our objective was to connect the fools to marketers flush with newfound abilities to sell them more and more meaningless shit thanks to the human-ness data they were giving us permission to mine from them. Users become the used — very inspired.

In any case, the human-ness angle gave the VC suits a damn good story for the investors, the cash poured in, and the options got doled out like scones with our morning lattes. Revulsion aside, much of the work was kind of brilliant, and we were stoked about it. Self-delusion is quite supportive of job performance as it can make you project beyond yourself and accomplish things. The realization that the accomplishments are valueless occurs much later. So in my case, everything was cool at the time.

And then ... well, it wasn't at all.

And then I quit.

It wasn't what you might think — me having some sort of ethical awakening. It was self-loathing.

What I did, you see, was destroy Larry Callahan, the founder of the company. Larry was that big-balled billionaire that bought out FreeScraper before it was Colloozit, merged it with PayRaid, and then sold out to Yahoo for about thirty-five times EBITDA. He later started, just for shits and giggles, that not-so-great wave-powered energy project off the coast of Oregon, which depleted his fortune by a smidge and made him a hero with the greenies. His next business — his last business — was this place where we worked. He was itching to make some real money again so he was being hands-on, at least for Larry, which made it not so surprising he recruited me personally to be the human being guy. Anyway, he's not around anymore. And that's my fault.

The end began about a year into the job when one day he asked to meet for coffee. I expected some kind of casual, Larry-style performance review. And yet he didn't pick the usual hangout around the corner from the offices, but a diner way down on Bowery. He was tucked away under deep shadow in the back corner, which wasn't his thing.

Larry was a warm Irish hulk — a toucher. Normally he'd sit close with his hand on your shoulder or kneading the back of your neck. His natural color was red-faced mirth. He was that guy that begins a joke with a laugh and gets you going before he's anywhere near the punchline. He had a talent that drew you to him, being one and the same talent that sucked billions out of investors.

That afternoon, though, it seemed like Larry left his charm in the back seat of the Uber. We were about ten minutes into the opening chitchat when I realized I was doing all the talking. Larry was staring at his napkin and wiping his trendy little glasses. It occurred to me I might be getting laid off.

So I shut up and waited for him to come out with it.

"Whit," he said, "I want you to build me an app that will make me forget things."

"Forget things?" I said, and he said, "Yes," and I said, "You mean, help you remember things you forget?" and he said, "No, forget things."

Why would people want an app that would make them forget things, right?

He said, "Not people, just me. I have some things I need to forget — some very specific things."

I said I didn't understand and he told me that understanding wasn't what he needed from me. I asked what sort of things he wanted to forget, but he got testy. "They're private and need to stay private before and after I forget them."

He gave me a thick NDA to sign and then he pushed an envelope across the table stuffed with a West Village one-bedroom quantity of cash.

I managed to eke a few more particulars out of him before he patted the table and stood.

I asked if this was why he hired me, so I could do this for him. I remember the disappointed smile. He said, "Come on, Whit, you're my human being guy."

On his way past, he gave the back of my neck a squeeze. "Keep me in the loop, Whit," he said.

I sat for a good hour drinking coffee and trading long stares with the envelope. Something off-base was happening with Larry and my gut told me to bow out. But there was the cush job, which would no doubt become someone else's if I refused him, and along with the job, I'd probably lose my friends back at the loft.

Gradually, I let rationalization wash me along. The project would undoubtedly be very cool. I knew I could do it, which was no small thing. No one had ever tried anything like this, let alone with an app you could use outside of the lab. And he was Larry Callahan, for shit sake. I wanted to please him because he just had that thing about him that made you want to. And fuck yes, it was a sick amount of money.

I texted Larry to tell him I'd do it, something I'm sure he knew.

I got right into it, since Larry had set me a three-month deadline. I needed to keep up appearances at work, so I only had nights. Things at home with my girlfriend, Karla, got dicey in a surprisingly short amount of time. I had to wait until she was asleep to work. And towards the end, I was testing it in bed at night, so that wasn't so sexy for her. Sometimes I'd miss work-work the next day, which didn't help relations in cushy-land either.

My first few weeks were full of sputters and mis-starts. I was after what's called an osmotic method — introducing suggestions to the mind when it's at its most vulnerable, meaning during sleep. About a month and a half in, I read a new paper on biofeedback and it finally started to pull together.

I went at it, seriously, like I'd never done with anything before. At a point, it stopped being so much about pleasing Larry and more about making it work. It seemed like the most important thing I would ever get a chance to do. And everything else got tossed by the wayside — Karla, my cushy friends, and the creepy feelings I had about the whole weird project.

If you've ever gone after a discovery, maybe you understand what I was going through. When your theory starts to work, you get this prolonged rush. Things, one after another, snap together and work. The feeling is beautiful enough that you tell yourself it transcends ego, which of course is just your ego fucking with you. I even made the app compliant with standard mobile OS, as if I was going to release it to the iTunes store or something. The self-delusion ran deep.

Technically, I'm still bound by the NDA, but I don't expect you guys care enough to tell anyone how it works.

You begin by firing up the app and talking into your phone — you describe the memory you want to lose. The program dissects your story and comes up with fourteen yes/no questions, which confirm what type of memories it's dealing with. But the questions are easy to answer and that's pretty much all the effort on your part — consciously. When it's time for bed, you put in your earbuds and put on your biorhythm cap. The app plays radiant trance music that lulls you to sleep, and then the voice starts. She runs through a set of hypnotic suggestions repeatedly for about two hours while the app tracks your biorhythms.

I tested it on myself first. I told Karla it was biorhythm therapy to help me sleep. The stickiest problem was finding something I wanted to forget. I settled on a vaguely homoerotic locker room incident from middle school. The next morning — pffffitt —totally gone. I downloaded the recording. Even hearing myself tell the story failed to spark the original memory, as if it had happened to someone else.

I loaded it on Larry's phone in November. I'd only tested on myself so I urged him to go slow. I warned him — he'd be playing around with irrevocable memory loss, right down to the synaptic plasticity. I mean, it's highly discriminate, but still.

He said, "I'm sure it's fine. I need to get started."

I did my best to put it out of my mind and get my life back together. I took Karla away to New Orleans for a weekend. I didn't spend any of the money, though. It didn't feel good, having it. It wasn't guilt. I was stewing about not getting the recognition I deserved. And yes, that's about as messed up as it sounds. I thought that I'd wasted the one halfway great thing I'd do in my life on some rich guy's wacko personal project.

Two, three months went by. At work, Larry was almost a total no-show and people were starting to talk. Then scuttlebutt broke out that our funding was drying up, which I of course knew was probably not the case.

One early April afternoon — this is like ten months after I handed Larry the app — Karla and I ran into him. He was walking with his wife up on the High Line. Larry looked like he wanted to sneak past me, but it was a narrow path and we were unavoidable.

His wife was beautiful. She was tall but delicate, with an honest smile. Her hair was up in back — red, but she was letting it go gray. After introductions, Larry made their excuses, but Gloria — he called her Glory — said she was starving. She let go of Larry and grabbed my arm, walking us down the nearest stairs to a place on Hudson.

She wasn't chatty. In fact, I don't think we said a word, but she didn't seem to mind, like we were a couple that didn't need to try anymore. We walked five paces ahead of Karla and Larry. I remember glancing back and seeing this look on Larry that read, weirdly, as jealousy.

We sat in a booth. The weekend brunch crowd was noisy. Karla did most of the talking, at nearly a shout. She managed to get some grunts out of Larry, but he was too busy glaring at Glory. She seemed unconcerned, just listening with her quiet smile. Meanwhile, there I was, absorbing all the tension, expecting any second Larry would stand up and drag Glory out of there.

The waiter came around. Glory hadn't opened her menu. She gave Larry a blank stare, so he ordered her a club sandwich. It got stranger from there. Karla, still trying to get a conversation going, asked, "Do you have a favorite restaurant in this neighborhood?" Glory looked at Larry again. He said they like Blue Hill. Glory nodded. Karla asked Glory if she worked. Again, she deferred to Larry — he said she was taking a break from her career.

As soon as we said goodbye and were out of earshot, Karla laid into me. "What the hell was that about?" I was damned confused too, even with all that I knew. She asked me if I saw the bruise on Glory's face, underneath the makeup.

"She's abused," Karla said. "That son of a bitch has her terrified. You did notice that, didn't you?"

Well, I was shaking at this point because Karla didn't know the half of it. I was convinced Larry was using the app on Glory to wipe her memory clean — beating her and intimidating her, then making her forget all the abuse. It all fit. I felt fucking sick.

And that feeling only got worse as the weeks passed. Karla didn't let it go. She asked if I had seen Glory. I hadn't. It seemed no one had. "You need to confront him, Whit. You can't just do nothing," she told me.

But I made excuses. "We have no evidence. And even if I could find some," I told her, "it's sure to lose me my job. And what about everyone else at work? It'll ruin things for everyone."

It was maybe six weeks later that Larry made one of his by then rare appearances at work. He was a mess — exhausted and about twenty pounds lighter. He skipped his rounds of the departments. He stayed clear of me altogether.

I was in sorry shape myself by that time and, seeing Larry, I almost lost it. The crew took me out for drinks that night to talk about what was messing me up. I didn't talk, but I drank plenty. I came home in a state and Karla unleashed her pent-up shit storm. "You're self-serving. You don't give a shit about people. You're immature. You're irresponsible."

At that early stage in our relationship, I had at least two I-can-change-I-swear cards to play, but I of course went with sarcasm. She split for her sister's apartment.

That began a murky couple of months for me. I started texting and emailing Larry, trying to get a read on how screwed up things really were. He wouldn't respond — nothing back from him for weeks. Finally in one bourbon-fueled email rant I called him out about misusing the app. The entirety of his reply read, "As per our agreement, stay out of this."

I knew what I had to do, but it took me a few days to pull myself together.

I stayed home from work and got started. I had to crack Larry's passcode, but that wasn't tough. I found a set of "Glory" digital recordings — 116 dating back to the beginning, and there were still new ones coming in.

I double-clicked the first file and waited to hear Glory's voice. But no, it was Larry. He recounted a time he spent with Glory. I listened to more episodes. In some, he recalled milestones in their life together — a miscarriage, eloping, her father's death — but most were just everyday things.

Larry spoke to Glory directly, and with such affection — Glory, we were here, or Glory, we were doing this. They were rich with personal details and impressions — smells, feelings, all spoken with such tenderness, soft and low.

He'd begin the same way each time — "Glory, Glory" — like he was summoning her — like a religious thing. Like an invocation.

The stories could be about the most mundane incidents, but

always a connection to his heart. In one, they were at their summer place. He said something like, "Glory, you'd stayed out too long in the sun, and we came off the beach for a nap and you asked me to put aloe on your sunburn." He described the white lines on her back when he pulled down her shoulder straps, how she rolled against him when he sat next to her on the bed, how he worked the gel into her back, feeling the heat of the sun and dry ocean salt. He described the scent of her and of the aloe — everything that was filling his head.

Many of the memories were sad, but nothing mean-spirited or bitter. In other words, all memories you would want to hold on to.

I was damn freaked. There I was, the pawn who had facilitated this senselessness, witnessing a good man destroying his most cherished memories.

I listened to every recording. I took notes, charted them out, trying to find a pattern, an insight. I thought maybe Glory had fallen out of love with Larry. Maybe he was forcing himself to forget out of spite. But no, Larry's devotion was obvious — in every episode, through dozens and dozens. I found no sense in it.

And then one Thursday in the offices — I hadn't been in all week — Lucy from marketing came to my desk in tears. Larry was in again. He had been acting so lost, she said. "He's wearing a pajama top under his jacket."

I found him sitting in the kitchen. He had his iPhone out, trying to untangle his earbud cords. I grabbed him by an arm and walked him to the elevator.

We wound up in Madison Square Park. We sat on a bench facing the reflecting pool. It was a gusty day, but warm there in the sun.

I couldn't think of how to help him. I remember how he watched the leaves — curled, brittle, orange and red maple leaves swirling on the path. They slid toward us. He watched them circle round his ankles.

Then, all of a sudden, he clamped down hard on my hand. He looked at me like a guilty kid. "You know, don't you?" I nodded, even though I didn't understand a goddamn thing. He nodded too and hummed to himself, staring at the ground again.

We sat for quite a while, mostly in silence. But he popped up now and then with scattered thoughts. He talked about his rugby days back at Dartmouth. He was fearless — "total abandon," he called it. "I took that into business, you know? Not one day was I afraid on the job. But now, he said, I'm the worst kind of coward."

I then asked him why he was doing it — why he wanted to destroy his beautiful memories.

He didn't answer, not for some time. Then, in a whisper he said, "I couldn't take it. I couldn't take having all of those lovely memories in my head knowing that she was losing them."

He said that after Glory was diagnosed, he worked with her every day, sharing memories with her to try to keep them alive, but one by one they fell away. They fell away from her, he told me, like leaves from a tree. "Soon, they weren't ours anymore, just mine. God ... those memories," he said, "but they turned on me, Whit, like thorns tearing away at me."

I asked him if erasing the memories had brought him relief. "No," he told me, "they're gone but the pain is still here." And the guilt of not being able to help her, that was there too.

Glory didn't last much longer. She passed about four months later. Larry disappeared. And I can't say I tried to track him down.

A year and some after that, I learned the news like everybody else. It was all over the papers, what had become of Larry. And I thought immediately of this one vivid passage from Larry's recordings — from his forgotten memories.

One night, he and Glory took a walk in the park during a snowstorm, one of their favorite things. Glory loved the special kind of quiet, but this snowfall was wet and heavy, soaking them both. Glory was shivering but insisted they go on. Deep into the park, they heard the terrible crack of a huge tree limb giving way. Huge clods of slush and splintered branches came down all around, but they didn't get a scratch. Glory laughed and took off running. He chased her all the way to Madison to a warm bar.

And so, yes, they found him, in the dead of February, sitting against a huge, red oak in Central Park — over by the Conservatory Water. The cops called me in for questioning. Seems they had an old report in Larry's file about possible spousal abuse. Karla had put in the complaint. And so they wanted to know what I knew. I said I knew nothing of it but that there was no way he would have hurt Glory. I didn't tell them anything more.

Kesi's arms are crossed over her head. "Really?"

Whit goggle-eyes her. His twitchiness has subsided to some degree. He has his hands clamped under opposing armpits.

"Well, come on," she says. "That was for real?"

"Incredulity. That's all you've got? I just butterflied my soul open for you."

"Well?"

Whit gives a you're-really-going-to-do-this-to-me chuckle. "You know, Kes, it's hard to say what's real when life is manufacturing incomprehensible shit. But the look of pain on Larry's face, sitting there on the bench, that was real for me."

"Yes," says Kesi, "I can imagine that would be a tough thing to forget. But no, wait — you can use your memory eraser."

Whit opens his mouth.

"Did you keep it?" Sam hugs his shins, chin on his knees. "The money?"

"I mean, technically, yes," says Whit. "But no."

Kesi laughs.

"Well, Whit, OK." Claudia arches her back, hands pushing at her lower spine. "You went back to an incident that's haunting you, or so you say. You show love for this man, and I can see that you're ... I don't know, let's call it provisionally repentant. Fine, whatever. But how is this helping us come to an understanding? Because this has got nothing to do with what happened here."

Whit unsticks a hand out from his armpit and nibbles at his thumbnail. "Right. Is that what we're trying to do? Understand what I did? Look, everybody knows what I did, Claudia." His throat is closing around his voice. "What do you want?"

Kesi mumbles something.

"I think Whit, he is being honest from his emotional standpoint of view," says Stefan. "Maybe is not his fault his view is so ... how do you say it? Is from his view only?"

"Self-centered and childish," Kesi's says.

"Yes. But is real at least, Whit's story. Is not like fiction like Andre's city story, but then maybe that is what Andre intended, who can say? Morals is the thing here, Claudia. His point is there are morals from his life that Whit is trying to figure out. Is not so easy — not so gray and white."

"There's no gray, Stefan," Sam says. "There's no gray in doing the wrong thing when you know it's wrong. There's no gray in assisted suicide. It leads straight to death, which is totally black, man."

"That's the way you see it?" says Whit, rewrapping his arms around his chest. "You think I helped Larry kill himself?"

"Slower than the better methods, but yeah."

Squeej locks his fingers around one knee and leans back to the full stretch of his arms. "For me, what's totally messed up is that Andre, well he's all about remembering, right? And here Whit's gone and made a forget machine. No doubt Andre'd be all up in your business, dude, about making Larry forget, 'cause memories are the narrative, narrative is life, and so on. You gotta admit, that soul suckin' app you made was whack."

Kesi's still looking at Whit like she caught him sleeping with her best friend. "But it's nice to know that after the Larry tragedy you learned your lesson," she says. "You stopped with the fucked up apps."

Squeej pulls himself forward. "Oh, right, like, how long after the memory eraser did you repeat offend with VoG?"

Whit shrugs, eyes downcast. "What can I say, Squeej? You've got to do something at least twice to establish a pattern of behavior."

TWO DAYS AND ONE HOUR PRIOR

I-81 Northbound, Troutville, Virginia

Kesi makes it under the rest stop pavilion's overhang just as the rain begins. The unwavering downpour fails to stir the dense evening air. As Kesi makes her way through the entryway, the thirty-degree temperature differential sets off a rush of air past her. She reaches behind and frees the sweat-soaked T-shirt from her back.

Aside from a few bladder-bloated travelers en route to the restrooms, the interior is inactive. The gift shop off the entryway, sparsely stocked with Virginia-themed paraphernalia, is unattended.

She heads into the central food court. A greasy mix of aromas drifts out of Cajun Jim's Shrimp Station, Asian-O-Vation and a Cinnabon wannabe named Sinful Buns.

Kesi cuts diagonally across the dining area, winding through the alternating lime and orange tables. She slows and narrows her eyes at Cajun Jim's back-lit menu board, its listings barely legible over faded photos of croquettes, shrimp rolls, and smoothies.

"Would you like to hear our specials?"

Kesi turns to a late twenty-something man seated just behind her.

"We have some lovely pan-seared scallops over a bulgur and oyster mushroom ragout. It's finished with a drizzle of parsley romesco balsamic pesto glaze ... foam ... or something."

Kesi fails to react.

"We recommend pairing that with a Kiwi Lime Blast Slurp Ice from Sinful Buns. We like to keep things locally sourced."

She takes a step back. The man's tousled hair and week-old scruff are not as telling of his condition as the bluish shadows around his eyes and body odor pungent enough to cut through the fast-food smells. He sits at a table strewn with flattened drink cups, balled wrappers, and a service tray that has captured the overturned contents of an anti-freeze green, 32-ounce drink.

"Sorry, I'm usually more clever," he says, drumming his fingers. He makes continual adjustments to the position of his neck and shoulders. "More handsome too."

Kesi looks beyond him. "Maybe you could just point me to the water fountain."

His eyes widen. He inhales, straightening enough to reveal the lettering on his T-shirt: GOD IS ALL IN YOUR HEAD. There's a logo on the sleeve — VoG.

He lets the air out with a sputter. "Nope. Nothing like that."

She nods at the table. "You look like you've been sitting here awhile."

He stands, shoves his hands in his pockets, and twists for a view of the wall clock. "Coming up on two days."

"What the hell?"

"More like purgatory. But I've had an enriching experience. I've learned some things — some profoundly useless things. Actually, I'm working on a pet space-time theory. Would you like to hear about it?"

Kesi steps closer and eases her pack to the floor.

"OK, so you probably plotted your trip today on Google Maps, right? But did it account for the time you spend in here? No. You've got to believe those Google nerdniks would if they could, but they're up against the time envelope in here. I'm convinced we are presently — wow, I'm not sure if there is a presently in here — but anyway, we're a half step removed from temporal space. People rush in, they deposit their bodily wastes, grab their caffeine delivery vehicles, then — *zzzrrrr-pop* — time latches on and yanks them back onto that ol' highway continuum. In here, they're only outtakes — like clips that didn't make it into the road movie, which is why I'm thinking I may not actually be aging ... you know ... shit ..."

Kesi, who was leaning in towards him, straightens and overcompensates.

He springs to her side and grabs her arm to keep her from toppling backward. "Wow, I really didn't want to move that fast."

She angles back to see his face. Her eyelids flutter. There's a film of sweat on her forehead.

"You should sit down," he says.

Her feet remain in place.

"Don't worry." He puts an arm around her waist. "I'm not a creep or anything."

Her knees give way. With some effort, he guides her to one of the orange bucket chairs.

"Christ." She lets her head drop to her knees. "You're the second strange guy today that's told me he's not a creep."

"You think I'm strange?"

"Equal parts smelly and strange, yes."

He jerks open his T-shirt collar and whiffs. "Who was your first guy?"

"My ride here."

"Someone dropped you off here? What kind of miserable human being would do such a thing?"

"He's not nearly as miserable as me after thumbing out there in the heat for four hours."

"Oh yeah, it's rough out there. And now you're stuck in here. There's no escape."

She scoots forward far enough to slide her cheek onto the table.

"Here, let me make some room for you." He piles the tabletop trash onto the tray. "How about some juice? And maybe something to eat. What's your name?"

She nods, her cheek adhering to the Formica. "Kesi. Juice, yes. No food."

He takes off toward the food counters, then spins and returns, sloshing green liquid onto the floor.

"Sorry. But do you have any cash? I'm, well, undercapitalized, as it were."

She squints at him, then wriggles a folded five from the front pocket of her cut-offs.

Kesi's color improves with the downing of her Snapple Orange Mango. She approves the purchase of a cherry Yoplait as well.

"Sorry to run at the mouth," he says as she eats. "It's been a few days since someone's recognized my existence. Don't worry, I'll lay off the space-time theorizing since you're most likely associating that with the onset of your vertigo."

She sucks on the yogurt spoon, her gaze drifting back down to him from the sliver of moon occupying the skylight overhead.

"So, I don't know." He drums his fingers. "Where's home?"

"Nowhere. No home. Your eyes are a weird shade of blue. They're blue, right?"

"They used to be. I'd have to check. My self image is a bit distorted at present."

She leans farther in to the table and mounts her chin on her forearm. "And I'm beginning to think maybe you're not insane."

"Insane would be too convenient an explanation."

"Shit, I'm wiped out." Her head flops to the side again. "What did you say your name was?"

"Whit, but I didn't ... say."

"Whit as in Whitney or Wit as in cleverness?"

"Only my mom calls me Wit as in cleverness. No, Whitman. I was named after my favorite uncle who died just before I was born. He was also my only uncle. Actually, his real name was Arnold, not Whitman, but he liked poetry. And he was also nuts. They sent him to Nam. He came home and threw himself off the Kinzua Bridge in Pennsylvania, which at one time held the distinction of being the tallest railroad bridge in the world. Wait ... yes, in that order — Nam, home, high dive. Come to think of it, that jump may have been a fairly rational response to Nam."

He stands, burying his hands first in his front, then back jeans pockets, then under his armpits.

He sits again, entwines his fingers, and bows them inversely for a crack.

"Are you always this —" Kesi says. "Sorry."

"What?"

"Never mind."

"Entertaining?"

"Twitchy."

He rubs his nose, skitters his fingernails on the table, and then presses the nail hand flat with the other. "No, well, yes if I don't have my anti-anxiety meds."

"Oh? What are you anxious about?"

"Nothing. I mean, I do worry about stupid stuff. It's not the kind of worrying that does me any good. It's just anxiety. It's a chemical thing. Worrying is a side effect."

"What stupid stuff?"

"Oh, like at the moment I'm stressing over how to tell you that I like your hair ... or lack thereof. There's really no social convention. 'I like your bald.' 'I like your head.' Doesn't work."

"No, but thanks."

"And I worry about the fact that my meds can be addictive, so when my anxiety gets bad and I really need them, I put off taking them, increasing the anxiety over how freaked out I'm getting, which in turn opens up a further range of options for what to worry about. It goes on."

"Do the meds help?"

"They don't get rid of the anxiety, really. It's more like you don't give a fuck that you're still anxious. It's like smothering the worries in warm caramel sauce."

"That sounds nice."

"It's very nice, which is why it's so addictive."

"No, the caramel sauce."

He stands again. "You're still hungry. Do you want me to —"

"No, no, I'm fine. Sit. And did you tell me why you're here yet?"

"Car trouble."

She lifts her head. "Car? Where is it? Is it in the shop?"

"I'm not sure. Three days ago I kind of parked it on its side in a gully along a country lane about fifteen miles east of here. I've always been a bad parker. I'm guessing it's been relocated by now."

She puts her head back down, cheek nuzzled into the crook of her elbow. "Shit."

"Exactly. I was just about out of gas, which I imagine is why I was looking for a parking spot at seventy-five miles an hour on a slick, windy road. It all made sense at the time, but I was asleep ... I think."

He looks for a reaction but she has closed her eyes.

"And you?" Still nothing. "During your bout of delirium, I think you said you're here writing a piece for *Travel & Leisure*? I'm joshing, I —" He reaches out to her shoulder but curls his fingers. Half standing, he surveys the interior of the pavilion, then drags his chair over to her side and hunkers down next to her.

"What? What are you doing?"

"It's OK." He backs off a few inches. "Go ahead and doze. I'm just blocking you from sight in case the little fascist assistant manager makes his rounds."

She sighs and re-closes her eyes. "Man, do you smell."

Kesi jolts awake, her eyes opening on a room empty of travelers.

"No, she's not ... Wait, yes ... yes, she is now taking notice of me."

Kesi turns into a field of vision dominated by a cantaloupe orange polo shirt struggling to contain the speaker's belly. His arms are propped at forty-five-degree angles, supported by melon-sized rolls of fat.

The man continues speaking to himself, his eyes expressionless.

"Sorry, did you ask me something?" Kesi's voice is sandy.

He grunts repeatedly. His spirited nods are setting off pudding-like quivers across his jowls.

Kesi checks the room behind her. Whit is nowhere in sight.

The visitor reaches up with both hands and presses bratwurst index fingers to ear buds. "Yes. Yes, she has initiated a conversation. Should I respond?" More pauses and nodding. "Yes. Right. OK."

Kesi stands. "Who are you?" She rounds the table away from him and pulls out the chair concealing her backpack. "Who are you talking to?"

The man's face comes to life. "Terry. I'm Terry. Sorry, don't you know V-o-G?"

"Who? No. V-o ... what?"

She grabs her backpack and turns toward the exit, almost colliding with Whit.

"V-o-G — Voice of God," says Whit. "He's talking to God."

The stranger, looking spooked, plods away, hissing into his phone.

Kesi looks up at the man who accompanies Whit, towering over him.

"Hey there, Kesi," Carlton says. "Let's get goin'."

ONE DAY AND TWENTY-THREE HOURS PRIOR

Roanoke, Virginia

"Kind of a shock," says Whit, his head in the refrigerator.

He comes away holding two brown bottles and begins yanking kitchen drawers at random.

"What?" says Kesi.

Whit finds an opener and heads for the couch, holding out a bottle for her.

"No, thanks. What's a shock?"

Kesi bounces with him as he drops onto the couch. He puts the bottles between his thighs and pops off both caps. She watches as he downs two-thirds of the first without a breath.

"Check it out." He swings the bottle in an arc describing the modest-sized space encompassing kitchenette, dining, and living room. "As expected, you've got your framed MEH-ga ..." belching, "Megadeath — excuse me — poster. You've got your disassembled Triumph engine on the dinner table.

"But the food in the fridge looks destined for a different palate. He's got Israeli couscous salad and swiss friggin' chard and goat yogurt. And celeriac ... I think, or maybe it's celery root ... or maybe those are the same thing."

"Not exactly a window into his soul."

"This ... " Whit polishes off the beer. " ... is a damn hoppy IPA microbrew. That says something about a man."

He holds up the second beer for her again. "You sure?"

"No thanks, I don't drink. Carlton is clearly not a predictable guy." She shifts her butt forward on the threadbare cushions and reclines farther.

"Are you Moslem?"

She ignores the question.

From the hallway to their left comes the sound of Carlton walking to and fro in one of the bedrooms. Even at that distance, his weight sends shimmies across the living room, rattling objects on the glass and chrome coffee table in front of them — a liter beer glass filled with change, a tire gauge, assorted bolts and cotter pins, a penlight-anchored keychain.

Whit whips his legs up under him and shifts sideways, leaning over her. "He's the first creep, right?" he whispers.

She drops her head back, closing her eyes. "Hmm?"

"You said that I was the second strange guy you'd run into today. Was he being creepy? Why'd you get in the car with him again?"

"I can take care of myself," she says.

"Good." He slouches into a position parallel to hers. "That makes one of us."

She yawns. "Aren't you tired?"

"Too wired. Wired-tired. The beers'll help."

Carlton's footsteps become more pronounced. The two lift their heads as he enters. He holds out a bath towel.

"Hope you don't mind," Whit says to him, holding up his beer.

"I told you help yourself to anything. Wouldn't of said that had I minded."

"Gotcha. You mean what you say. Takes a little getting used."

Kesi nods and lets her eyes close again.

Carlton snaps his fingers at Whit and holds the towel higher.

"Subtlety lost on you? There's whatever you need in the shower. You can't stay here smelling like you smell."

Whit takes another guzzle and plants the beer on the table before hopping over to accept the towel. He heads straight for the hall bathroom.

The seat cushion expels its air as Carlton eases his weight down into the black faux lizard-skin armchair across from Kesi. The silence is soon interrupted by a faint squealing of pipes and a set of thumps as the shower water sputters on.

A much louder thump signals the shower's conclusion. Kesi awakens and eases open an eye.

"Where you headed?" Carlton asks, still in his chair. "I haven't got 'round to asking you where you're headed?" He twirls an Allen wrench around his fingers like a magician's coin.

"Oh Christ." She sits up, yawning wide. "Look, Carlton, what's this all about?"

He narrows his eyes. "Meaning?"

"Why are you being so accommodating? You circle back around to the rest stop to get us — me — hours after you drop me off. You let us crash at your place. It's kind of unnatural."

He sniffs, continuing his finger motions.

"And don't give me that 'I have nothing particular to do' shit," she says.

"It ain't shit. It's true."

She waits him out.

"But, yeah, I was worried about you is all. I got this friend, Lucas. Lucas went through the rest area. Said 'some bald black chick' — which is his words — was out there hitchin'. Must've been a couple hours later, meanin' you weren't having no luck. I got worried for your safety's all, with night coming on."

"Touching. And you do this often? Rescue total strangers?"

"You ain't total." He scratches behind his ear. "No, it's the first time, if you gotta know. I'm doin' a lot of first-time stuff lately."

"Oh, like what else?"

He tosses the hex key onto the coffee table. "Like toleratin' ungracious questions from a person who's in my place, accepting my hospitality."

Kesi slumps forward until her chest hits her knees. With both hands, she rubs the stubble on the back of her head. Then she sucks in a breath and straightens.

"I don't see that happening anytime soon, Carlton, understanding each other. But thank you ... for letting me stay."

"I ain't lookin' for thanks. I would appreciate a' answer to my question about where you're headed, though."

She stares at him for a long moment.

"New York State."

"OK." He relaxes into his seat. "Whereabouts? And why don't you take a bus or somethin'? You're looking for trouble out on the road like that."

"I'm out of cash. I've been staying at collectives and the people there — we — live off what we can scrounge and grow, so ... well, my cash ran out a while back. I'm heading for a similar place that I heard about."

"Whereabouts?"

"Greenport. It's in the Hudson Valley."

He nods, tugging on his ear. "OK, I can take you. Your friend going there too?"

"Slow down — what?"

"Haven't been up that way and I like drivin'."

Kesi's mouth opens.

"Cool. I'm in."

They turn in unison. Whit, clad in a towel skirt, combs back his wet hair. "When are we leaving? Oh, just so you'll know, big guy, I worked the soap down to about the size of a toenail. I had to ditch it, at that point. I have this unnatural fear of soap when it gets that small — childhood thing. What?"

Kesi stands, covers her face with her hands, and growls.

"Jesus! What am I doing here? Did I say you could come? Did I say I wanted a ride? I've got to get some fucking sleep — some real sleep."

She shoulders her way past Whit, then turns back.

"Where can I fucking sleep?" she asks Carlton.

He points over her shoulder. "First door past the bathroom. Made up the bed in my daughter's room."

"Daughter? Seriously?"

"Yeah, for when she's visiting. And what is that s'posed to mean?"

She shakes her head and turns again for the bedroom.

"Daughter's are great, man," Whit says as he enters the room.

Carlton stands. "You got the couch. Keep it quiet. Clean up your empties."

Whit watches him walk to the end of the hall and close the master bedroom door behind him.

"Can I get a pillow?" he says, under his breath.

"Huhyuh... hungh... uhyah..."

Whit's cries from the living room are at the same time agitated and subdued, like those of a panicky, pillow-muffled dreamer.

Kesi lies still at first but pushes herself upright as the complaints grow more insistent.

Then a strange voice from the living room — a puzzling whine in a register octaves above Whit's. "Terryyy. Oh Lord. Terry!"

Carlton pounds past Kesi's room, footfalls spaced at a dead run.

Kesi stops at the entrance to the living room. Carlton is by the couch, struggling for a grip on the intruder, a slight man throwing himself from side to side in an effort to make his escape.

Whit, still prone on the couch, clutches at something covering his head and lashes out with his feet. His left heel hits home with a thud.

"Unggg .... mother fucker." Carlton releases the intruder and doubles over, hands to his groin.

The wiry intruder spins toward the door, taking the coffee table edge across his shins. Bolts, tools, and miscellany scatter as the table twirls into the back of Carlton's knees. The big man falls, flailing at the intruder on his way south.

Whit pries the drawstring loose and snatches the laundry bag from his head. He leaps to his feet onto the cushions just as Carlton and the intruder crash through the table glass, producing a sound horrific enough to spook Whit laterally from the couch. He comes down ass-first against Kesi's legs.

Kesi is thrown into a floor lamp, which follows them both down.

"Terry! I need you to get —" The intruder howls like a feline amid the body pounding and skittering glass. "Noooo, no, stop!"

Kesi pushes off against Whit and regains her feet.

Carlton too has risen. He lifts the stranger in a bear hug and rotates him to horizontal in preparation for a body slam.

"Carlton, no. Wait! You'll kill him." Kesi jumps onto Carlton's arm and puts all her weight into wrenching the man loose.

Carlton throws both arms back, sending Kesi rearward toward Whit and the wall.

The front door whips open. The invader, silhouetted by the night sky, lunges through, his footsteps hollow across the porch and down the wooden stairs. Hulked like a chimpanzee, he cups one hand over his ear. "Oh God oh God oh God. I need your guiding hand. Oh Terry, please! Abort Terry. Now."

"Damnit." Carlton takes chase out the door. "Come here you little som'bitch."

Whit, still on the floor, finds the switch on the lamp beside him.

Kesi, alit from below, stands in T-shirt and sleeping shorts, braced against the wall.

"You want to tell me what the hell just happened?" She stares at the doorway.

The slapping of Carlton's bare feet recedes down the front walk. A car door pounds shut, then a gravelly peel-out.

"Fuck. Mother fuck!" Carlton calls out from the roadside.

Kesi turns to Whit.

"Wow," he says.

"Wow? Does that mean something to white people?"

"No. I don't know."

She cocks her head. "OK, Whit, let me see if I can help." She points outside. "Some silly little loser just tried to kidnap you. You want to tell me why someone would want to do that?"

"Right. That could be."

"Oh, could it? You in hot water with the people around here?"

"No, they're not from here. They found me. They followed me — us — here."

"Are you serious? Who?"

"VoG. The VoG idiots. Voggers."

"Wait. You mean —" She watches Carlton reenter. "Oh shit, look at you."

Carlton's chest heaves. But for his briefs, he's naked and bleeding from any number of cuts on his elbows, knees, and feet. Small shards of glass protrude from some.

He wraps his hand around his scrotum and glares at Whit.

"Oh, damn. Sorry, man," says Whit. "You alright?"

"I'm sorry too, Carlton," Kesi says. "I couldn't see. I mean, I thought you were going to kill him or something."

"Yeah, pro'bly, or something," he says. "Fuckin' amateurs. Little turds had no damn idea what they were doing."

THREE WEEKS, TWO DAYS AND TWENTY-TWO HOURS AFTER

The Colony, Greenport, New York

Sam sits on the stool, head dipped at forty-five degrees, scratching away at his notebook with a hand-whittled No. 2, when the others enter the multi-purpose room. They find their lounging spots in silence, all except for Stefan, the last to arrive.

"Hey, my brother." The ka-chunks from Stefan's work boots return across the floor in off-beat echoes. He goes straight for Sam and puts an arm around his shoulder. "Wow, look at how busy you have been writing. Looks like this has become serious business for you."

Sam nods a number of times, finishing a sentence before looking up. "I figured out how to work in Andre's story. It's about the future. It's about what happens here in the future." He turns his pages back to the start.

Stefan lifts his eyebrows. "The Colony, here? Cool, cool. And perhaps foreboding, no?"

Stefan heads for an open area in front beside Portia. "I am going to sit here beside my beautiful Venus of love because I know she will comfort me if Sam's story it becomes too frightening."

Portia smiles and pats the rug beside her.

Claudia, Whit, and Kesi sit behind, spaced apart adequately to avoid the possibility of contact.

Claudia scoots over a few feet to get a clear view around Stefan's unruly hair. "So you're comfortable with this, sweetie?"

Sam looks at her as he slides the pencil into the wire spiral of his notebook. "I'm doing it, Mom. You want me to be comfortable too?"

"No. OK."

Sam pulls his hair back behind his ears. "This is going to be long, I think. So I have just the first chapter, anyway."

Sam's Story

Anybody driving by might question the wisdom of me looking for rides along what's left of this highway. But the thing is, the rare person with the wherewithal to have something in drivable condition is generally out here looking for Tellers, and with me being a Teller looking for a ride, there's some logic to it. After a day, a night, and most of another day, I'm still trying to convince myself of that, anyway, when I hear a truck.

With the road surface being roughly equal parts pavement and pothole, it's about all the driver can do to find a path to ride on let alone spare an eye for what's by the roadside, but then watchfulness isn't exactly an optional personality trait these days.

As it nears, I make out a four-by-four that's been rebuilt so many times out of mismatched parts it looks like some kind of underworld junkyard beast. It's black, mostly, and loud — huge tires. What's chugging out of the pipes is mostly black too, indicating a probable fuel mix of used fryer oil, lard, and a possible drop or two of kerosene. The driver is white, mostly.

"Seen you before," he says when he pulls up alongside.

"Yeah," I say back to him, "I seen you. I guess it was reciprocal.

Your name's Carlton."

"Yup," he says. "I know."

Carlton's got brutal written all over him, from the barbed wire tats to the ritual facial scarring. His one eye's straining wider than normal to compensate for the one that's been beaten into droopiness. He's got arms the size of legs and, as I recall, legs about as big as me.

I climb in without formalities since having a Teller on board is the only reason he'd of stopped. I go for the back seat because shotgun is occupied.

She's got her feet up on the dash, his partner, arms crossed, all business as usual. She's lean and probably about chest high on Carlton, but by the air about her, she's tough enough to keep him in his place, not that she's beastly like him, far from it.

"Hey," I say. She doesn't budge.

Carlton asks once we're rolling what better story I've got than Revenge of Sabertooth Sasha, the one I told last time he'd been present.

I ask him what problem he's got with it.

"I'll take that as a no," he says, just as he passes the southbound exit for Poughkeepsie.

"What are you doing, man?" I say. "It's a good fifteen miles 'till the next turn around exit and we've only got a couple few hours to get to the Colony."

"You never been there, have you?" says Carlton, to which I admit no.

"Well, if you had, you'd know it'd be a waste going tonight, the waste being of my time and effort and fuel and entry token, being you ain't close to being Colony material."

His partner turns now enough for me to see a fairly sweet face, I have to say, though it wouldn't be obvious to just anyone given the general derisiveness coloring her looks and hair like a raven shredded in an updraft. She's backhanding Carlton in the right pec to get his attention on a figure up ahead. Without a pause, he veers back into the left lane.

The subject of their interest is a good ways off but is doing his utmost to be noticed. He's shadowed against the dirt-pink sky atop the Jersey barrier in all his wind-blown, dreadlocked extravagance, legs planted wide like he owns what's left of the interstate and eyes upward instead of looking for danger, which as a party pulling up on that road, we just might be. His palms are raised upward too, like checking for rain, or maybe asking for it.

Carlton lets up and drifts to a stop a bit shy of him.

"The System has collapsed, my friends. Can you see the glory?" The guy looks our way now and bellows like a champion. "Civilization has ended!"

I'm not thinking about a response, being that the whole effect is serving as a sort of coherent-thought retardant. Glory Man's arms are still raised and his gray-hairy chest is puffed like a rooster. He's got his shirt tied around his waist. There's no sign of shoes and, considering the look of his feet, they've been lacking for some time. He's got bluish military pants on, his empty cargo pockets filling up in the breeze like windsocks.

Carlton's eyes are locked on the guy. He cracks his neck, snorts long and noisy, and sends one gobbing end-over-end out his window. "Civilization dead. Who'd a thought?" he says, mostly to himself. "Thanks for clearing that up. I was wondering what become of my dry cleaning."

The old man nods at Carlton with a commiserating kind of smile. He takes his time getting down off the barrier and putting his shirt on. He minds his step on the road rubble between him and us, though not grimacing like I'd be doing were my feet in that condition.

Carlton, I notice, checks with his co-pilot for an opinion, but nothing's forthcoming, so he asks the old man straight out if he's a Teller.

The old dude throws his hands up high and brings them down on the truck roof — *batta batta bat* — like an introductory drum roll.

"Oh, yes, brothers and sister, I can tell. I can tell of a world that our good Mom Earth has in mind for us. For there is a mind present in the world, my friends, and we are part of that earth-mindfulness. Now that we're liberated from the System, we have only to open ourselves to the mindfulness and we will all join in the great clearing and rebuilding. The System fed on our living information, you see, on our dreams and our intimacies. It suckled at our essences, draining us of our human-soul-nourishment. It left us dry and faint and racked with craving, not for nourishment, but for soul poisoning addictives. But mindfulness, yes, that is the manna that falls now from these spoiled heavens. We need only gather it up. What do you say? Will you gather with me?"

We're all a-goggle, that is, Carlton and me, as his co-pilot, from what I've been noticing, isn't the fazable type.

"OK, we're gonna go with yes," says Carlton, which I'm taking as him thinking he's got the Teller he's after, not an affirmative to the manna gathering, mindfulness, rebuilding, and so forth.

"What'll we call you?" says Carlton.

The old man straightens and turns to the sun, a disdainful smear a couple hands above the horizon. "My given name is Lawrence, but it's been Andre for a good number of years. Lately, I have taken the name, Olorun. It means Sky Father."

Carlton shakes his head. "Nah, can't see any of that working with the gristle-for-brains at the Colony. How about Oracle?"

I point out there's like a good dozen Oracles out there or Dark Oracles or Reckoning Day Oracles or variations thereof.

"Yeah, damnit. What is it you go by, kid?"

"Satyricon."

"Right. What's that mean, anyway?"

"No idea," I say.

Carlton mulls it over a while.

"Fuck it. Let's go with Father Andre for now. Maybe something'll come to me."

Carlton's associate administers to Father Andre's feet with some non-potable and manages to locate a pair of ragged sneaks in the cargo area. Carlton meanwhile engages the guy in what you might call a conversation if either was responding to what the other was saying. Suffice to say, Carlton agrees to whatever it takes to get Andre into the back seat, including promises to gather, rekindle, be mindful, eliminate bio-hygienically, and whatnot.

I slide over for Father Andre. Carlton peels out and gets the truck moving at a good clip. At the first opportunity, he swings a wide U-ey across a stretch of median covered with a long-ago dried up mudslide.

Father Andre is out cold and snoring like a rusted bilge pump before I can offer him a drink of half-turned cider, which is all I got. The man smells of woody sweat and something medicinal, and I see he's got a hunk of tawny bar soap jammed into the breast pocket of his shirt. Even saggy with sleep, his face is deeply lined, and every crease looks insistent, like he willed it into place to make a point.

His hands too look purposeful. But something's odd — odd enough to give me willies, and I'm no stranger to odd. Father Andre's left hand is callused, popping with gnarled veins and criss-crossed with a thousand wrinkles, as you'd expect with his age and all the scavenging. He's got white scars across his swollen knuckles, and one half-gone nail and another split. But the right hand ... well, it's youthful. The palm is smooth and pink with health. The fingers are plump and mocha-colored like they've been babied under soft leather and sunflower oil. Father Andre's got the hand of a boy, though it's the size of his other.

I want to ask Carlton about the curiosity but think better of digging up something that might be better left un-dug. I'm not getting the ride I planned, but there's at least a skinny promise of something, which is a heck of a lot more than I had just previous.

Carlton's companion, I see, is getting a little shut-eye too.

I lean forward. "So, can she talk or what?"

Carlton snuffs. "Trini? Can't. Won't. Whatever... she don't."

"How come?"

"Why don't you ask her?"

"I guess she must've gone through something traumatic or something, huh?"

"Ha. Yeah, might say that. She did get fairly traumatic that one time when they was cuttin' her tongue out."

I lean more forward to check his expression. I'm not seeing anything but serious.

"Mother," I say. "What the hell'd she do to deserve that?"

"Didn't tell a good 'nough story at the Colony."

I tell Carlton he's full of shit, but he just clucks his tongue. I tell him he's not scaring me and I'm still going.

"You really think you got a Teller in Father Andre here?" I say. "Sure, he's got the sonorousness for it, and with all his wing-nut preaching he might keep them awake, but without a story, it'll end quick and distasteful. He's got no telling experience like me. You bring me along and I'll back him up when he falters, which he will. And I'll only take an eighth share of the winnings, assuming there is any, which there might be if you'd just go with me instead of him, but whatever."

Carlton sits me out as I go on about stuff he's already no doubt contemplated.

"Look, Scout," he says finally, "here's how it's gonna go. I'm damn hungry. Trini's hungry. We got a couple hours to smack some sane into Father Andre, if that's what it takes, and make sure he's got a story to tell. Tonight's the two-month gathering at the Colony and I ain't missing the opportunity. Man Ray Carney said he's bringing two new Tellers, but if they's the hack road kill he gen'rally scrapes up, Father Andre's got an outside chance of taking 'em. You leave the experience part to me and keep your mouth shut and maybe you'll get a full stomach and maybe you'll get primed for Three Rivers or maybe Muck Bottom next month."

I give him lip about how neither Muck Bottom nor Three Rivers is worth the entry token, but I can see the only voice he's hearing is grumbling up from his stomach.

"Yeah, we'll eat good tonight with some luck, Scout. Drink too. Damn, I'm hungry."

I settle back, satisfied at least that Carlton's "we" now includes me and, though I'm about a day beyond feeling pangs, find my mind is afloat amongst images of what food might get awarded at the Colony where it's said they have 'baga root fields growing and plum trees and hens and even some goats, raising the possibility of milk and cheese and other clotted by-products, tangy and toothsome.

I might have nodded off because next thing I hear, Carlton and Father Andre are going at it.

"They ain't comin' to hear no sermon, Father. You hear me?"

"Sermon? You take me for a religious man?"

"Might be tough avoiding that impression, what with your manna from on high and benedictions and such. And that's all well and good, as far as it goes, meaning as long as it goes toward getting us through a story."

Father Andre puts a grip on my leg, addressing me and Trini along with Carlton. "Religion has no part in this, friends. The truth is our only story at a time like this. We have a new start — an opportunity now to be truly human, free of the System again."

Trini is all slouched down sideways against her door. At the re-mentioning of the System, she runs her fingertips across her throat.

"We were a world caught up in pointless, repetitive fictions," the old man goes on. "The System sensed our need. It took control, friends, because we were willing to cede it as long as the stories kept coming. And in our neediness, our souls were laid exposed for the taking."

Carlton's jaw is aclench. "And another thing, old man. The Colony crowd ain't got patience for this System shit of yours and what it perpetrated upon us nor even how it brung itself down. Past is past. Netways is gone."

"Networks," I say.

"Whatever." He looks at me. "We got a geek on board?"

"No," I say, "but they were networks is all."

"Any case, all the digital whatnot is gone, as is all the geeks what made 'em. And with 'em went the power, water, and wherewithal to keep the world in some semblance of livability. As I look at it, when you got a world ruled by geeks that's got too complicated for even the geeks to comprehend, it's an epic cluster-fuck waiting to happen, which is exactly what did happen, thereby once and forever sending everything down into this present sinkhole of total, irreversible use-lessness.

"Only sweetness in it was watching that mother of a netways crash suck most of them pathetic, keyboard-poking mothers down with it — all testament to how damn useless and self-impressed with their own significance they were."

"Not to mention what those bio-coders did," I say.

"Yeah, and that," says Carlton. "And what I'm tellin' ya, old man, is that people for damn certain didn't want truth back then. They didn't want to understand how things worked. They just wanted their stories which, despite losing the God almighty digital stream, is all they want now, meaning not the truth but the cowardly avoidance thereof.

"You got visions of future glory and easier days and Momma Earth, you go with that. And if you can muster up sunshine-farting heroes streaking down from the heavens to set things right, so much the better. Dig deep, old man. Come up with an engagin' shit storm of a story or you'll be deep in with your precious Mom Earth from a six feet under perspective before this time next week."

Andre raises a fist above his head — the old, battered one — but lowers it with a slow grumble. He goes sulky-like for the next hour, but I can see he's giving Carlton's lecture consideration. He's a man of principle, that's plain to see, but he's hungry like us. Principles might make you a better man, but hunger puts you in the same soot-spewing vehicle as the rest of us shameless hacks, lurching northward along a busted-up excuse for a highway toward a plateful of edible promise ... you know, so to speak.

Sam lays the story on his lap. He rubs at the impressions left on his palm from the notebook's wire spiral.

"That's it," he says. "At least, that's all I've got so far. I guess I'll go again when I have some more."

The sun is down and the room has dropped off to near darkness beyond the circle of candle glow that surrounds him. A buffeting sound fills the silence as the blow from the two oscillating fans intersect in their rotations.

"That's assuming it's worth going on," Sam says. "I'm not at all sure what the hell I'm doing or what for. You guys awake?"

"Yeah," says Whit. "Listen hard and you can hear the collective 'hmmmm'."

Sam stretches his T-shirt sleeve up and wipes the sweat off his lip that is more the effect of the mugginess than nerves. The overhead fluorescents buzz on.

He squints at Kesi, hunched forward over her crossed legs, picking at the calluses on her hand.

Portia, sitting board straight, seems twice Kesi's size. She beams a smile that forces Sam to avert his look toward Stefan, who has started out to the hall for the twins.

Whit slaps barefoot back to the group from the far corner of the room where the light switch is located. He has his fingers wrapped around the back of his head, elbows up. His T-shirt reads, IT'S NOT A BUG, IT'S A FEATURE. He arches his neck, revealing a pink scar ring and some faded bruising. He passes Stefan, who fakes a gut punch, getting Whit's elbows down fast.

"Oh my goodness, Sammy," says Portia in her little girl gospel voice. She fans herself with a flattened cereal box, her smile uninterrupted.

Introducing themselves with a burst of machine-gun giggles, the twins appear at full run across the open floor. Augustina is in front. She stops just before the group, makes a dramatic little hop onto the carpets, and falls into a somersault, flopping over against Squeej, stretched out on his side. Squeej springs up to his knees and delivers a punishment tickle to her exposed potbelly. Arthur, close behind, leaps onto Squeej piggyback, hugging his rangy neck.

"Oh my goodness," Portia says again. She looks over her shoulder to Claudia. "What do you think of this boy of yours?"

Claudia has a questionable smile going. The heat-flush on her cheeks has subsumed most of her freckles. "It was fine."

Portia pulls her chin back. "Oh, come now. It was wonderful."

"Fine's as good as it gets from her," says Sam.

"Well, I think it's a hell of a thing you got started there, man," says Whit. He drops rearward into Stefan's vacated space on the carpet, aiming his head for Portia's accommodating lap.

"But what?" says Sam.

"But, well, you're clearly messing with us. I guess it's the meta-ness. Here we are only three nights into it and you've already leapfrogged the storytelling into post-ironical ... ness."

"I think it's the way you worked Andre and everyone into the story, sweetie," says Claudia. "And yourself, I assume you're narrating. One might find it disconcerting."

Sam shrugs. "I guess disconcerting 'one' person isn't so bad."

"I find it impressive, man," says Whit, "in that it shows your capacity to project, although you've managed to project yourself into a world of apocalyptic shit."

Whit looks up at the ceiling because the fat, first drops of a summer shower are popping against the chicken wire glass skylights. "You're asking yourself, WWAD, assuming the world is heading for shitsville."

Sam shakes his head.

"What Would Andre Do?" says Whit, still examining the ceiling. Everyone except Portia, in fact, looks anywhere but at Sam.

"This is hard, doing this," Sam says. "In a way it came easy, but ... I don't know — it's hard."

Portia is nodding and fanning.

"I think it's dope, bruh," says Squeej, struggling to talk with Arthur tugging at his ears. "You and Andre and Carlton in the future. I'd pay to see that, shit. I'd, like, like to be with my homies there, just ripping 'round in that raucous truck along with you."

"Yeah, I don't know," says Sam.

Squeej rolls the twins back and lays himself out spread eagle, nose to the carpet. The toddlers attempt the route from Squeej's calf to opposite forearm without toppling, squealing at each of the cook's groans. The group watches, except Kesi, still digging at her palm.

"And Trini?" Kesi says in a whisper, drawing all eyes. "Is there a reason no one's commented on a certain character named Trini in your story?"

She looks up at Sam. "Andre would say to 'build the collective narrative.' Is that what you're doing?" she says.

"Andre'd say, 'Build the collective narrative to connect with the trauma,'" says Sam. "I know. I'm trying not to think too much, to be honest."

The wind is up and the rain is coming down hard, splattering against the panes and onto the floor through the open windows.

Kesi looks at Claudia.

"We can mop it up later if there is a lot," says Claudia.

Stefan yawns and burrows through his beard fluff for a scratch. "Sorry, Sam, I'm rilly beat. Hard day, and this rain it sounds like is going to wash out the damn chard seedlings I just plant, so will be like very long day tomorrow too, as well."

He scoops up his twins, an arm around each waist. They dangle, heads down, as if on playground swings. Augustina squeals and runs in space. Arthur twirls clockwise in an attempt to grab the elastic waistband on her PJs.

"Enough now, little monkeys. Is time for bed." He takes them off toward the hallway.

"But my goodness," says Portia. "I love your story, Sammy, and I hope we do go on to chapter two."

Whit reaches back and tickles her big toe. "But Portia, dear, if he continues on, Father Andre will tell his story within the story and we'll be into sub-meta, which has been known to cause the mind to fold in on itself."

Portia laughs and slaps at his finger.

"But Sammy Boy," he goes on, "you go for it. And yes, I'm hereby granting you limited use rights to my character, in case you've got plans for me in your story. And I know Kesi would like to take part as well for the chance at some hang time with Carlton again."

Kesi stretches over to Whit, hand raised, triggering a full body cringe. She sits back and waits for him to relax his knees down from his chest before diving back to slap her palm down on his gut.

ONE DAY AND FIFTEEN HOURS PRIOR

I-81 Northbound, Near Buchanan, Virginia

Carlton leans toward the wheel and eases his T-shirt away from his back, popping it free of his wounds.

"We should pull off and find someone to stitch those up," says Kesi, watching him settle back against the seat. "They'll just keep opening up."

"I clot fast," he says. He checks Whit in the rearview.

Whit thumbs through web pages on a smartphone, slumped too low in the back seat to appreciate the Shenandoah Valley views off the east side of the interstate. His window is presently about three-fifths of the way down, sucking in enough of the morning humidity to negate the effects of the air conditioning. Since occupying the seat, he has tested window positions from whistling-sliver to full-blast and about a half-dozen in between. He reaches again for the window toggle.

"Hey, Opie, let's leave that be," Carlton says, "and I said go easy on my damn phone battery too 'cause I forgot the car charger. You ready to get into this?"

Kesi turns to the back and raises an eyebrow. "Yeah, how about it, Whit? You have sufficient time to concoct some elaborate bullshit for us?"

Whit rouses with a sharp breath. "Sorry? Oh ... no, I'm not going to shit you." He sits upright. "Hey Kesi, this place you're taking us in

New York, I'm seeing mentions from a bunch of folks about a place up there which —"

"Let's get something straight in case it wasn't clear the first two times," says Kesi. "I'm not taking you there — either of you. I don't exactly have an invitation myself. You want to drop me off? Fine. I'm at a loss for how to get there otherwise since that little incident last night convinced me thumbing around here is now a lousy damn idea."

"Which brings us back 'round to it, Opie," Carlton says, "being what the hell was that about?" He checks the blind spot over his left shoulder before switching lanes to pass a Ryder step van.

Kesi looks past Whit out the back window. "Carlton, what's with these guys in the Jeep?"

"What Jeep?"

"The tan Jeep, or what the hell ... bronze Jeep behind us. They just followed us into the passing lane."

"That's a Toyota Land Cruiser. Ain't a Jeep."

"Whatever, Carlton, I call them all Jeeps."

"If you're asking if them's the little turds from last night, then no. They're in a Lexus GS — silver."

Kesi looks at Carlton. "That's a pricy car, isn't it?"

"A good fifty K. Struck me odd as well for such little, incompetent shits. What you say, Opie? That seem odd as well to you?"

"Not so much." He rubs his throat, still engaged in the phone. "Kesi — it's the Colony. They call it the Colony, am I right?"

She closes her eyes and leans her head back against the rest.

"There's an old guy who founded the place," says Whit. "The Colony comes up in search results for stuff like 'self-sufficient-eco-city-as-alternate-natural-bio-energy-organism'. Actually I think it's a hyphenation movement, is what it is."

"Some sorta cult?" says Carlton.

"No, a cult would never hyphenate. Cults are singularly ridiculous.

This is more like stitched-together philosophy. Philosophies tend toward horizontal thinking. Cults are totally and perversely vertical, singular obsessions — categorically and dogmatically vertical. Cats and dogs, you might say, shorthand-wise."

Whit picks up the phone again. "The thing about this old guy, though, there seems to be some confusion about his name. Some are calling him —"

"Whit, Jesus, focus," says Kesi. "Who are the kidnappers?"

"Right." He adjusts the window again. "Well you know, that whole business you witnessed was really kind of stupid — cult-style stupid, as it happens. It's an embarrassing, complicated tale of woe is what it is, but it's my woe and no point in troubling you guys and I'm sorry about last night but it's really not worth your time to —"

"Woe or whatnot, we ain't stupid and we got time," says Carlton. "It's a good eight hours to Greenport. But make it simple, Opie, 'cause I'm already out of patience."

Whit rubs his window-side ear. "Well, OK. It's a mess. I'd much rather wait until I'm clear of it and can explain how lame it all was, but anyway —" He takes a second to roll up his window.

"Wow, did I tell you about the dream I was having when that Vogger woke me up last night?" He sits forward. "I'm a kid back home ... or sort of ... like, vaguely home-esque, and ... hey, did you guys have a laundry chute when you were growing up?"

"Swear t'God, man," says Carlton.

"No, seriously, so I'm in the chute but it's not going well. I'm stuck."

"You want to pull over?" Kesi says to Carlton. "Maybe you can beat it out of him."

"And the towels reach up for me and wrap around my neck and then, like some kind of crazy-plushy animal snake, one jumps down my throat and I'm screaming but nothing's, you know, emitting."

"We get it," says Kesi. "It was a very bad dream. And then you woke up with a laundry bag on your head."

"Right, but I mean, the mind's amazing, picking up on the laundry reference and fashioning a whole story in a split second. Must have been the smell of the bag. So I take it neither of you knows much about VoG."

"Nothin's exactly what I know about it," says Carlton.

"I know it means Voice of God and seems to appeal to pathetic losers," Kesi says.

"Correct," says Whit. "That's about the size of it." He turns his eyes to the scenery and reaches for the window button.

"Hutt!" Carlton narrows his eyes. "You're gonna lose that digit, dammit."

"Sorry." He turns back. "Where to start? OK, VoG is sort of like GPS. Ever use GPS, Carlton?"

"Got one. It's in the glove compartment. Couldn't stand the sound of 'er voice."

"Sounds about right for you. Most people, though, generally like GPS because they're in constant need of direction. They're lost, in other words. The Voice of God app is designed for folks who are lost in a spiritual sense. VoG is like GPS for the soul. The big difference, though, is that unlike GPS, VoG guidance has no connection to reality."

"So it doesn't work?" says Kesi.

"Oh, no, it works alright. It's just not based on science. It's based on religion. In other words, it's pure crap."

"Hey, you wanna watch that?" Carlton shoots him a look.

"Ahh, I didn't realize we were in the presence of a believer."

"Just need to have some respect's all."

"I don't, but it's on my to-do list."

"Cut the shit," says Kesi. "You're saying VoG is some kind of website that gives you directions?"

"Antoine ... Antoine was one of them."

"What?" Kesi turns to him.

"Antoine, but some other bloggers are calling him something else French like that." He thumbs the phone again. "And he's African American."

"They ain't French," says Carlton. "Them little turds weren't French and weren't Black neither."

"Christ," says Kesi. "Whit — the directions. How do they get the spiritual directions?"

"Oh, you know, it's a phone app. It helps you make decisions. You talk to it — to God. You ask God a question. You express your uncertainty, your yearning, your need for, you know, whatever you're needing. God points you in the right decision. It's the Voice of God giving you guidance."

"Sweet lord." Carlton shifts in his seat, wincing. "Who'd be fool enough to make such a blasphemous damn thing?"

Whit lowers his head and raises a hand.

"Shit," says Kesi.

"Shit," says Carlton. "So those wing nuts last night —?"

"Yup, God-fearing Christians seeking out my profane, damnable ass. And it's an old aerosol can factory or something, right, Kesi?"

"What?"

"The Colony — it's an old factory complex that they're squatting in, Antoine and the back-to-earthers."

"They're not squatters. They bought the place. They formed a co-op and bought it. So these people, are they looking to string you up?"

"What?"

"The little turds."

"No ... maybe, but more likely they want to — and Carlton, man, I'm not trying to dis you now — they want to kind of, you might say, follow me. I'm not talking like Twitter. I mean like a disciple."

Carlton's foot grazes the brake. "Just what're you sayin'?"

"Yeah, a goodly number of these fanatics — sorry, I mean to say these believers are convinced VoG is truly what it claims to be. And that sort of makes me the Deliverer of the Word, so to speak — AKA the Right Hand of God."

"Son of a bitch," said Kesi. "So it really works, I mean, well enough to fool people?"

"Absolutely. I know it's hard to comprehend, but I'm pretty clever when it comes to these things."

"Yeah, well your as'nine. What would inspire you to do something so as'nine?"

"A joke — a farce. People download the app, get a good laugh and I get publicity. It was the logic loop I was trying to promote. I figured it would help me get backing for my next project. Unfortunately, people didn't exactly get the joke."

"Count me in on that," says Carlton.

"What's the loop thing?" says Kesi.

"The logic loop? It's the way the VoG questioning works. OK, so some wayward soul reaches a tough decision point and resorts to prayer. 'Please God, I just don't know which way to turn.'"

"This is horse shit," says Carlton. "Just because a person's religious don't mean they're crazy like that to think they're gonna hear from God."

"Most of them, you're right, realize God won't actually speak to them, but they may ask Him for a sign, right? Or they'll ask for the wisdom to see the light or the strength to carry on, that sort of thing."

"Yeah, well those is just what Kesi here'd call figures of speech. They ain't meaningful."

"True, but prayer has a strange psychology to it. They put their faith in something that on some level they know won't result in anything and somehow feel like they've accomplished something. It's remarkable."

Carlton taps the steering wheel.

"Hey, whatever works for people," says Kesi.

"I can see that it does work, yes. And is that because God provides answers? Of course not. But over the centuries, the clergy have gotten truly skilled at making it seem that way. They've perfected the art of pulling these lost souls into an absurd kind of logic loop. It goes something like this:

"Layperson says: 'I don't know which way to turn, Father.'

"Priest: 'Let your conscience be your guide, for God guides your conscience.'

"Layperson: 'But that's the problem. I feel that either way, I'll be screwed. Or, I should say, I'll be hurting someone either way.'

"Priest: 'And yet by not acting, will you be causing more harm?'

"Layperson: 'Well, yes.'

"Priest: 'Then you must choose and have faith that God is guiding your actions.'

"Layperson: 'So whichever decision I make will be the right decision because God is behind my decisions?'

"Priest: 'Yes, if you've truly put your faith in the Lord.'"

Carlton huffs. "You got a damn lowly opinion of somethin' you obviously ain't been raised right to appreciate."

"Now that's not true," says Whit, "I think the logic loop is a thing of beauty."

"So this prayer logic loop is in your program," says Kesi.

"Yes, ask VoG pretty much any question and it ultimately leads you into the loop and toward a resolution. You wind up feeling like God's got your back ... that is, as long as your faith is intact."

Kesi sighs. "I'm still having trouble understanding how people could get sucked into believing in an app."

"You and me both, but like I said, I'm good."

"Give me an example. What does the app tell them?"

Whit rubs his nose. "OK, it's cold and rainy. You fire up the app and ask your question. 'The roads are slick. Is it really worth the danger to go out to visit poor, ailing Aunt Mindy tonight?'

"VoG says, 'Has this question bothered you for long?'

"You say, 'No. Well, I mean, I do make excuses not to see Aunt Mindy.'

"VoG: 'Of course. Then you must weigh this matter carefully.'

"You: 'I mean I could actually get hurt, right? Aunt Mindy wouldn't want that.'

"VoG: 'Is that what is of most concern to you?'

"You: 'No, I suppose I'm worried about Aunt Mindy more than I'm worried about me. But if I bang up the car, my wife's gonna be so upset.'

"VoG: 'Remember that God guides your conscience.'

"You: 'I do remember. And I think I feel guiltier about not seeing Aunt Mindy.'

"VoG: 'Faith brings freedom from care.'

"You: 'Yes, maybe it does.'"

"That's pretty messed up." Kesi turns forward again and lays her head back.

"It's not my fault that religious people are so gullible. It's like they're just hanging out, waiting for the next Lazarus miracle."

"Hey, again," says Carlton, "people like you lookin' down your noses who most likely never even read the Bible. I bet you never even read it for all your professing. I bet you don't even know what book Lazarus was resurrected in."

"Sure I do. It's from the Gospels."

"Which one?"

"Luke."

"Wrong. John."

"Yeah, but note how confident I sounded when I said it."

"You know, it's sarcastic jerks like you gets people around them hurt. Ain't hurting me, mind you, 'cause I can spot you coming, but innocents. They count on you for something serious and they wind up getting hurt."

"Andre!"

"What?"

"The old Colony guy — it's not Antoine. His name is Andre."

THREE WEEKS, THREE DAYS AND TWENTY-TWO HOURS AFTER

The Colony, Greenport, New York

Sunset is happening and the room has gone rosy. Sam holds fidgety little Augustina up under her armpits so she can light the candles on the folding table. Portia sits on the stool next to them, waiting.

Augie finishes and makes a big show of blowing out the pocket lighter. She sucks in another lungful and goes after the three candle flames. Sam tosses her up a foot, all squirmy with giggles, and catches her around her tummy. Augie squeezes free and runs out to the play area.

Sam goes back to the carpet and sits with the others, rubbing at the sticky remains of Augie's cashew butter and banana snack on his cheek.

Portia is ready to start. She somehow radiates a smile without smiling, aided by the warm candlelight on her honey-brown moon of a face.

Portia's Story

You all may know that I hail from Detroit where my momma raised me alone, although my older brother Reggie was a help to her, but

Reggie was born with a hole in his heart and we didn't know about it and he passed when he was just fifteen, which you might think is awfully unfair, but it wasn't so much if you'd known Reggie and how full he made his time with us. That was my poor brother, Reggie.

I got big fast — full-grown by twelve — though not as filled out as now. My voice, it stayed nine. My momma would say, "Portia, there's nothing but thanks to give God for having a voice of an angel. It will draw love to you." And she was right because a beautiful love found me there in Detroit at seventeen and that was my Jameel. He was twenty-three and I was only nineteen when we were married but it might have lasted forever, that's how much we were the right ones for each other.

Jameel, when we were married, already had a pretty good job driving forklift and would deejay at clubs and for weddings and sweet-sixteens. He took to music like he was born without a choice in the matter. In the clubs there in Detroit, it was all House music and Techno they wanted to dance to, and Jameel played it, but otherwise you would hear him singing Al Green and Teddy and Marvin, and I'd just sigh and hum along with him because his smile was so sweet and his voice fine enough to stand up to it. "You're all, you're all I neeeeed to get by."

I was good in school and I liked it well enough, so I went to Wayne County Community to learn dental hygiene, and I might have stuck with that but then Jameel heard about an opening in Lansing at the GM metal stamping plant, so we moved out there. I was doing temp work when his cousin, Darnell — he's the one got Jameel into the plant and was a real live one, that Darnell, able to talk the paint off a post, my momma would say — Darnell told me they were hiring clerical for operations and, to my surprise, I got a job with benefits and we were so happy with ourselves.

In just two years, I got moved up to coordinator. We were doing fine. We had a nice apartment and Jameel set up a sound system even before we got a TV, which wasn't for the first year at least. I missed my family, but Detroit was just an hour and a half and we had an extra bedroom so my mother came and stayed sometimes, which didn't bother Jameel all that much. He could get along with anybody.

Jameel was so proud of his LeSabre, all sparkling metal-blue. He worked on that baby out in the apartment parking lot. I'd bring lunch out and sit on the grass and we'd have the apartment window open with the music going. We could do that most warm weekends and be happy. We drove to work together each morning and he'd use his car cover on the LeSabre in the plant lot, no matter the jokes he'd get from Darnell and the others. We had lots of time together. It was fine, and we were even saving for a house.

But then came 2005. Management put out a memo about plant closings and sure enough ours was on the list. Just like that, all of us were standing there in the cafeteria hearing this from some vice president.

Jameel got laid off in the first round in May 2006, and they kept me on eight months longer and then that was it for me too. I should have just taken my severance when Jameel got laid off because, with me needing the car for work, Jameel couldn't get around as easy for interviews or day work. And things got worse with him than I knew. He made out he was fine when I'd get home, but he wasn't.

He talked about taking our savings and going in with Darnell to start a proper deejay business. They'd need a van and more equipment and Darnell with his talking could get the jobs, but he put it off. Other men would not have thought twice about gambling with our savings, but that's not the way Jameel was. He worried all the time and always put me first in his thoughts.

So by the time I was let go, I was one of the last and there was nothing left in Lansing as far as work. And we even talked about taking the leap and buying that van but then, such as things happen, my momma had a stroke, which put her out of work too. With the hospital bills, that was the end of our money, and that hit Jameel hard.

When Momma got out of the hospital, we moved in with her back in Detroit. Then we had to sell the LeSabre and one thing led to another with Momma's health ... on and on ... and then she passed, not more than four months later.

And then Jameel —

Oh no, it's OK. It's just I haven't said it out loud since I had to tell Darnell that Jameel took his own life.

That was it, you see. That's what took all the strength out of me. All so quick, things slipped away without me having the will to hold on. And so homeless, homeless, homeless, that's what it all came to there in my proud, sad city of Detroit — I was out on the street.

I did have family but I suppose, like Jameel, it just got too dark around me and I couldn't face them. There were a few awful nights, which I can't go into, but then, thank God, I had the luck to fall in with some good squatters, and I have to tell you it was just easier there with people who understood the shame of it. Do you understand what I mean? Well, of course you do.

The squatter house was off of Schoolcraft out near Highland Park. It was a perfectly regular street lined with ranches, one after another. People had made them their own with different siding or maybe a walk that curved or a wishing well, which is what was in front of ours. A lot of the lawns had gone to weeds and a lot of windows were boarded up, but still you could stand out on the sidewalk and picture couples coming home at night to their kids, them watching TV and giving their momma backtalk while she threw together dinner. They just walked away like there was a great plague, leaving their homes there still perfectly fine.

We were front-door squatters, meaning it didn't seem like we needed to hide, the neighbors on the one side being squatters themselves. In our house, there were five bedrooms because of the second story added on and one in the basement, and my housemates said when they got there, everything was spotless and left with pride.

And so there was a wonderful man there named Gordon Arneau. He'd worked most his life in the city engineer's office, but always meant to be an architect. He had the whitest hair and fine, delicate hands. Gordon was the one actually told me about this place here, but that was later.

When I arrived, all around the house there were drawings Gordon had done. They were just pencil on white butcher's paper, but his lines were so very thin and exact. Usually there were three or four together, with a floor plan of a building and a drawing of the outside and the insides of the rooms, looking so perfect you couldn't believe the beauty and care that was possible with just a pencil.

So I asked this girl Kaley, who was just a fragile thing — it was her asthma and the house sometimes got damp without proper heat — I said, "What are these buildings?" because there were all different types, some being regular row homes and some as roomy as concert halls or tall as water towers. And there were buildings that I couldn't even begin to describe, one floating in the air and one twisting like a sewer underground, as confusing as a maze. I said, "Are these places that Gordon wants to build?" And Kaley said, "No, they're homes from our dreams."

Yes, I know, it was such an astounding thing. Kaley brought me in the kitchen to where her own dream was tacked on the wall. I couldn't make out what Gordon had drawn at first because it was so unusual until she explained it was a houseboat — broad and tall, with three or four stories above the water and two below. Her family, you see, had a cabin on Lake St. Clair and it was her beautiful memories of childhood bringing on her dreams of a houseboat that, of course, never was.

Kaley showed me rooms she walked through in her dream. Gordon filled them with furniture and even people sitting on the furniture or cooking dinner or taking a shower, all from what Kaley remembered.

But other rooms were left sketchy because, she said, she hadn't been in those rooms — didn't even know they existed. She said Gordon put them there to make the house right. He said buildings have laws you have to obey, even in dreams.

I was there maybe two months before I told a dream to Gordon. I don't remember my dreams much, generally. Gordon was patient, but I could see him waiting. I don't know why the man was that way, wanting to know about the places inside you, but it was a sweet thing, really. You wanted to tell him because he was just a lovely person. But I had nothing to tell him for a while.

Then one night I woke up from a dream that frightened me for being so clear. I was at work at the plant, in the dream, and Darnell was there. But later that morning when I tried to tell Gordon about it, there was almost nothing left, it faded so quickly.

Gordon gave me a note pad. "Put it beside your bed," he said. "You won't want to sit up, but try hard. Write as much as you can."

The dream came again, just like Gordon knew it would. I thought I sat up and started writing but I didn't. I just dreamed I had done. But the next time it happened, I did wake up. I swung my legs out of bed and lit a candle and wrote and wrote.

In the dream, I was with Darnell in the office in Lansing, although everything was wrong, like in dreams. There was a kitchen stove across from my desk and Darnell was making huge waffles, him talking away like he did. I sat at a counter beside other people, though not exactly the ones I knew from work. They were piling canned fruit and peanut butter and pouring cream on their crispy, brown waffles as wide as pizza boxes. I cracked mine up into little squares and scooped up thick, sour rhubarb jam.

And then Darnell was leading me through dark, narrow halls, down toward the plant floor, leading me into rooms and through to more hallways to more rooms like he was my guide and my protector, walking with a stick out in front of him.

We came to a room full of clothes, all swinging on hangers from the ceiling. Darnell swatted at them to make room, but the clothes swung back in my way, reaching back at me like arms.

We walked through a room filled with plates, stacked on the floor and displayed on shelves. I walked round and round looking at the colors and designs. Many had faces on them, people shouting with joy or crying.

We climbed a steep stairwell so narrow I could hardly make it up, to a room with a low, low ceiling. I got down on my knees, the floor all padded like a mattress and smelling of lavender and pee.

There were many rooms and I wrote about a few more. At a point it got harder to remember things because the fading had begun. But I knew that at the end of the dream, I'd been very upset. That's what woke me up, my own shouting in my ears.

We sat out back, Gordon and I, when I told him my dream, on a low brick patio wall that bordered the lawn. There was spring sunshine and the smell that I love of cut onion grass.

While I read from my notes, Gordon sketched, laying them out on the ground in front of us. He'd stop me each time I got to a new room, asking me to close my eyes and look around. He'd ask if there was a refrigerator next to the stove or if there were stairs to my left or if I could reach out and touch both walls. I couldn't answer all that much but things came back. I remembered what Darnell was wearing — a purple flowered shirt — and on the floor in that padded upstairs room there had been a patchwork quilt.

Gordon was patient. He knew I was starting to understand. The building wasn't my old office at all. It was my momma's house. It was her yellow Frigidaire beside her old electric stove. And Darnell's purple shirt was my momma's housedress, with its purple lavender flowers, the scent from the room upstairs being lavender too. And it came to me Momma being in that room, lying in her sick bed, telling me, "Be the woman you need to be, Portia."

After a time, it was just me talking and him sketching without any more questions. I saw that the plates with all the pictures on them, they were record LPs. It was Jameel's collection, although no sign of Jameel. And all of a sudden seeing the hallway path that Gordon was drawing I could picture my poor brother, Reggie, and that Darnell had led me to him in my dream.

Reggie was working away on the boiler down in the basement — an awful, monstrous thing. Darnell was saying to Reggie, "You got no idea what you're doing there, Reggie." And Reggie was all indignant saying he could fix things himself, which was not unlike him. And they fought, which I found upsetting, which is why I left them and without Darnell's guidance got lost.

The room with all the clothes hanging, I guess it was plain enough that was a closet, like the one I hid in when I'd done something my momma didn't like.

And then, as I said, I made it to my momma's sick room, which was really very comforting being with her.

But then came the end of the dream with all its confusion, me going from hallway to room to hallway. I was looking for Jameel, with Momma's voice saying, "You be a woman now, Portia. Go find your Jameel. He needs you." And I had it in my head he was back in Lansing and I needed to get out of that building to get to him.

Gordon, he gathered up his sketches and rolled them up all neat and said, "Don't worry, Portia. We're going to find your way out of this building," as if that's all it would take to make things right. With all I'd remembered, I was left with this aching feeling. I thought then that it's better when dreams fade away.

Next couple of days, though, the cloud that had covered me since Jameel passed started to clear, like a cold leaving my head. I found reasons to go out and about and even went to visit my aunt, though I was firm about not burdening her.

For a good five, six days, Gordon worked away in his room in the basement, asking not to be disturbed, which I didn't. And, feeling much better, I got three days of temp work and was busy with that. I bought a couple of chickens and we made Gordon and everyone a nice stew that lasted a couple of days, so that was nice.

Then that very same week, we lost the house. The neighbors, they were mostly good people, like I said, but there was one down the block not so good and he brought up complaints. The police had been by twice but no one thought much of it to tell me so I got a horrible shock when I got home on that Friday night and everyone was gone, Gordon too. The house was padlocked and dark, and I don't even know what happened to Gordon's drawings.

Yes, but it was alright. I had to get on with things. I made up my mind to come here, to live with you all, because I thought maybe Gordon had come, being he talked about it so much, how good it is here.

First, though, I went to say goodbye to Darnell. I told him about the dream and how I wouldn't ever find my way out of that building, and Darnell, he said, "You know that some dream map's not going to lead you to Jameel, don't you, Portia?" I said of course I knew that. And Darnell said, "And you know Gordon just wants to give you the strength within yourself to set off on your own way again."

Portia folds her hands in her lap.

"You go girl," says Squeej, sloppy with crying.

Portia laughs. "Oh sweetheart, that's all there is."

"Yeah? Oh." Squeej wipes his nose with the back of his hand. "That Gordon. Damn."

"Yes." Portia straightens herself on the stool. She's smiling for real now. "I wanted you all to know that's what brought me to you, for which I'm so grateful to Gordon, and I'm also so grateful to have come to understand Andre's dream too, which is the most beautiful dream I've seen in my life and worth spending a life working for."

Kesi darts a look over to Whit, no doubt quashing any urge he has to comment.

"And so are we, dear," says Claudia, after a second. "We're grateful for you, Portia."

ONE DAY AND SIX HOURS PRIOR

The Colony, Greenport, New York

Whit snatches his hand back from the rusted chain links as the dog crashes into the opposite side of the fence, all claws and snarl. She falls back hard against the ground with a whelp. In a blink, she's up and resuming her patrol of the factory yard.

She is meaty and built low with a tigerish brown coat and a quarter-sized notch out of her left ear. She canters along the front fence, her eyes locked on Whit as she makes her turns.

Kesi has taken refuge from the heat in the shade of an elm about ten paces back from the gate, using her backpack for a seat cushion. "She wants at you in a horrible way."

"Nah, she's warming up to me, aren't ya girl?" Whit stoops low and wags an index finger through the fence.

The dog, on a lap heading away from Whit, spins and comes for him at a dead run, foam winging out from her jowls. Whit rises and retreats to Kesi's position. He crouches beside her, protecting the index finger in his palm.

After a while, he turns to Kesi. She waits with eyebrows raised.

"Oh, shut the hell up," he says. "If I could just get in there for a minute, I'm sure I could make friends."

"Right. That dog's at least half pit bull. And she's serious ghetto, not one of your inbred Greenwich Village pussies."

"East Village pussies."

He shoulders her over and takes half the backpack.

"Besides," Kesi says, pointing, "the gate's not locked. Go on through. Nuzzle up with the bitch."

"Hey, I'm just trying to keep this situation from descending into the miserable. I'm not the one who dismissed our ride. It's what, like six miles back into Greenport?"

"Which from the looks of it, only exists on maps. I didn't see a town, did you?"

"No. And I thought you had a cell."

"Not now, not ever. And who is there to call? Carlton the Barbarian?"

Whit hums an annoying tune.

"What?" She nods toward the factory complex. "I suppose you think these people would invite him in?"

"You may be passing judgment on Carlton too quickly. He has some fine qualities."

"Such as?"

"Such as the ability to maybe save my ass again."

"Save your ass? From who, Opie, your worshipers?"

"Oh God, please let's not let that nickname stick. And yeah, among the multitude of directionless Voggers are some decidedly whacked ones, and among the whacked are some dangerous ones, I have no doubt."

"True that."

"And besides, what makes you think these Colony people are going to welcome you into their brick shit yard, anyway? Or me?"

"I have experience living in collectives. I know how to be useful. You, I can't speak for."

Whit rubs his face and leans back against the tree. From their seat, he has a view through the fence of the low structures standing on both sides of the factory yard. Anchoring the complex at the far end stands a wide manufacturing building, its four floors fronted by dozens of tall, mostly broken, multi-paned windows.

Closer, spanning the width of the yard from rooftop to rooftop, is a steel trellis intertwined with rusted pipes, taking the journey in a confusion of right-angle turns and dips. The old company sign hanging from the center of the trellis has a single word remaining — COLONY.

"Shit, I'm tired," he says after a while, eyes closed. "But I'm finally getting feeling back in my psyche after laundry bag night. And the anxiety's on the wane, which is a relief because for the past week I've been feeling like a jittery little gutter rodent."

"Well, thanks for that sexy image."

He sits up and looks at her.

"Don't get excited," she says.

He leans back. "For a guy like me, that's close enough to a come-on. And from a beautiful woman no less."

She doesn't respond.

"You're blushing," he says.

"I'm not. And your eyes are closed so how would you know?"

"You're too dark for me to know anyway."

"And, what, women don't go for you? Is there a problem I should know about?"

"Nothing mechanical."

"Maybe it's your line of work. Maybe women don't want to date heretics."

"Funny. I study social relationships, you know — that's what I do for a living."

"No shit? Well, see now, that's a useful skill for a collective."

"I know it sounds like an enviable profession, but it has its down side. A guy doesn't like bringing his work home with him at night."

"Likely excuse."

"Not to say my relationships never work out."

"Have they? Ever worked out?"

"Actually no, never."

"Hey, listen —"

Whit stands at the distant sound of a woman's voice.

The dog retreats toward the call, cutting between the second and third buildings on the left, then reappears, leading the way for a young woman.

She is about five-four and slim with medium-length hair black enough to reflect the sunlight. She has it gathered loosely behind her neck. The sleeves of her work shirt are rolled up past the elbows, revealing caramel skin that transitions to chalky-beige from the wrists down.

Kesi approaches the gate with a raised hand. "Hi."

The dog, panting hard, drops to the ground about ten yards shy of the gate and watches the woman continue on.

"You teasing her?" the woman asks. She puffs at a lock of dangling hair off her face.

"No, no," says Whit.

She waits for more.

He clears his throat. "Is she yours? You know what they say about women with aggressive dogs?"

She turns to check the animal. "Yeah, they say their no-good, strung-out, cocksucker boyfriends take off and leave them with worthless mutts."

He scratches the back of his neck. "Well, yeah, I suppose they say that too."

Kesi steps closer. "Sorry, we tried to make friends with her but I guess we just got her pissed."

She nods. "It usually takes a lot to get her this worked up."

"Yes, really sorry. I'd like to ... we came to see about joining you for a season or two. We'd do a trial, of course, or whatever."

The woman picks up her shirttail to wipe her hands. "Did you let anyone here know you were coming?"

"I tried. I heard about this place from Marian Garvey. She gave me a Gmail address but no one got back to me. You know Marian?"

"No."

"Marian was here up until about four years ago, I think."

"I wasn't here then. And the internet's been out since March."

"Artist?" says Whit.

She looks at her hands. "Potter. OK, so no, I don't think we're accepting any —"

She turns at the severe sound of a creaking hinge. A tall young man emerges from one of the sheds on the right side of the yard. He lays down some empty plastic crates and joins them.

"Hey, what's up?" He tosses his head to the side to clear his eyes of his ragged blond hair. He's wearing a tattered Gang of Four T-shirt, cut-off khakis and plaid Converses.

Whit pulls the latch up on the gate and pushes through, hand extended. "Hey, I'm Whit. This is Kesi."

Kesi follows.

"Sam. You here for a stay?" He looks at the young woman. "They staying, Trini?"

"Hi Trini," says Whit, hand out. Her eyes remain on Sam. She continues to wipe the clay from her hands.

Whit steps past them and drops to one knee a few yards shy of the dog. "Hey girl, you want to make friends now? What's her name?"

"Rosa," Sam says. "Say hi to Whit, Rosa. It's OK."

The dog snaps up and walks to Whit, head down, tail in motion.

"OK, so 'Rosa' doesn't work for this dog, you realize that."

"Right, but no, you just got to get to know her. She's a sweetie pie." Sam gets a disapproving look from Trini.

Rosa accepts Whit's attention, curling around to rub her ribs on his knee.

Kesi repeats her pitch to Sam and they chat about her time spent at other collectives.

Whit takes in the surroundings. Three rusted storage sheds stand to his right. The sky blue door from which Sam emerged is patterned with scratches that indicate a long history of entry by men bearing clumsy tools. A sign remains above the door — THINK AFETY.

Dislodged bricks, splintered plywood, and discarded factory mechanics lay strewn about the yard, but to Whit's left, in the vicinity of some recently renovated buildings, the grounds have been cleared and swept. All three are flat-roofed and built from red and gray brick. Their exterior support girders are painted safety yellow up to about eye level. The windows — all in good repair — are well over ten feet tall and, in many cases, topped by arches.

"Look," says Kesi, "we've been on the road for a few days getting here. Maybe we can just spend one night and get to know each other. If it's not to be, we'll understand. But we're really wiped out."

"Sure," says Sam. "There'll be plenty for dinner. How did you get here from Memphis? Did you hitch?"

"Mostly. Wasn't too bad. But we were kind of —"

"Did you say you lived in the Riverview section?" says Trini. "There was nothing but squatting in Memphis, last time I was there."

"Squatting, yeah, but we had a pretty good situation for a while," said Kesi.

"This isn't squatting," Trini says. "We have ownership rights."

"Of course, yes, I know."

Trini looks at Sam, her expression unreadable.

Kesi steps back. "I'll just grab my backpack and maybe we'll —"

"Look, I don't know if —" says Trini.

"I can see about fixing your internet." Whit stands with his hand down, rubbing Rosa's neck. He looks up at Sam.

"Shit yeah," says Sam. "That would be great."

"I'm not just sucking up, Sam, when I tell you that it's exceptional in here," says Whit. They pass from Building 6's narrow entry hall into an odd-shaped anteroom. "And I've seen some pretty cool loft renos. Or was it like this when you moved in?"

Kesi follows, running her fingertips along an interior wall that has been paneled with repurposed oak floor planks. The room and the hallways leading off it are airy and cool despite the abundant light passing through the tall windows.

"No, I mean, yeah, thanks. Materials-at-hand is what Andre keeps beating into us, which makes a shit-load of sense since it's all we've got. But Andre, yeah, he had all the ideas. A lot of the stuff used in here is harvested from the other buildings, so they're getting pretty torn up, but ... anyway."

Kesi moves across to a half-wall partition and taps on the corrugated steel surface. "I love it, Sam." She looks down. "What's this floor?"

"Just the cement that was here, but we lacquered it. That sucked as a job but it turned out nice, I think."

Sam depresses a half-deflated soccer ball with his toe, then with sharp back spin, pops it to his shin for a shot against the metal-faced wall opposite. The bang resounds fully in the space.

"So anyway, we don't have a name for this room, but the twins play in here a lot."

"Twins? Whose are they?" says Kesi.

"Stefan's. Yeah ... and his girlfriend, but she's not here." The ball, on the rebound, rolls to him. He uses the same trick, this time lofting it to his hands.

"Hey, by the way," he says, "Trini's not really as bad as all that."

"I totally get it," says Whit. "I'm sure she's here because she likes being left alone."

"You can't assume that," says Kesi. "This isn't a convent."

"It's true. She doesn't trust people much," says Sam. "She's cool to be with once you ... well, once she decides she wants to get to know you." He looks at the ball in his hands, then stoops and rolls it into a nearby corner.

"Smart girl," said Kesi.

Whit walks to the windowed side of the room where the floor is covered with old area rugs. "Cute too," he says, "which combined with that bitch-on-wheels thing she's got going is pretty hot."

He sits on a toddler-size riding toy and duckwalks around to face Sam and Kesi, maneuvering among scattered Legos and Polly Pockets. "Which is strictly a clinical observation. You two a couple? I'd guess she's the only reason you're still here, am I right?"

Sam looks down, sending his bangs forward.

"Fuck, Whit," says Kesi.

Sam shrugs. "No, it's OK. I mean, we're sort of ... I like it here. What do you mean?"

"You said your mom's here. I assume she's the one who committed to being here, not you. But now you're older and ready to bust out, right?"

"No, I like it here. I like meeting new people is all, more than Trini ... and more than Claudia ... my mom — and, well, more than the others."

"It's a great place," says Kesi. "You could do a lot worse."

"Absolutely," says Whit. "Goes for Trini too. Believe me, I've seen worse and —"

Kesi reaches out with a foot and gives the trike a shove, nearly knocking Whit over. "This would be a good time for you to take a break from being an asshole."

She nods toward a set of double doors. "Sam, you say this is the old research building? That where the lab was?"

"Yeah, but no, that's the multipurpose room. Originally, originally, I guess it was a part of a lab sort of thing. But they'd cut it up into little offices so we cleared all the non-supporting walls. The lab, which is now the kitchen, is on the other side of the multipurpose room. We found some industrial kitchen stuff in the old cafeteria in Building 8 and dragged it in. Squeej got it all working."

"Is Squeej the mechanic?" says Whit.

"Mechanic?" Kesi gives him a look.

"Nah," says Sam. "He's a chef — good one, too. Used to work at some fancy place in New York."

"Yeah? Which one?" says Whit.

"Something Kitchen ... I think. Something like that."

"That narrows it down."

"Squeej's food is awesome," says Sam. "Dinner's like a big thing here. Not much in the way of entertainment though. You'll find yourself heavily into board games if you stay."

Kesi and Sam push through the swinging doors. Whit bears down on his handlebars and pads the floor, knees up beside his ears. He makes it through, accepting a mild smack in the rear from the backswing.

Whit's eyes rise toward the double-height ceiling. Sunlight cuts down in streams from four wired-glass skylights through a network of iron pipes, wooden struts, and electrical conduits. The room is big enough for full court basketball. There is a netless hoop mounted on the far wall.

"Sammy, can you help me with this?"

Whit stands. A fifty-ish woman, her elbows up, bands the frizzy, graying hair off her neck. Her middle has lost most of its shape but her arms look fit. Her jeans and work boots are fully lived in. She stands beside a tall wooden stepladder, laid out on the floor.

"That thing's rickety as shit, Mom."

"Yes, that's why I need you to hold it, sweetie. I replaced this fluorescent yesterday but the damn thing's still flickering. Who are your friends?" She has her eyes on Whit and the riding toy.

After introductions, they involve themselves in Claudia's task.

Whit suggests replacing the ballast. They recover one from a stockpile of scavenged parts in a basement room and find it solves the problem.

Claudia leads the way through the doors at the far end of the room into the kitchen where they find Squeej, dish towel on shoulder, earbuds implanted, rolling out dough.

The kitchen is far shallower than the multipurpose room but runs the same width. On three walls, crackled subway tile runs up to a height of five feet. Windows dominate the exterior wall and are open to their maximum. Two oversized, forties-era ceiling fans whoop above, flapping the earthy smell of boiling lentils back down and dampening the metal-on-metal cooking sounds.

Whit and Kesi pull metal stools up to the chef's workspace, a black-surfaced lab table that reveals its origin in the Bunsen burner nozzle protruding from one corner. While Squeej works — pivoting between his cutting board and the industrial range a step behind — he instructs Sam on the production of iced chai lattes, in particular, frothing milk with a hand-cranked mixer.

"Why would you think to come all the way up here?" Claudia leans back against a deep steel sink with her glass of water.

"It wasn't we, it was me," Kesi says. "We met on the road."

"Oh, I assumed you were together," says Claudia.

Squeej keeps track of the conversation without interruption to his chopping pattern. An errant spurt of milk draws his attention to Sam's wild action on the hand mixer. He yanks his earbuds and flips the cords over a shoulder. "Whoa, easy my dude. Stefan likes it creamy, not stiff."

"This is for Stefan? You doing take-out now?" says Sam.

"No, man, he'll be in from the field in a sec."

Whit straightens on his stool. "But Kesi and I have come to know each other quite well, Claudia, and —"

"I've been planning to come here for a while," says Kesi. "The Colony is kind of legendary. I've wanted to see for myself how you do things."

Claudia raises her palm and freezes Whit. She turns to Kesi, closing her eyes. "What you're saying is they talk about Andre."

Sam looks up from his mixing bowl.

"Andre?" Kesi's voice tightens. "No, I didn't mean per se, no."

She turns to the chef, who gives his sautéing shallots a few flips. "So Squeej, that can't be what your momma named you."

"Nah. Chef Sanford, he done that. Ran a tight, tight shop." He dumps a bowl full of diced carrots in with the shallots and gives the mixture four rapid tosses. "See, when we effed up, deal was we got duty wiping down front-of-house. I always got stuck cleaning these huge picture windows an' shit."

"Well, it suits you," says Whit. "You're a Squeej if I ever saw one."

"True, true. Tags you get when you're grown's usually good ones."

"Likely true with the names they call me," Whit says.

Kesi taps Whit's chair with her toe.

"So what's your real name, Squeej?" Whit says.

"Ah, nah, we don't do that."

Whit laughs. "Come on. How bad can it be?"

"He was Mennonite," says Sam. "His name's Esau."

"Ah, nah, dude, seriously, let's lay off that."

"Sorry," says Sam. "I just find it amazing."

They sit in silence for a while, watching Squeej slice ribbons of dough, then weaving lattice patterns.

"But yes, people online — or at least what we're meant to think are people — have interesting things to say about Andre," says Whit. "I expect lots of folks down there in Memphis heard about him too, right Kesi?"

She digs into his ankle with the edge of her sandal. He squints the eye not facing Claudia.

"What do you mean? Who wants us to think they're people?" says Sam.

"Oh ... bad joke. You know, a lot of those comments you read on blogs are fabricated. Doesn't necessarily apply but —"

"We couldn't get on the internet in Memphis, you know," Kesi says to Claudia. "But Marian did talk about Andre. She had kind words."

Claudia looks surprised. "Marian? Marian Garvey?"

"Really?" says Sam to Whit. "So you think people would, like, put fake comments up there about Andre?"

"Yes, that's right." Kesi's eyes are set on Claudia. "Marian recommended I come here."

Squeej sputters his lips. "Damn, go figure. Never'd guess you'd get a kind word out of Marian about the Colony."

Claudia pushes some curls behind her ear. "It's just that Marian didn't leave with such a high opinion. Maybe she's feeling nostalgic. Who knows? She's a changeable person."

"From bitchy to bitchier, then back again, yeah," says Squeej.

Kesi drums her fingers on her thigh. "Maybe ... I don't know, it was just the impression I got. Nostalgic, yes, maybe."

Claudia gives a small laugh. "So you made this long trip — hitch-hiking no less — based on a few off-handed remarks from Marian Garvey. Are you an impulsive person?"

"Mom," says Sam.

"No," says Kesi, "not normally. But it's not like I could order a brochure or something. I wanted to see this place for myself."

Claudia drains her glass and puts it in the sink. She heads for the door. "OK, I'm getting the idea. Well, glad to be a source of curiosity for you two."

Whit turns to Kesi.

"What?" she says.

"You know, my father used to say, 'Whitford, the last thing the world needs is more ambiguity.'"

"Sorry?"

"To which I would of course reply, 'Why don't you just come out and say what you mean, Dad?'"

Sam laughs, continuing with his work.

Kesi looks toward the wire racks and stainless steel carts behind Sam. They hold eccentrically shaped flasks, jars, and metal pans. "I thought your name was Whitman."

"Yeah, Dad always had a hard time with that."

"My old man was always saying wise freakin' shit too," says Squeej, turning back to the stove.

"Squeej," says Kesi, nodding at the shelves, what you fermenting over there?"

He glances over his shoulder. Six large jars contain a variety of substances in tones from amber to plum, most with a layer of froth near the top.

"We got, this week, hibiscus and blueberry kombucha, pickled pattypan squash, and your standard cabbage kraut, 'cept with ginger and radish and burdock root, just 'cause I could."

Kesi hops down and goes to the shelf for a closer look.

"Challenging aroma," says Whit.

"Thanks, man." Squeej dips to adjust a burner. "Fermentation's a gift from Mom Earth and the smell's free too, yo."

"Anyway, guys," says Whit, after an inhale, "I can assure you that Kesi, while a bit nebulous, is a sincere individual, so I sense Claudia's got the wrong impression. As for me, despite my foul luck and generalized ambivalence, I'm sincere in my curiosity about this place too, and while curiosity for me is often the prelude to disaster, I'm gonna go with it, and by the way, no offense, Sam, but what's with your mom?"

"Yeah, right? Claudia," says Squeej. "But we seen that, Sam and me, right, Sam? The chatter online like Whit was saying. That's just some lame shit they talkin'."

"Lame?" says Whit.

"Besides lumpin' us in with squatters, which we're not, they say we steal electric, while meanwhile Andre's got the wind turbines goin' pretty nice. And they say we dumpster dive, which is like totally fallacious, though I've been in that ass in the air position and there's nothing to be ashamed of, but here, we grow our own."

"Right, right, clearly," says Whit. "By the way, how many people live here? I expected more, I don't know ... numbers of people, or is everyone out working?"

"We're down to, what, ten now?" says Sam, looking at Squeej. "That's if you count Stephan's girlfriend, assuming she's coming back."

"Was twenty-nine, like a year ago last winter," says Squeej. He snatches the dish towel from his shoulder and swipes scraps of dough off the cutting board.

"Really?" says Whit. "You lost all those people?"

"Yeah," says Squeej. With the towel guarding his hand, he grabs the lentil pot and dumps its contents into a colander in the sink, releasing a steam mushroom soon sucked into the fan's updraft. "See, Andre, well, he calls out this dude, Cliffy, for having bad intentions, know'm sayin'? And then these other brothers and sisters get presumed into being in on what Cliffy was intending 'cause they were tight with Cliffy and then Andre starts officializing rules that was mostly just kinda assumed. And Lori, by the way, she'll be back after she gets some sorting out done, is what Stefan says."

"Right. Except no way she's coming back," says Sam.

"Yeah, but maybe yes she is though 'cause Lori, her leaving, that was a different thing, not a Andre thing. It was a Stefan and her thing. And mainly it was just Stefan being too possessive, what with all the loved ones he lost in Croatia and all."

"Right," says Sam, "meaning Stefan is likely to tell you she's coming back because it would crush him to think otherwise."

"Oh dude, yeah, that would be sad."

Whit waits for more, then nods. "So, Sam, you and your mom have been here for, what?"

"Going on eight years."

"Wow — and another place before that, you said. You prefer this to regular domestic life?"

Kesi turns back for her stool. "Oh, Sam, you know, Whit's going to keep bugging you with questions until you tell him to fuck off."

Sam scratches his nose with his T-shirt sleeve. "Yeah. But no, I don't think we ever had anything resembling regular life. Mom's got no family. My dad wasn't all that awful a human or anything. But, well, he had this nasty bike accident — spinal injury and all — leading to a bad Vicodin habit. And so Mom kicked him out. She's not one for putting up with excuses.

"And so Mom was always butting heads with the powers that be at the school where she worked and we were living in some chipboard garden apartment where people didn't even say hello in the hallway. She saw communal as giving me a family, I guess. I think she was right, mostly."

"You think this gave you a good life?" Kesi says.

"Sure, I mean I went through shit, but what kid doesn't? And when I did, I had people to talk to who cared."

"Straight up, that." Squeej slops the wet lentils up and down in the colander. "Got your friends, got relations, but people here living and working together, 'specially when it's working toward a thing."

He high-fives Sam.

"Sounds nice," says Kesi. "It's not like that at all collectives."

"Nah, quality of people is real important." Squeej slides the contents into a large mixing bowl.

"But Kesi, I mean, what were people saying?" Sam switches places with Squeej to rinse his hand mixer in the sink. "About Andre, I mean."

"Good things ... really. A visionary ... right?" Kesi does a lot of nodding. "In urban sustainability and self-sufficiency, you know? It's one-hundred percent ... well, it's totally out of respect that they bring up Andre."

"Andre got no shortage of vision, for damn sure," says Squeej.

Kesi looks down at her hands, now clenched in her lap. "I think Andre's vision comes from down deep, from the life he lived. He knows what city dwellers need and what they never get ... and what they could accomplish if they knew how."

One of the ceiling fans buzzes and falls for a moment into a clackety wobble, startling Kesi. She brings her hands up to the table.

"You can see it here," she says, "in what he's done here ... what you've done — using what's available, turning industrialized land back to farmland. Sure, it's not as much of a challenge as in Philly where —"

"Philly?" says Sam. "Andre's from Philly?" He looks at Squeej.

"No shit?" says Squeej.

"Yes, I mean, I think so." She wraps her arms around her chest. "Didn't you know he —"

"Nobody knows where Andre's been and nary a shit 'bout what he's done," said Squeej. "You ask, and he just plain shuts you down. Claudia, she maybe knows some things, but she ain't letting on."

"Oh?" Kesi stands and puts her hands in her pockets.

"Who told you Andre was from Philly?" Sam dries his hands on his T-shirt.

Kesi stares at him for a moment. She smiles. "You know, I don't even remember who told me that? I could be totally off. I feel funny talking about it if he doesn't like to."

Whit tilts his head down and scratches the back of his neck. "Unambiguous," he says in a whisper.

"Whoa, OK." Squeej for the first time is devoid of motion. "So you never met Andre but you don't want to, like, betray his confidence with us, who are truly his true brothers?"

Kesi's eyes widen. "No. Look, that came out wrong."

Whit leans toward Kesi. "Do we need to talk?"

They turn. Stefan enters, carrying a faded plastic laundry basket bulging with bean pods and leafy greens. "Oh my Jisus, talk about foul wind," he says.

Stefan's ropey arms are sun-browned and slick with perspiration. Below his beard, dark lines run across his throat where the dirt has collected in moist creases.

Trini is close behind with a milk crate full of tomatoes in various green to red hues. A fat joint dangles from her lips.

"How is my mustard greens doing I bring you this morning?" Stefan says. He nods to the visitors as he lays down his basket. "Why you aren't cooking them, Chef? You know don't you that Black people, they like mustard greens, so maybe cooking with them, you could maybe finally find this Black soul you seem you want so terrible. But, no, instead, I smell from outside, even, the foul sauerkraut."

He removes his distressed baseball cap and lifts his T-shirt, wiping across the red impression left on his forehead. His belly is matted with damp hair.

"What you mean by that?" says Squeej. With one hand, he cracks an egg into a petri disk while reaching for a fork.

"I mean, mustard greens — delicious for you, at least is potentially. Kraut — ugh, foulness."

"They is gonna be inspirational damn mustard greens," says Squeej, "especially if I, like, deliver them to you courtesy of my kickass thai pickled red pepper dressing, but they ain't happenin' tonight, dude. And, by the by, it be our damn greens, collectively speaking, which also be true about that spliff, Trini mi hermana."

Trini lays the crate on the floor, squints, and sucks in a lungful before handing the joint to Squeej by way of Sam. "Except, Squeej," she hisses through the expelled smoke, "I'm the one taking loving care of the plants."

Stefan steps close to Kesi. "Squeej, he love this collective sharing but you won't catch his collective ass out in field when comes to helping me."

"Well, I can do that, bruh. I can do that sometimes." He stretches his long, fully tattooed arm across the table to Kesi. She shakes her head at the offer. Squeej sneaks another toke before handing the joint to Whit.

"Sure, good deal, you can help me with tomorrow. But, man, this not good smell in here. Hi, I'm Stefan." He extends a hand to Whit, who shakes and then, pinky extended, transfers the dwindling butt to Stefan's thumb and forefinger.

Stefan lifts the joint as in a toast. "You look wise I can see, friend. I guess you hate kraut too, I can bet."

Whit, exhaling, shakes his head hard. "But if hating it will bring me greater wisdom, I can easily do that."

"There you are. Our guest, he finds kraut is detestable too, Chef," says Stefan. "Detestable ... and undigestible. Is that word, undigestible?" He surrenders the joint to Sam's snapping fingers.

Sam shakes the hair off his face and clamps an eye shut. As he prepares to suck between his fingers, Trini leans in with a wicked grin and whispers in his ear. He coughs out a laugh. She snatches the remaining roach and runs giggling for the door.

"Hey." Sam chases her.

Squeej slides the last of the pot pies onto a baking sheet and wipes his hands on the towel. "It ain't its fault it smell, dude. You know why kraut smells?"

"How am I to know? Is certainly unnaturally odorous," says Stefan.

"Actually, ain't nothing naturaller. Know why it smells?"

"No, why?"

"For the benefit of the deaf."

Stefan lifts the crate onto the table, shaking his head. "Farts, man. That is the joke. Is not friggin' kraut. The joke, it is about farts."

Whit laughs.

"Yeah, bruh, but I'm not into that. Too damn easy. Dudes just say fart and expect a laugh."

Whit laughs more, drawing a disapproving look from Kesi.

"But Squeej, man, kraut, it don't make noise. And this is why what you're saying it isn't funny. Is not funny for that very particular reason."

"Whit's laughing," says Squeej.

Whit laughs again.

Sam reenters, grinning and glassy-eyed. He faces Kesi, then diverts his look with a shallow cough. He makes his way back to his frothing bowl.

"Well," says Stefan, rolling the tomatoes out onto the counter. "Whit is polite audience, apparently. And you, Sam, you will today present me with my iced chai, is that not right, brother?"

Sam scoops an extra dollop of foam out of the bowl, plops it onto an already overflowing mug, and slides it to Stefan, leaving a white comet trail on the black tabletop. He hands mugfuls to Kesi and Whit.

Stefan takes a big draw of foam. The mug comes away leaving a fluffy dangler on his mustache. He smiles at Kesi and Whit. "You two — you have met Claudia, yes? And Andre?"

"Woof. Um, yes. I mean that would be yes to Claudia, no to Andre," says Whit.

Kesi smiles and sips her drink.

"Ah. I see Claudia just now and I had feeling you had met, yes. She seemed preturbed. Is right word, yes? Preturbed? Was there something wrong?"

Whit's smile goes south.

"Whit," Sam says, clearing his throat, "could you take a look at the computer now?"

Whit stands. "Yes, we should do that. We should do the internet now because I promised ... that we'd do that."

Kesi turns and joins them.

"Hey, I don't have any conversation yet with you. Why not stay and chat?" Stefan says.

"It's cool, Stef, really," says Sam, one hand guiding Whit toward the door. "They'll be at dinner. And they'll meet Andre. And I'm sure it'll be cool."

"Ha. Yes, could be," calls Stefan after them. "Anything is possible in this world here."

"Nice to meet everyone," says Kesi without turning back.

ONE DAY AND THREE HOURS PRIOR

The Colony, Greenport, New York

Whit and Kesi are the last to arrive at dinner. They walk first to Andre seated at the head of the table. Andre puts a finger to his lips and gestures for them to sit. The room is silent, although the twins can be heard giggling and skittering about their play area in the anteroom outside.

The skylights above allow for a late-day, lemony radiance in the room that also benefits from an assortment of sputtering candles positioned along the dinner table.

The group sits at two mismatched folding tables butted together to a combined length of about ten feet. An embroidered heirloom tablecloth struggles to cover the stretch. At the far end opposite Andre is Claudia, anchoring the scene with assured domesticity.

The kitchen door swings open and fluorescent light paints the dinner party. From Whit's angle, it produces a cool aura around Andre's Rasta braids and estimable goatee.

Once Squeej, aided by Trini and Sam, ports all the food to the table, he sits, completing the party of nine adults. He pulls the bandana from his head and mops his cheeks, looking uncomfortable in his forced state of inactivity.

"Mom Nature, my Family offers your bounty this evening to our guests." Andre has risen. His eyes are on the newcomers. He holds his hand out to Kesi, seated to his right. She submits to a squeeze from his meaty palm.

"We have produced food that honors life and we would like to share it with you."

Andre pauses between thoughts as if soaking in his own resonance.

"Friends, this is food grown by us — outside of the System. The System, you see, reengineers its food for the addictive appetites of its citizens as surely as it does with its instruments of alcohol and narcotics. This Distortion of our food sources is but one of the System's many agencies of oppression. Growing Mom Nature's food with respect for all moving things and sharing our food within our supportive Family, these alone are profound revolutionary acts. And so we ask you to join us in this meal with reverence and revolutionary spirit."

Kesi's eyes are wide, a queasiness in the curl of her lips.

Andre stands waiting.

"Yes, of course," says Whit. "Certainly."

"Yes," says Kesi, her voice unsteady. "Of course we do."

Reaching out with his left hand, Andre joins with Stefan. The others at the table follow suit. Whit takes hold of Kesi's and gives it a little tug. She squeezes back.

Stefan puffs out his chest. "The squash it is so sweet from all that rain which we have in June."

"Sorry?" says Whit.

"The iron in the spinach always leaves grit on my teeth," says Trini, ignoring Whit. "It's cool to think of the plant like a little refinery mining that iron out of the dirt." Her black eyes glimmer in the candlelight.

Continuing clockwise around the table, Squeej, Claudia, and Portia take their turns, each offering a thought on the food before them and the land that produced it.

Sam thanks the dairy cows for their contribution, mentioning six or seven by name. He tweaks his eyebrows at Whit.

"OK," Whit says, "well I feel privileged to have witnessed Squeej preparing this meal, which in itself was inspirational."

Squeej half-stands and takes a bow.

"I hope to begin helping soon." Kesi's voice is barely audible, eyes down. "I hope to help soon with raising this beautiful food. Thank you for sharing it with us."

The conversation loosens with the passing of plates to Squeej and Trini for serving. Claudia fills in Stefan on new accomplishments she has witnessed from the twins during daycare hours.

"I see Arthur getting more verbal, Stefan," she says. "He was frustrated again today with our word game, but when I asked him to tell me what he didn't like about it, he said, 'I don't like are.' I thought, 'Oh boy, he's taking a step backwards with his verbs.' But it dawned on me he meant the letter R. He always writes it backwards, you know, which is nothing to be concerned about at their stage in development."

Stefan hangs on her words but has to excuse himself to handle a skirmish between the kids in the hallway.

"You're a teacher, Claudia?" Kesi says.

"By profession, yes."

"She's a wonderful teacher," says Portia, patting Claudia's hand. Portia's braids are bound behind her neck with a flowered scarf, opening her broad face to the room light. "And I hear you and Whit are looking to stay on. I don't mean to be blunt, you know, but do you have skills?"

Kesi swallows. "Plumbing," she says.

"Tight," says Squeej. "Sorely could use that."

Whit catches Kesi's eyes. "Plumbing?" he mouths.

"Trini, your slop sink," says Sam through a mouthful.

Trini's eyes narrow at Sam.

"She's got a bum faucet in her studio," says Sam.

"Well sure, I'll have a look," says Kesi.

Portia smiles. "And how about you, Whit?"

Whit puts a big scoop of kraut in his mouth and holds up a finger, making "yum" squints as he chews. "Squeej — props, man. The kraut's life-altering."

Squeej directs a boastful smile at Stefan, returning to his seat.

"Yes, is not necessary. I will eat your miserable kraut. Where I grow up, you don't have luxury to turn down food, even when foul."

"So where do you teach, Claudia?" Whit says, avoiding Portia's look.

"Just here," Sam answers. "She taught me. I didn't go to school." He raises his fork to Portia. "Whit knows networks and programming and stuff. He got the internet working this afternoon."

Her mouth falls open. "It's back up? Oh, I have some things that long ago needed doing."

"You tell people you didn't go to school, Sam?" Claudia says. "Ours was a school, in a real sense."

Sam pops his eyes at Whit.

"Claudia has instilled fine values in this young brother." Andre's cadence downshifts the conversation. "She raised him to attend to the earth with open eyes. He'll be a good man of the Family and of the earth."

Sam is involved in his plateful of adzuki bean and celery root salad. "The earth needs good men," he says between swallows. "But let's not overlook Venus."

Andre glares at Sam. Then he laughs and slaps the table, causing Kesi to recoil. "You do your work here, young brother," he says, poking a finger at Sam, "and then Venus can have you."

Sam folds his hands in prayer. "Space is the place, brother Andre. All hail Sun Ra."

"Indeed," says Andre.

"And as for work to do, Sammy," says Portia, "how about we

begin with getting your lily ass on that internet and you can help me with the tax accounts."

Claudia lifts an eyebrow. "I'll thank you to keep your mind off my son's ass."

"Yeah," says Trini.

Portia pulls her chin way back. "Well, I'm sorry, sister Trini, with the tight little Ecuadorian, cradle-robbin' ass. Ain't always easy when one's not petite."

"Petite is not especially always desired," says Stefan, stabbing the carrots out of his pot pie. "You have truly profound behind, sweetheart."

The men grunt in assent.

"Why thank you, baby," Portia says in all seriousness. "It's not that I didn't know it."

"Well, in any case, Sam," says Whit after some silence, "you didn't miss much at school, unless you were the kind of kid that thrived on disillusionment."

Stefan, Trini, and Sam groan, reacting not to Whit but to the sight of Portia's overstuffed management looseleaf. She lets it fall to the table and licks a finger before leafing to her chosen spot.

"So ... brother Andre dear, I had a talk with Tracy at Ashford's about bartering for her lovely goat milk, but she wants cash. She'll give us wholesale, but that in any case means we'll definitely need to pull in more sales out of Hudson and Rhinebeck and maybe we could manage one more farmers' market, and there's also that roadside stand in Tivoli. He said — Werner, from Tivoli — he said he'd love any kind of heirlooms, Stefan sweetie."

Andre makes deep-throated sounds as he eats, rocking his head.

"Dude, we're for sure gonna have surplus on the goose beans." Squeej is winding and unwinding his bandana around his wrist. "I already canned enough for the Second Coming."

Stefan nods. "How has Trini done with her pot selling in Red

Hook? And how short are we this month? I mean, sure, surplus we have, and even we can quick put in more heirlooms, but this means I'll need about maybe ten, maybe twelve more hours in each week from Sammy and Chef and might need some extra hired hands come in September."

This sets off a belabored exchange, with Trini supporting Stefan's argument for more outside help and Portia insisting on first paying down their debt with the power company and county tax bureau.

Kesi's hand goes up, elbow on the table.

"Yes, dear?" says Portia.

"When I was at Penn, they sent the undergrads out on internships. They'd spend a few weeks working on a local farm. Why don't you do that? You have plenty of room. It's probably good money, right?"

"Yes, we've looked into that," says Portia. "That means qualifying as an organization and I don't know —"

Andre raises both palms to the group, eyes closed.

"This is a good path, Sister Portia. Bring the young ones here to learn from our Family. And you know that you can come to me if you need more funds to keep the System at bay."

"No, Andre," says Claudia, "we agreed we'd make it on your thousand a month. We need to be disciplined. Your money's not going to last forever."

"Well, Kesi and Whit, I will hope you have strong backs," says Stefan. "Or how about maybe you can throw pots?" He shoulders Trini.

"At your head, Stefan," she says.

Whit passes his plate back to Squeej and points to the pot pie. When he turns back, Andre is eyeing him.

"I approve of your advice for young Sam, brother." Andre lays his hand on Kesi's forearm as he speaks to Whit. "No doubt, in your school years, you got your fill of the System and its disfigurement of our children's souls."

Whit eats on, nodding. "I can't deny that a disfigured soul could be responsible for my current state, Andre. It's not a condition I would wish on Sam."

Andre opens his arms toward Sam and Claudia.

"Young brother Sam, you were not taught, you see, you were allowed to learn. Your mother simply showed you how to remain open to earth's love. And for that reason, you are ready to be one of Mom Earth's facilitators, ready to balance the transferring of energy. You can cultivate her soils and resolve the energy media we know as cities. You can inspire others to do the same through your creative emanations. You will pulse with her love and join all true, living entities in the reestablishment of the earth."

He lowers his hands and turns back to his plate.

"Andre?" Sam says. "Creative emanations-wise, I've been thinking that I want to write. I'm thinking that could be my contribution to the ... whatever — energy media."

"That's fine, brother," says Andre through a mouthful. "As long as you feel the pulse of her love, self-sufficient earth cities will spring up from the word-seeds you cast about you."

"What you writing 'bout?" Squeej rocks in his chair, his eyes flashing between Andre and Sam. "Cast us some word-seeds, dude."

Sam cocks his head and rubs at an ear.

"Oh yes." Portia is aglow. "You can read us something tonight, Sammy."

"Look, I'm just saying — I haven't actually written anything down yet."

"Well, that's fine too," says Andre. "The oral storytelling tradition is supportive of loving culture and restorative when there are injuries to the soul."

"I have a question, Andre." Whit leans back from his empty plate.

Andre looks his way but his gaze is adrift.

"The things you said, Andre — you're committed to the transformation of cities. But here we are, out in the country, in this old plant —"

Andre nods. "We've turned this remnant of an industrial facility, brother, into a laboratory for our urban ideations — a microcosm, you see. As in the city, this land was devastated by the System's industrial process. Do you know what the biggest culprit was?"

"Overextended distribution," says Stefan without looking up from his dinner.

"Exactly. Distance. The System's demand for mass production drew raw materials to this plant from hundreds, thousands of miles away, ported by wasteful vehicles." He refills his water glass from a pitcher. "Here, the plant chugged away, pumping poisons into the eco, in turn ravishing the food-producing potential of the soil and leading to local poverty and spoiled lives. So, here in this laboratory, our Family is tackling the same problems faced in our desecrated city-organisms where the connection with Mom Earth has been severed."

"OK," says Whit, "but still, why not do your experiment in the city? You could get a lot of neighborhood involvement, I'm sure."

Andre drinks, wipes with his napkin and leans forward with a new intensity.

"Yes, brother, there's a great, great need in the city. But with our small numbers, the city-system would co-opt our energy." He slaps his palms on the table, rattling the flatware.

"Now, Andre," Claudia says.

"It would divert our energy into its parasitic grid," he says. "And could we resist? No, we would be powerless, brother. We need to build our strength in bases such as this and then, when we move back, apply our principles of self-sufficiency, neighborhood by neighborhood."

"I get it, Andre, really," says Whit, "except maybe for the energy transfer thing."

Andre's eyes are fiery. He addresses Kesi. "How about you, sister? Do you understand?"

Kesi freezes for a moment. "Yes, I think so. You're talking about the transfer of energy between living things — from the earth to plants to people."

Andre's face softens. "Yes, my sister, it's a self-sustaining transfer, with each participant contributing energy in shares equal to what they draw from the air, water and food produced by the soil."

"Ah. OK." Whit looks at Kesi.

"You see my meaning?" says Andre. "City pavement blocks the essential energy transfer from water, sun, and air. And this is why sustenance has to be shipped from far away. The energy used in the transport, in fact, eats up half the food benefit, and the packaging often requires more energy to produce than the food itself. Then on to huge refrigerated supermarkets — so wasteful, brother. Blind waste."

"So you're advocating self-sufficient neighborhoods in the city?" says Whit.

"Yes, but we can't expect to return to a balanced exchange of energy any time soon. No, not in my lifetime, surely. Maybe in Sam's though, right my young brother?"

Andre sits back and brushes his goatee with his knuckles.

"You know, Future Man of the Earth," says Whit, turning to Sam. "I sat on an MIT task force last fall. It was about using people as sensors, you know, within an urbanwide network. This could totally sync with Andre's plans for energy balance. These guys were talking about up-clouding all of the data from people's mobiles, from mass transit, waste collection trucks, water and power meters —"

Whit, turning back, is shaken by a stern look from Kesi. Andre has his eyes squeezed shut, head down.

"What I mean to say, Andre, is that .... well, this would be a way to monitor individual energy consumption. And then each city dweller gets feedback back down from the cloud so they can work towards the balance you're —"

Andre's head is swinging from side to side. "No, no, no. Do you have any concept at all what that would do?"

"Well, I can sort of see what you mean. There's somewhat of a creepiness factor but —"

"Into the System? Don't you see that this is how the System fuels itself? On our living information, brother."

"Now Andre, dear." Portia has turned up the tunefulness in her voice. "Whit, Andre believes natural law is all we need."

Andre stands. He takes a deep breath before opening his eyes.

"That's right, sister, we do not need a man-law to tell us to blink, to be hungry or evacuate our bowels or to crave the love of others or to love Mom Earth without reservation. But, you see, the System fabricates laws to shackle our natural instincts. If we were to feed our whereabouts and our consumption habits into the System, the administrators could easily exploit us. What you describe, my brother, would be too susceptible to the System's unconstrained greed mechanism."

"Sure. Greed mechanism. Just a thought."

Andre hurries for the hallway door, head bowed, scratching at the back of his neck. "Perfectly alright, brother. It's just your learning."

Whit stands, looks at the assembly, and sits again.

Stefan mimes a whistle.

Kesi's arms are crossed, eyes on the ceiling.

Squeej claps twice and stands.

"Attention, my Family — there is dessert. Got ginger peach crumble with a wild blackberry syrup drizz. But fore that and just so you'll have a proper appreciation by way of the syrup —" He pulls a folded paper square from his back pocket.

Portia bounces in her seat and squeals. She claps with her fingertips.

Squeej unfolds the paper with exaggerated gestures.

"I have for you sibs and new-gained relations," he says, "a ditty spun from today's observations."

He lifts the paper.

"On my morning stroll by Rotterman's grove,
Seeking out blackberries ripe nough for baking,
With the bugs still a-snooze and the breeze down low,
I heard Mom Earth grumbling with the effort of waking.

"In that brook neath the bridge, her stomach was a-gurgle,
And her old knees creaked in the swaying of branches,
And with scents inter-circling from the bay leaf and myrtle,
Her morning breath whistled tunes through the grasses.

"Sure enough, berry-wise, I spotted the bounty,
And while plinking them into my handy receptacle,
Up bounds Rosa, in her maw displayed proudly,
Some varmint that surely only she'd find delectable.

"But even as gloomy as that possum's eyes was,
Nothing today could'a gotten me moody,
'Cause Mom Earth bestowed upon me a buzz,
Persisting far longer than any morning woody.

"And so — bros and sistas, though but a sampling of occurrences, this will hopefully serve, being not the most but the most chill of what your humble chef with his own eyes ... this day ... has observed."

He swings the paper wide and bows.

As the applause peters out, Trini stands and grabs two of the mostly spent serving platters. "Squeej, you want to kill off the last of the adzukis?"

"Nah, should chill on the roughage. Yo, what's it mean when

your shit's got fur on it?"

Trini scrunches her nose and turns for the kitchen.

"It means go to see the vet," says Stefan.

"No, dude, really." Squeej looks hurt.

"No, really, because you are fucking animal."

"By the way you two." Claudia, smirking, wiggles a finger at Kesi and Whit. "You're staying in this building, just down the hall from Andre. He's usually all alone here. I thought it would be a good chance for you to get acquainted."

Portia cracks up and throws an arm around Claudia's shoulder. "Oh, girl, you're bad."

THREE WEEKS, FOUR DAYS AND THREE HOURS AFTER

The Colony, Greenport, New York

Sam waits on the stool, the silent subject of discussion.

"You don't think he's taking a rather circuitous route?" says Claudia.

"To where?" Stefan whispers because Arthur is conked out on his lap. Augustina, lying beside him, is nearly there, dragging a fat crayon in circles around a piece of cardboard. "We are maybe assuming too much there is an object which we are doing here, but maybe is not about getting to someplace."

"Oh hell, someone's going to say 'journey' soon," says Whit. "When you find yourself deep into a senseless undertaking, you can bet somebody claims it's all about the journey."

"Yeah, and though didn't some dude say once, 'Making sense is a sure sign you're wrong?'" says Squeej.

"I think that was me," says Whit.

Portia, of course, defends Sam. She advises that he follow his heart around in circles if that's where it tells him to go.

"Well, I admit I'm warming up to his story," says Whit. "But he should insert some musical breaks. We could call it 'Post-Apocalypso: A New Dystopian Caribbean Musical.'"

Squeej cracks up. "Ho, Post-Ska, dude. Got ol' Andre with his Rastafarian shit raging. He walkin' dee earth, mon, spreadin' dee love-seeds."

At the pleading in Sam's eyes, Kesi stands and claps to shut everyone up. "You all have great suggestions for Sam. What you really need to do is just listen."

Sam's Story, Cont'd.

OK, yeah, so, Chapter 2.

Come late evening, Carlton and Trini and Father Andre and me are moving still, though at a crawl, the black beast being stuck in a queue of similarly bastardized vehicles strung down the denuded country lane that leads to the Colony.

The night's thick and hot and we've got all the windows down. Carlton's elbow is out his and he's upright and chesty, projecting airs of casual fortitude as we chug by the rabble pressing close on either side. From the road shoulder, they're packed like last-boat out refugees, down into the drainage gullies and a half-acre deep into the barren fields. The most audacious of the crowd form the roadside gauntlet — grumbling, feet shuffling ne'er-do-wells craning for a look-see into the vehicles, some making snatches for whatever they can get off the occupants, some content just hocking spit in the truck's wake.

Carlton is trash-talking, purely for the challenge it seems of perfecting the art since clearly somebody his size has got no need to. "Lean in just a bit closer," he says to one guy. "We'll take that pocky for a ride and leave your skull with your neighbors to pick over."

As we roll, we're encountering indescribably horrid smells, some registering as human stool and decomposition, and the rest that much worse for being unrecognizable. We can hear dogfights underway in nearby encampments, the snarls and whimpers nearly drowned out by the hoots of encouragement.

I try sneaking my window up but get a look of disdain from Trini, so I clear my throat and leave it be, wondering at her insistence, like Carlton, on appearing unperturbed by the roadside lowlife and puzzled by my own inclination to give a shit what she, in particular, thinks of me, cowardice-wise. Meanwhile, Father Andre, who's fortunate enough to have me between him and the pawing maulers, is lost in his preparation for the Tell, at least that's what we're hopeful he's doing — there's no real sign other than a phrase or two surfacing up out of his mumbles.

I hear some lines of poetry, which I ask him about.

He looks around first like he's re-getting his bearings. "Yes, young brother, sacred texts of the Yoruba people of Nigeria. It's an origin story: the creation of man."

"What's that name you keep using?" I ask.

"Orisha — a great, knowledgable god. Before there were men, it's said he longed for their presence. The passage starts this way:

"Orísha, the Creator, yearned, and called
To him the longing shades from other glooms;
He threw their images into the wombs
Of Night, Olókun and Olóssa, and all
The wives of the great Gods bore babes with eyes
Of those born blind—unknowing of their want—
And limbs to feel the heartless wind which blew
From outer nowhere to the murk beyond."

Father Andre recites for me the whole poem, his head laid back on the seat. Images tossed into the wombs of night. It was enough to cut my mind adrift ... babes with eyes of those born blind. Me being a storyteller, I couldn't help wondering what got told and retold all those years by those people, all their stories now likely lost, save for what's still etched into the firmer parts of Father Andre's memory.

Trini taps Carlton on the shoulder and then, failing to disrupt his preoccupation vis-à-vis the roadside scum, sharp-knuckles him in the ribs.

"Hey, shit Trini."

She nods diagonally back toward Father Andre.

"Ah, damn, yeah. So hey back there," says Carlton. "What'er you going on about with that?"

Father Andre is still reciting. "And where is Evening? Oh! where is Dawn?"

Trini reaches back and puts a vice grip on his big knob-knee.

"So Father Andre," Carlton tries again, "if that's what you're going with — and I'm not saying there's not a deserving turn of phrase in there — if you're going with that, it'll need some sexing up."

Nothing but nothing from Father Andre. We wait dry mouthed, fighting back visions of food.

"Oh no," he says finally. "Tell the Orisha legend? Well no, I wouldn't think creation myths relevant to my story."

"Relevant meaning...?" Carlton pounds his left elbow down on a mostly complete set of fingers sneaking their way through the window in search of his inside door handle. The would-be intruder opens his mostly toothless maw to protest but instead accepts in that space the butt end of a long-ago emptied Fanta can, deposited by our driver along with a fare-thee-well smack to the forehead.

"Don't misunderstand — these are ancient, ancient life lessons, brother, that have emerged out of our collective selves. But, no, as we discussed earlier, at a time like this, we need to see the world as it is, not veiled in allegory. Legends give us a common mythology, useful in more comfortable times, but the truth — that is the only story worth telling just now."

Carlton rubs his temple. "Look, old man, I gotta tell ya, I'm seeing more truth than we need these days from what you'd call a supply and demand standpoint. Lack of such is what got us here, I'll grant you, but today you got a run-rampant damn overabundance of truth, by which I'm speaking of starvation, pestilence, butchery, molestation, and general inconvenience. Truth ain't what your eager listeners'll be investing their entry tokens in tonight."

Father Andre looks Carlton's way but it's hard to say for sure what he's really seeing.

Trini stares at Carlton too, but in a narrow-eyed kind of way.

"Don't even," Carlton says to her. "This is the hand we been dealt today, girl. Play it or fold." And then he nods toward the Colony entry gate just coming into view. "Got our token?"

Trini looks behind us like she's wondering if it's too late to reverse course but then lets out a slow breath and leans back toward her window to dig into her hip pocket. A blood-and-God-knows-what-clotted hand appears and rakes at her scalp, its leprous owner faltering along sideways to keep up with the truck, throwing his opposite elbow into anyone on the roadside impeding his progress. Fortunately, Trini's hair is sufficiently oiled. She twists out of the grip and jabs forth with three knuckles, making a meaningful impression on the attacker's windpipe. Carlton neither speeds up nor gives the tussle more than a rotation of the eyeballs. And Trini doesn't bother to check back, as do I, to witness the now disabled assailant boot-stomped into the roadside muck by those he had so discourteously displaced.

"Look," I say, "what Carlton's getting at is the same thing, seems to me, what's in your poem." I'm looking at Father Andre, but his eyes are off somewhere. "Because this god, Orisha ... well, he yearned men onto the earth out of nothing. He made us up, like you'd do a story. So we're fiction, the stuff of us. And that's how we lived back before the geeks brought everything down, just couch lounging fictions feeding on non-stop episodes. The circumstances changed but we haven't. Reality can go blow itself, is what they'll tell you tonight."

I haven't yet gotten so much as his eye contact.

Carlton lets out a hoo boy. "I can tell ya from personal experience, kid, based on the beating my knuckles have taken on their skulls, that people ain't fictions."

Trini twirls her finger in a wrap-it-up way.

"Yeah, Trini, yeah. I'm on it," says Carlton, taking a pause to readjust his shoulders. "So here's the deal, Father Andre — you might not see it, but you got the bones of a story in this myth of yours. Granted, you need more drama, but that's easy to fix. And but be mindful, goddamnit, that this audience's got no tol'rance for anything stinking of what-the-world-needs 'cause they got their fill of that with the geeks who, as the kid here alludes, took it upon their foolish selves to make the world a better place. Ain't gonna be nobody listening tonight what didn't suffer deep from all that improvement."

I notice Father Andre's blinking now and even making deep throat grunts in appropriate places, and I can see Carlton notices too. Carlton goes on about what kind of carnal details and bloody elucidation works best on the gristle-brains in the seats.

"They want a vacation from the misery of their pathetic non-fictional existences in an awful enough way," he says, "to die tryin' to get it or no doubt take you down with 'em if they don't."

I'm thinking at this point, had I a couple few hours, I might maybe help Father Andre unravel his myths from his personal memories so as to pull off the narrative coherency we're in need of, but we're coming up now on the Colony.

And so there stand the gates, looking exactly as threatening as intended — layers of welded iron and corrugated steel capped off with another four feet of twisted rebar and barbed wire, the latter extending likewise atop the chain-link fence that surrounds the complex. And for further defense against the hordes, there are all manner of scavenged railroad ties, stripped autos, concrete sewer pipes, and major kitchen appliances piled aside the last thirty yards of road and laterally along the fence line for eighty more.

From a set of gun towers, flood lights bare down on a dozen or so Cyclops-sized guards, most of them only a tad more presentable than the roadside hoi polloi. As Carlton comes to a stop, Trini slaps the token into his palm. A guard steps up — in her case the term Cyclops being medically accurate — and shines a torch on the copper piece, then into Carlton's face. She pauses and stoops down toward the window, squinting with her good eye at Trini.

She snaps her head back up, looking disturbed, and waves us through.

"Tellers!" she roars so as to be heard above the obstreperousness, sending shudders through this poor narrator's bowels. Father Andre tenses too, I see.

Carlton, meanwhile, slaps the wheel. "Ha! Ol' one-eyed Nattie remembers you and your stick, don't she Trini girl?"

Trini I can tell wants to smile bad but hates worse giving Carlton the pleasure.

Carlton finds a spot for the truck. Trini hops out first and pops the back hatch. She grabs for herself a five-foot wooden staff and tosses another to Carlton as he swings down from the side runner. Then she beckons Father Andre out of the back seat, keeping a wary eye on the surroundings.

"That all you carrying?" I say to Trini.

"Only implement allowed inside," says Carlton for her. "But short of a flamethrower, you don't want to go up against Trini with that stick, which is why that charmer back there's without a eye and her compatriot's shy one 'nad."

With that, Carlton jogs off into the dark factory yard.

Father Andre stands by the truck all mum, arms adangle. I give him a nod but his eyes are only about half with me. Trini flips her stick back and forth between her hands and peers into the deep shadow that Carlton disappeared into. She loosens her stance when he returns less than a minute later accompanied by a grimy, wild-eyed urchin, maybe twelve. Carlton fishes around in the back of the truck and pulls out a jar of pickled whatever.

"OK there, Scooter," he says to the kid, "we done this before. You get this jar and another later. But if I find any challenge to the integrity of the vehicle upon our return, I'll break ya down into parts and render your fat for soap."

The boy nods like he's heard it before, which he has. "Don't call me that, damnit," he says.

"Hey," I say to the kid, "so what is your name?"

He glares back through a knot of curls and pulls the jar tight to his chest. "Ain't Scooter, is all."

Our sentry in position, off we go toward some old brick monster still identifiable as the Research Building, with Carlton taking the lead, firm grip on Father Andre's sleeve, then me, then Trini sidling along in the rear, looking near, yon, and lateral, her staff at the ready. We come up on the entrance where one of the three guards raps once, then three times on the door.

Carlton and Trini lower their weapons and wait for the usher, who turns out to be what looks at first like a particularly well-fed she, but soon damn obviously a full-pregnant she.

Trini's eyebrows are up.

"Yeah, been a while since we seen someone openly sporting that business there, h'ain't it Trini?" whispers Carlton to her.

"What's that?" the usher says. She's leading us down a dim hallway.

Over her shoulder she asks what name the Teller's using. She turns to look at me dead on, then at Father Andre, then back at me.

"Father Andre, in your house," says Carlton, nodding to him.

The usher's all self-amused. Trini's knuckles go white on her staff, her not being one to be smirked in the general direction of by someone dumb enough to be in this woman's condition.

Father Andre keeps pace with us and walks steady, but that's about all the outside connection to current events he seems to be making.

"Not much of a talka, your Tella," says our usher, managing to crack herself up.

"So Suzie," Carlton says to her, "what you serving up there? Girl or boy?"

"Fuck ya. And who told ya my name?"

"Well yeah, I met you with Loathsome Carl last winter," says Carlton, shit-eating a grin. "You and he was later entwined in view of the whole assembly up on one of them catwalk couches. Looks like something came to fruition," referencing her payload.

She throws her head back for a high laugh. "And damn right ya are. Being fruitful is one of my best attributes is what Loathsome likes to tell folks."

The dank corridor feeds us out into a lobby that's got some actual working bulbs going, and then it dawns on me the blurbery hum I've been hearing must be some sort of generator churning away below. In the wavery light, I get a better look at Father Andre's condition and it's not encouraging — ashy and hunger-woozed.

"Hey," I say to the usher, "someplace I can take our Teller to freshen up? I think a splash of something cold might be just the thing before his debut."

Me being not much better from lack of hydration, I realize as it's leaving my parched lips how dumb that was and can feel a dual cringe emanating from Carlton and Trini behind me.

Suzie pulls up short, looking serious. "Debut? He never done this before?"

"Not here, Suzie," says Carlton with a stiff throat. "He ain't done it here yet, is what the kid means by that."

"So he ain't heard the Credo?" she says.

"Nah, Suzie. Nope."

She takes a breath, looking up at the moldy drop ceiling and then eye to eye at Father Andre, him rocking back a bit on his heels and then mustering himself to attention.

"Fatha' Andre, you listening? Because this is the Credo and the Foundas need every Tella's 'knowledgment on it."

Trini, Carlton, and I are sharing a communal gulp, but here's Father Andre with a passable nod of ascent, enough to bring air back to our lungs.

"Good," Suzie says. "Goes like this: The rules inside the Colony is different than what's that on the outside. And the rules is called the Rule a Law, which is all historic and olda than all get out, being thought up by ... shit, I used ta know the fella who —"

"Aristotle," Father Andre says, like it was nothing.

"Right ... right. OK, so the Rule a Law works inside the Colony, see, because there's things at stake in here. Outside, they got nothing to lose, nothing at stake, so they show no respect for the Law. Outside, hope's gone. Inside, hope lives on for folks in stories. And for the Tellas, hope's still breathing in the promise of bounty enough to keep on living. And so the stories keep coming. So here's the Rule a Law ..."

Suzie — giving it more spirit than you'd expect from someone who'd no doubt done it on a nearly daily basis — recites sixteen dictates pertaining generally to guests of the Colony and another eight related in particular to Tellers, followed by the penalties meted out for violation of each. When she's done, she asks Father Andre if he understands.

"Yes, little sister."

"Well, better hope ya do old man and ya better make it a damn good story because you won't find me standing between them who failed to and them administratin' the punishment."

To this, Carlton taps Father Andre on the shoulder, waggles out his tongue, and nods over at Trini, who mutely flips back a bird.

Father Andre's still looking at Suzie. He reaches out and rests his hand — the freakishly young one, as it happens — on her little hand, which is resting on her for all appearances ready-to-give-way, natally speaking, belly.

"Beneath your bluster, young sister, we can hear the fear," he says to her, all soft and deep. "But you can feel, can you not, that Mom Earth is guarding this child. And within these walls, in this sanctuary, you practice the Rule of Law as well. Yes, children are food, my young sister. That's what it's come to for those lost ones outside. But when it's your time to bring this child forth, you'll feel the loving hands of Mom Earth around you, as all mothers do who open to Her mindfulness."

Suzie's eyes are wide and pooly. She narrows one down to a slit, letting flow a stream, and yanks her hand free of Father Andre's to forearm the snot off her nose. She looks round at us, ready to slap the snigger off our mouths but sees only curiosity. She points our way forward and heads the other, back the way we came.

"Make it good, Tella," she says as she waddles down the echoey hall, all the vinegar gone from her voice.

Squeej has a groan rumbling before Sam has lowered his notebook. "Sooooo cruel, yo. Nasty to leave us dangling again, my bruh."

"Sorry. I'll keep more coming."

Whit is flat out on his back, feet radiating from the heels like a penguin. "Wow, so Sammy — whole new meaning for the term baby food."

Kesi stretches her legs out, making sure to accidentally pop Whit's ear with her heal. "Whit's just pissed because you didn't put him in the story."

"Whit's not in Sammy's future because he no doubt be one of them geeks that's been aforehand expunged by the hordes," Squeej says under a grimace as he attempts to double his half lotus.

"Guilty," says Whit. "I'm on the endangered list. Sammy you're dead on about the fate of geekdom, but you know what threw me?

The Aristotle. Sure, Andre professed some cool shit, but Aristotle is so ... I don't know — "

"White," says Kesi.

"Yeah."

"Not so strange, so much," says Stefan. "Andre, he wanted the Colony to be its own city. And so, for a city-collective, you need Rule of Law. He is revolutionary, Andre, and socialist, but not anarchist."

"I see a collective, OK, but only as far as it was convenient for Andre," Kesi says. "He was good at getting you all working hard so he could dream away all day about his cities."

"It can be done, Kesi, our little city. We saw it almost happening when there were more people here."

Kesi stands and straightens her T-shirt. "You mean before Andre ran them off, Stefan? Sam, you ever hear Andre talk about collective ownership?"

Sam shrugs.

"Obviously," says Kesi, "he decided he'd stop short of handing over his shares."

Stefan shakes his head. "Hey, now, Andre, he was real generous. Yes, maybe he didn't split the shares in property, but he never asked for rent, did he?"

She steps toward him. "And for all the sweat you've put into those fields, did he promise you he'd cut you in? Ever?"

"Hey, Kes, come on," says Whit.

"Guys," says Portia. She puts a hand on Stefan's arm. "This isn't what we're after. I think Sammy's story shows both sides of Andre's dream, including the pain the poor man went through. Andre said, Sammy, that you've been raised with your eyes open, and even with all his torment, you show his love for people."

Everyone else watches Kesi, who shakes her head.

"You know, Portia, what I saw with my open eyes when I got here was everybody excusing Andre's behavior because of those dreams of his. You blow fucking dream dust on all this, but sometimes a good fight is good for people." She turns for the door. "All this open your heart, bullshit. Sometimes the only way to resolve things is to fight it out."

Arthur awakens cranky. He shoves off Augustina, who makes a play at sharing Stefan's lap.

"I wasn't fighting, Kesi," says Stefan. "Is not fighting to just to say what is true to you." He wraps an arm around each twin and stands. Augustina goes limp, slithering down to his ankles.

"Auggie, please." He calls after Kesi. "Sorry. You got a right, I would suppose."

"Yes, she does, " Portia says, pushing herself up to her knees, "as do we all."

"Yeah, all 'cepting for one maybe," says Squeej.

ONE DAY AND TWO HOURS PRIOR

The Colony, Greenport, New York

Whit stretches out on the bed, one foot dangling low enough to tap out an arrhythmic beat on the floor. His studies a rusty water stain in the plaster overhead that has meandered along a network of hairline cracks and bloomed into neuron-like blotches at the intersections.

Whit's eyes drift shut.

The soft slapping of bare feet draws near.

"How is it?" he says, pushing up onto an elbow.

Kesi has a white towel draped over her head. "Not at all bad. Remarkably, tons of hot water from the solar, but need a better shower head to save on water."

She raises her arms to dry the inside of her ears. exposing her belly between her slight T-shirt and slighter sleeping shorts. Whit's gaze drifts down to her long, smooth legs.

"What?" she says.

He flings his other foot to the floor and sits up. "I guess they assumed we wanted to co-bunk."

She sits on the bed beside him and flips a foot onto her knee. "I seem to remember you correcting Momma Claudia on the 'together' thing. Why didn't you say something when she brought us down here?"

"Same reason you didn't, I suppose."

The towel slips down Kesi's back as she leans forward. Her head is cleanly shaven. Chin nearly to her heel, she uses a fingernail to dig at the site of a splinter.

"Right," she says after a delay. "I'm not sure about that either."

Whit reaches. "Mind if I touch?"

"Why?" she says, involved in her toes. "Are you good with splinters?"

Whit's fingers pad along her scalp and back around to the nape of her neck. She draws her shoulders up to meet his hand, her own fingers pausing in their activity.

"It feels wonderful," he says, sliding up to the back of her head. "I can see why you do it."

She straightens and eases back onto her elbows. "Yes, it does," she says.

She looks up at him for a moment.

"Why did you get into it with Andre?" she says. "I'd think you're smart enough to know not to challenge someone like him."

"Is that what it sounded like? I thought I was agreeing with him, at least up to the part when I was feeding our souls into the System's digestive ... um, system."

"Sure, joke, but his theory seems like the most grounded thing about ... Oh shit."

Andre can be heard approaching from the far end of the hallway, treading heavily.

"... I ask you, what will it take? .... with all the planning and sweat we've put ... just damned clowns and pawns of the System ..."

He passes by their open door, arms raised at contorted angles, dreads bobbing about his face.

"Well no ... no, brother, we will not tolerate your nonsense here."

They wait for his voice to recede.

"Wow, who's he pissed at?" says Whit.

Kesi is on her way through the door.

Andre's voice is booming by the time they join him in the kitchen.

"I ask you again, have you truly committed to this Family?"

Squeej cowers on the opposite side of the cutting table from Andre.

"Is Mom Earth just a source of pubescent amusement for you?" With each point, Andre pounds the table within inches of a ten-inch chef's blade, triggering corresponding facial tics from Squeej.

"Nah, Andre, c'mon." Squeej is close to tears. "Shit, I only meant to say that —"

Andre opens his fist and reveals a ball of paper. He flicks it off of Squeej's chest. Then, dropping his head, he resumes his grumbling posture and stomps out.

"Brother, I've simply no time left for puerility tonight ... fool interrupted my preparations ... a critical test ... you'll need to do some serious maturing ..."

The three wait as Andre's voice travels through the multipurpose room next door and is swallowed up in the hallway beyond.

"Duuu...uuu...uude," says Squeej. He picks up the paper and tries to flatten it on the table.

"What was that about?" Kesi says.

He wipes his nose. "I wasn't meanin' disrespect. It was my lil' ode to Her, right?"

"I think you better ..." says Whit, pointing over Squeej's shoulder. A thick fog rises from a pan of sautéing leeks and garlic.

The chef pivots, all reflex, and removes it from the burner.

Whit twists his head to see the note. "Ah. Today's observations." "Yeah."

Kesi picks up the paper and reads to herself. She smiles.

"Well hey, Squeej, we all loved it," Whit says. "And I know it's meaningful to you."

"Yeah, très meaningful."

"To hell with Andres. No accounting for taste."

Kesi irons the paper between her fingers. "Andre always come down that hard on you, Squeej?"

"Nah, he be chill, gen'rally, you know? Lately, he's buggin' out like this sometimes. Never at me, though. Claudia, she totally needs to get with Andre and see what's up."

Squeej for the first time seems to see Kesi's attire.

She crosses her arms over her chest. "So Claudia and Andre, they're close?"

"Was, more than is. But, yeah, still tight in their way."

Squeej looks past them toward the sound of claws clicking on the floor. "Oh, hey Rosy. Com'ere girl." He walks around the table and kneels, welcoming the dog with a neck hug.

Trini enters, leash in hand. "You burning something in here, Squeej?" She nods hello to Kesi and ignores Whit's wave.

"Nah." Squeej's cheek is pressed into Rosa's ear.

"Something's burning. Can you smell that?"

"Nah."

"Hey, what's up with you, homey? Somebody break your crayons?" She goes to the frig, leaning back to yank open the heavy door.

"Ain't nothing." Squeej pulls his face back and accepts a flurry of licks.

"Can I give Rosa some cheese? What variety of nothing?"

"Sure." He stands and wipes his face.

Trini lays a block of feta on the table and breaks off a two-inch chunk.

Squeej passes her, returning to the stove.

She looks at Kesi.

"He and Andre got into something," says Kesi.

"Yeah? Over what?" Trini lobs the cheese toward Rosa, who meets it at the apex of its arc.

Squeej cocks his head toward the doorway.

"Right," says Trini. "Now the smoke detector's going off. I knew

I smelled something." She leaves, Rosa at her heels.

Squeej slides his skillet back on the burner as Kesi and Whit turn to leave. "Prob'ly just Andre smoking some blaze. He could use some mellowin', for damn certain."

The smell of burning paper becomes pronounced in the multi-purpose room. In the hallway, a white haze hugs the ceiling. Kesi and Whit break into a trot.

Rosa's frustrated barking echoes back to them. As they round the corner into the far corridor, Trini fades through the smoky doorway into Andre's room.

Kesi and Whit follow through, stopping just inside. Orange flames rise from the center of the room. Kesi clamps on to Whit.

Trini grabs Kesi by the wrist and yanks her to the right. "Help me get the sheets off the bed. We can soak them down in the sink."

Whit rubs at the claw marks on his arm as Rosa, yapping, passes him on a tear around the room's perimeter.

The flames spread. Whit waves an arm, hacking.

Much of the smoke coalesces and swirls toward an open window. Andre, kneeling on a low counter, strains to open a second pane.

"Wait, Andre. Christ." To Whit's left, Sam runs along the wall toward Andre. "Keep the windows shut."

The flames, encouraged by the draft, leap higher.

"No, no, it's fine." Andre's voice is barely audible beneath the dog's racket. "I need to see my experiment."

Whit moves to follow Sam but comes to a halt as the extent of the scene registers. In the garish illumination of the flames, Andre's vast cityscape spreads before him across five hundred square feet of open floor space.

"Somebody get over here." Sam pins back Andre's elbows. Rosa circles them, yelping.

Whit heads around to them.

Distracted, Kesi, with a dripping bed sheet held high, cuts

straight across the sprawling model toward the fire. She bounds from toe point to toe point in an attempt to avoid the cardboard structures.

Andre breaks free of Sam's hold. He waves his arms at Kesi. "No, sister, please. You'll ruin everything."

Concentration broken, Kesi trips on a length of aluminum gutter incorporated into the design. She pitches headlong into the flames.

Trini screams and takes off across the model toward her.

Kesi lands on her left shoulder and rolls clear of the fire, but she remains on the floor, struggling to get the sheet over herself.

Andre pounds through from his direction, leaving flattened materials in his wake.

Andre reaches her first and helps her up. Kesi's T-shirt is burned through in areas. Steam rises from her shoulder and chest as Trini apply a wet sheet.

As Trini walks Kesi to the side of the room, a loud hissing breaks out.

"There! There it is." Andre claps as the flames subside beneath a thick smoke plume.

Kesi, attended by Trini and Sam, stands hunched and shaking by the open window. Andre, chuckling, paces the sidelines around the model, watching the water jets, integrated throughout the model, do their work. When the mechanism cuts off, he screeches and skips into a victory dance.

Whit has Kesi straighten and helps Trini remove the sheets. "Do you people have anything we can use on this?"

"Sure." Trini leashes Rosa and goes for the first-aid kit.

"Damn, Andre," says Sam. "You could have let us know what you were up to. I mean, what the fuck?"

Kesi gapes at Andre.

"It's fine, children. It all worked fine." Andre tiptoes to the burned-out area and stoops to examine his handiwork.

Whit turns back to the model as the air clears. Andre has

modeled his town from an eccentric mix of found materials —
terraced housing projects fashioned from stacked cereal boxes and
segments of plastic paint buckets. The mass transit system is made up of
old hoses and twisted aluminum conduits. The intricate detail extends
to shrub groupings and vegetable gardens. Andre has installed aluminum foil solar collectors, oatmeal box wind generators, and yogurt cup
waterwheels throughout the town.

His design accommodates about a dozen semi-autonomous neighborhoods, each anchored by marketplaces, schools, clinics, and arts
centers, bounded by canals and swaths of public green space. Homes
and businesses spiral outward along with parks and waterways.

Despite the damage, there is no mistaking the harmony of Andre's
plan. In some sections, jagged diagonals stagger out as in a rocky
coastline. Elsewhere, the curves suggest the sensuous tangle of a
forest floor, with walkways and bike paths rising over streams and
obstacles in sweeping arcs only to spread back down, forking and
flowing along green spaces like ground-hugging vines.

Back in their room, Whit sits on the bed and snaps open the blue
plastic first-aid kit. He pats the mattress beside him.

Kesi follows instructions, eyes blank.

"I think it'll be OK," he tells her. "Let's get that shirt off."

Kesi narrows her eyes at him, then raises her arms and waits.
Whit sucks air through his teeth as he inches the remnants of her
T-shirt upward.

"So how about Andre, coming for you like that?"

Her eyes reveal nothing as they disappear under the shirt.

"Were you thinking 'Godzilla' when he rampaged across those
little cardboard buildings?"

Kesi is biting her lower lip when her face reemerges. "Actually, I
was thinking, 'Shit, I'm fucking on fire.'"

"Yeah, that sounds about right."

Whit guides her arms down. He takes her left elbow in his hands and turns it, examining her side and chest.

"You really think you know what you're doing, don't you?" she says.

"I am a doctor, you know."

She nods. "Ph.D. in cognitive neuroscience. Not sure if that's relevant."

"It is relevant to all things," he says. "But I confess I only made it through pre-med before deciding doctoring wasn't for me. What a fool I was. This is so rewarding."

"Shut up."

"I mean in a purely professional way, of course. To us doctors, looking at a breast is no different than looking at a toe or an elbow."

"Really? Would you like me to explain the distinction?"

"Maybe later. I'm busy."

He lets her arm down and lays two fingers across her wrist. "I should get some ice water and soft towels. I think you'll be OK. These are mostly first degree."

She rests her other hand on his shoulder while he counts her pulse. "I have a confession to make too."

"Yeah?"

"I saw Trini in the shower room earlier and told her to tell Claudia that one bedroom would be enough."

He puts her hand down and leans in to examine a section of reddened skin just below her right collarbone. He clears his throat. "This part looks like it's going to blister." He circles the area with his finger just above the surface. "And your breathing is getting more hurried. Are you in a lot of pain?"

"The fire, it was really fucked up."

Their eyes meet. "Pretty damn scary," he says.

"Seeing the flames made me feel kind of ... funny." Her eyes widen momentarily.

She pivots her head and kisses him on his cheek. With her freed hand, she finds his and brings it to her left breast, then touches his lips with hers.

"So, it doesn't hurt much," he says.

"No."

With an index finger, he traces a line under her breast and then down to her navel. "You're very warm."

She helps him with his shirt and jeans, then leans in and kisses him. Without removing her lips, she rises to kneeling on the bed, arches her back, and slides her shorts down. Whit wraps his hands around her narrow hips and eases her down onto him, skin to skin.

SIXTEEN HOURS AND TEN MINUTES PRIOR

The Colony, Greenport, New York

Whit slips out of bed and drops to the floor to search beneath the bed. His bare ass is oriented ceiling-ward when Andre enters unannounced.

"Good morning, brother."

Whit spins and hops back on the mattress. He jerks the sheet over his lap, uncovering Kesi's bare back.

"And how is the young sister feeling?" says Andre, scratching his shirtless belly.

Kesi twists her head and opens an eye toward Andre, then groans and yanks the sheet over her head, exposing Whit.

Whit drops back to the floor, this time finding his shorts.

"She's going to be OK," Whit says as he rolls upright on the floor and dresses himself.

Andre stands watching the two of them. He smiles and bongoes his belly with his fingertips.

Whit settles back against the bed frame. "So Andre, your demonstration was quite a hit last night."

A muffled whine comes from Kesi's direction.

Andre steps over and drops onto the bed. He puts a hand on Whit's shoulder.

"I was very pleased, very pleased. Let me ask you, brother, what does one do about firefighting when there are no vehicular thorough-fares?"

"Sorry?"

"You noticed, I'm sure, that there is a complete network of pedestrian walkways and bike paths in my city, but nothing broad enough for cars, and certainly none broad enough for fire engines. In fact, there are no streets. So how do you extinguish a fire?"

"I don't know. I guess you need some pretty good sprinklers."

"Yes, yes, brother, quite so. But we don't want to rely on the pressure from city water lines because in an emergency service can be disrupted. I've devised a gravity feed system that distributes the water from roof-top collectors by way of an aqueduct network. Of course, the model is crude, but my test last night showed—"

"Oh, for Christ sake." Kesi sits up, eyes still closed, sheet clutched to her chest.

She turns away from them for her clothes. Whit leans forward, studying her lower back.

"Wow, Kesi, your tat."

"What's that?" says Andre.

Kesi twists back to face them. "Old man, how about you give Whit a tour of your damn city so I can get dressed?"

Andre's face brightens. "It would be my pleasure. Come, brother." He launches himself off the bed and leaves the room.

Whit stops at the door and turns back to her. "Let me see it."

She bares her teeth.

"Kesi."

"You're a pain in the ass." She drops the sheet and brings the tattoo into view. Flames lick their way up her spine to her shoulder blades. They rise from a single word positioned in the small of her back.

"Does that say MOM? You have a flaming mom tattoo?"

"It says MOVE, you idiot."

"Move? Really? I don't get it. What's —"

"Can I just get dressed?" She stands, avoiding his eyes.

"Sure, but shit, after last night, fire all over your back is —"

"Look, genius, you know what? Ask Andre. Ask fucking Andre Africa what it means."

THREE WEEKS, FIVE DAYS AND TWENTY-TWO HOURS AFTER

The Colony, Greenport, New York

Sam tightens the wing nuts on the standing fan and gets the racket from the grill down to a buzz. After a few seconds, the clatter starts again.

"I think I'd rather sweat," says Whit.

Sam turns back and yanks the cord from the outlet. He retakes his spot beside Portia, angling himself to catch the air she's moving around with her flattened cereal box.

Whit lies on his side, studying Kesi, who has been on and off the stool twice.

She sits again. "OK," she says. And then again, "OK."

She shakes her head as if answering "no" to something she has asked herself, looking up and away from everyone.

"I don't do this sort of thing, talk about myself," she says. "People think they're the authority on themselves. In truth, they're in the worst position to know who they really are. They babble on and on while all the time you can see right through them. I can't stand the thought of doing that — of being that.

"But yeah, I know I have to."

Kesi's Story

Some time back — I guess soon after I finished middle school — at a time when a lot of kids were getting a feel for who they were, I slid the other way.

I remember not knowing ...

Shit, this sucks worse than I thought it would.

OK, when I was seven, I was into yellow. That was me — a yellow wool coat my mom found at the discount store, yellow sweatshirts with ruby sequins in star designs, yellow backpack. My room, every-thing — sheets, walls, lamp — yellow. You got to know my mom hated it, but she did it for me. And I have trouble thinking back to that time and remembering anything bad.

I do remember the day it ended, though. It was when Clarissa Turner tripped me on the sidewalk on the way home from school and hung over me with her nasty-ass friends, foot on my stomach, telling me all the things yellow reminded her of.

Yellow was just the first of the me's, strung out like beads on a necklace, one me knocking into the next. There was the me loving American History, of all things, the me telling my teacher I'd be the first Black woman to be mayor of Philly, then the fool me who got nearly raped by her cousin, and the pissed-off me looking for some-thing bigger and more important to be pissed-off at.

But instead of these little lives building towards something, each undermined me a little more. And, by and by, I fell apart.

And so I was lost in a way I won't get into, and I didn't get back on track until just recently, if you can call this a track.

When I got to the Colony and heard Andre talk about stories, I clenched up inside. Because throughout my early yellow times and even through most of my lost times, I did have a story that was important to me.

The story came from my mom, and she was a damn good storyteller. She'd come up with one at the drop of a hat, but soon she was telling this particular one most every night because I wouldn't stand for any other. She fancied it up more with each telling. Over and over, Mom told it until I wasn't sure if it was part of me or me part of it.

In western Africa, Mom would say, stood a deep forest — the Red Forest — that gave way to a flowing, grassy plain, and beyond that a putrid swampland laced with streams that trickled into a river that snaked this way and that. And in the widest crook of one of those turns was an ancient city called Nok, long past its days of glory.

Over the centuries, those who came through the forest and survived the journey across the plain and through the infested swamp would settle in Nok, building their homes, workshops, theaters, and temples. The structures rose and fell with the centuries, some built so shabbily they crumbled before the end of a lifetime, some outlasting many generations. A number of the stone foundations remained from ancient Nok, although few citizens treated the relics with respect.

A high wooden tower stood in the center of town, built on the base of what had once been a huge stone edifice. The foundation was wide enough to enclose a whole marketplace, which it had at times. The foundation's walls were six feet thick and, had you been a bird overhead, you would have seen that they formed the shape of an enormous leaf — rounded at one end and tapering to a tip at the other.

High up in the wooden tower lived a woman, old beyond anyone's recollection. She was said to be the daughter of a great shaman, the builder of the structure. But few had even caught a glimpse of her. Her father was the source of legends. His name was Sangoma.

In his youth, Sangoma the Healer, it was said, made the arduous journey to Nok. His ambition was to take up the life of a musician in the city and to find the love of a woman. And so on his journey through the Red Forest, Sangoma practiced his music, performing on a wooden flute and dancing over roots and stones along the path. He was unaware, however, that his playing had drawn the notice of the mischievous Red Forest faeries. So entranced were the creatures by Sangoma's tunes that they trailed him as he exited the forest and continued on farther, across the plains, mimicking his dance steps as they went.

But once they moved from the grasslands into the swamps, the mucky ground and undergrowth made travel tiresome. They became angry with Sangoma for luring them from their home. They believed he sought to gain an advantage over them, when in fact Sangoma remained oblivious to their presence.

The faeries threw themselves on Sangoma, stinging him in the fashion of the pests of the swamp and inducing horrifying visions. The torture went on for days until the faeries grew bored and turned for home. But it was too late for Sangoma. He had been rendered mad.

Hope seemed faint to the boy, and fainter still as the delusions persisted. He felt insects swarming over his body. Shrill chanting filled his ears. Worse of all was the breath of the fire demon that seared his back. He was in constant torment, but the flames in fact drove him onward in the direction of Nok.

Sangoma struggled on for days longer, dragging himself through the muck, his limbs torn by the sharp reeds. After a time, as he pushed onward, the stinging and burning eased. The harsh voices aligned and took on more gentle tones. The language was foreign, but with concentration, Sangoma came to understand that the chanting was instructive. He was hearing the spirit of the grand Red Forest shaman, Nommo, teaching him about elemental forces in the world.

Through Nommo's lessons, Sangoma was shown many things. He learned the secrets behind the cycle of birth, growth, death, and decomposition. He learned how ailments of the body and spirit resulted from an imbalance in receiving the natural elements. He learned how to restore the balance, and the path to mastering the elements themselves: water, earth, and fire.

Weeks later, Sangoma made his way into Nok. At first he kept to himself, but as he gained confidence, he revealed his newly acquired learning to those he found trustworthy. Before long, his reputation spread and he was given a shaman's title.

Sangoma practiced his arts for nearly ten years, taking on apprentices and servants to help him with his work. But as he matured, he thought back on his original ambitions. He tried to take up his flute again but this talent was apparently lost to him, as if stolen by the swamp demon. As he looked into the adoring faces of the young women who came to him for cures and advice, he imagined a simpler life and mourned for the love that seemed impossible for him.

Sangoma became disillusioned with his calling and with the passing of time withdrew from human contact, immersing himself in his studies of the elemental arts. Early one morning, hazy from lack of sleep, he experienced a premonition — a huge, tree-like tower springing up from the stone leaf foundation that lay in the center of town. The vision was clear in its instruction and yet Sangoma was troubled by the symbolism. In the leaf and tree structure, he saw only an earth sign. Where were the other natural elements that would bring the tower into balance?

The project took four years and all the influence he could muster to rally workers and artisans of the town. The wooden tower rose high into the air. Its staircase was magnificent, spiraling around the inside wall through multiple chambers to an observatory at the top from which one could see all the way back past the swamps to the Red Forest, its tallest trees rising above the haze in the far distance.

During the first year after its completion, Sangoma gave the townspeople permission to enjoy the tower. They climbed the stairs and flew banners from its windows. They held concerts inside and feasted in the gardens they had planted around its perimeter.

All during this time, Sangoma awaited more instruction. How was he to make use of the tower? At the end of each day, he locked the tower doors. Deep into the night, every night for many months,

Sangoma stood on the altar in the great ground floor hall performing incantations. He petitioned the gods of the forest for guidance, but no new knowledge came to him.

Finally, late one night, as Sangoma tried yet again, he was disturbed by thunder moving in from the distance. It came closer and sounded more frequently until Sangoma could no longer hear himself chanting. Enraged, he gathered powders from the altar and climbed to the deck at the top of the tower. Standing at the edge above the town, he scattered the powders to the wind. Arms to the sky, he screamed admonitions at the god of thunder.

As if in reprisal, lightning struck just beside him, tossing him against the parapet. He pulled himself up but fire erupted, blocking his escape down the stairs. Just as he feared he would perish, a down-pour burst forth, extinguishing the flames.

All the next day, Sangoma lay on the deck lacking the will to pull himself out of the sun. The people of the town had heard Sangoma's tantrum and had seen the lightning strike. His sacrilegious actions frightened them. Fearing the gods' wrath, they stayed clear of the tower.

But as the sun began to set that day, Sangoma was roused by the sound of a sweet, pleading melody far below. He made his way to the parapet's edge and saw a lovely young woman standing at the tower gate, her head shaved in the tradition of the most devout of his followers. In one hand, she held her flute; with the other arm she lifted a girl of six or seven years.

"Healer! Healer!" the woman called. Something in her voice stirred him.

Sangoma descended and joined them just outside the gate. He was taken by the woman's beauty and the pure gaze of the child.

"I am the widow, Isoke," the woman said. "My daughter woke last night just before the fire broke out. She came to me and said you were calling to her. I told her she was still dreaming but she went on into the night and all day today asking for you."

Sangoma held out his hand to the girl and asked her name.

"Kesi," she said. "It means I was born in a time of great trouble for my father."

"Yes," said Sangoma. "I know the meaning."

He asked the mother what had become of the child's father.

"He was dozing under a tree when it was struck by lightening. There was nothing left of him when we arrived."

"Do you remember your father?" he asked the girl.

"No, but I know about the tree and the lightning. He did not know enough to survive the lightning." She looked up at the tower.

"That is because he did not understand the balance of the three elements, Kesi," said her mother.

"Is that true?" the girl asked Sangoma.

"Perhaps, yes," he said.

"Can you teach me about the balance?" she asked.

"Yes," he replied. "But despite what happened to your father you mustn't be afraid of this tower, even though the base is shaped like a leaf; even though it is so like a tree in stature."

"How do you mean, shaped like a leaf?" she asked.

Sangoma knelt and drew the tower's leaf shape in the dust.

"The leaf is an earth sign," he told her. "It is a riddle, you see. Why did the gods instruct me to build this tower that represents only one of the elements? I have failed to find the balance."

The child giggled. "I love riddles. This is a simple one, though."

"Oh?" Sangoma winked at the mother. "And what is the answer to the riddle, my wise child?"

The girl looked solemn. "Will you be my father?" she asked. "If I can answer your riddle, will you marry my mother and be my father?"

Sangoma was taken aback. Before he could think further, he heard himself answer. "Yes, there would be no choice but to do so."

The girl smiled. She pointed to the drawing. "That's not only the shape of a leaf. It's the shape of a raindrop. And it's the shape of a flame. The balance is already here in the tower, Father — earth, water, and fire."

Sangoma and Isoke laughed. They embraced the girl and rocked her with delight.

Sangoma fulfilled his promise, marrying Isoke and raising the girl as his own. He taught the girl as best he could but her curiosity was insatiable. She studied on her own and surpassed him in her understanding of the elements. After her parents passed on, she lived on in the tower. Some say she lives there still, maintaining the balance of the city.

Kesi stops. She looks off toward the windows and hugs herself across the chest. "That's it."

"Nice," says Whit. "You did great."

"You have a fitting name, dear," says Portia. "But you know that, don't you?"

"Sure," she says. "Sometimes, it's about all I'm sure of."

NINE HOURS AND THIRTY MINUTES PRIOR

The Colony, Greenport, New York

Whit finds the improvised gate cut through the rusted chain links at the rear of the factory yard. He exits and takes a foot path along the edge of the fall root field, cutting through a border of dogwoods and gray birch into the "Western Ten" acres. In the tall grass between patches of leafy greens and squashes, a tractor and its hauling cart sit idle. Stefan is nowhere in sight.

He continues on and explores the adjacent fields a while before returning to the compound.

Back at Building 6, the Colony flatbed is absent from its spot in the yard. Through the kitchen windows come the sounds of dishware and chatter.

Claudia and Sam are in conversation when Whit enters.

"I don't think you mean force, sweetie."

Sam stacks plates and returns them to their shelves. "Yeah, I sort of do because we owe it to him. He's slipping, Mom. So let him fight us, you know?"

Claudia scratches at a dried mud patch on her jeans. "How exactly are we going to force him to help himself? We've been through this."

"You know," says Whit. "I spent most of the morning with Andre.

And yes, yesterday's fire was whacked, but today he was fully lucid, his base level of paranoia notwithstanding. And I'll tell you, the man's no lightweight. I can't see any reason why his city plan wouldn't work, other than it being a grand idea and this being the real world, two things that rarely get along. Is that coffee I smell?"

Sam turns to the coffeemaker. "Sure. How do you like it?"

"Black and bitter."

"Like you like your women?" says Claudia, looking up.

Whit's eyes widen. "Claudia — you made a joke."

"It was your joke," she says, straight-faced. "I was avoiding having to hear it from you."

Whit accepts the mug from Sam. "Hey, by the way, what's MOVE?"

Claudia glances at Sam before answering. "Excuse me?"

"Kesi said to ask Andre about MOVE," says Whit, taking in air with his first sip, "but in that endearing way of hers that tells me it would be a stupid damn thing to do."

"Where is Kesi, anyway?" says Sam.

"I don't know. I thought she might be helping Stefan deliver something ... or something."

"Yes, Trini went too," Claudia says. "I thought I just heard a truck. Maybe they're back."

"So anyway — MOVE?" He takes a slurp.

Claudia turns to the fridge and opens the door. "Back up a minute," she says to the tub of yogurt positioned at eye level. "Andre seemed paranoid?"

"No wild outbursts or anything. But as you know, he blames all our ills, whether socio, economic, psychodramatic or otherwise, on the System. It's got that 'they have eyes and ears everywhere' thing going for it, it's got the faceless, robotic bureaucrats — you know, fully certified for consumption by registered paranoids."

Sam is pressing the thumb lever on the coffee pot, flipping the lid up and down. "You think Andre's city plan is just a pipe dream, don't you?"

"Naaah... not a dream, a paranoid fantasy — and it's a valiant battle plan in the ongoing war between the unfortunate and the System. But as we know, it never ends well for the unfortunate, hence their name. Andre's deeper intellect is telling him it's a losing battle, which is too painful for him, which accounts for the euphoric flights of utopian fantasy — which I totally love, don't get me wrong — but it's escapism."

"Still not getting if you think it's bullshit."

"It is and it's not. It's complicated."

"No cars," says Sam. "I love his plan too, but in what universe, right? Andre says cars killed the cities and led to the exploitation of the poor."

Claudia closes the frig door, empty-handed. "He won't get in a car." She moves closer to Whit. "So there you go. How are we going to get him to a counselor if he won't get in a goddamn car?"

"It's extreme, yes. But still, I think he can maintain his equilibrium if we ... if you just let him do his thing. The fire yesterday, that was a misunderstanding."

"No, man, you have no idea," says Sam. "Andre's getting worse by the day." He looks toward the front of the building with the sound of a door clanging shut, then back at Whit. "Complicated how?"

"OK, complicated because, sure, his ideas are wacko, but the world needs wacko. It's like what mutations are to evolution — wackos prod civilization forward. That's because wacko idea-hatchers have an ability to latch on to these pure, beautiful beacons of truth, which often outlive them. It's the easiest thing in the world to dismiss wackos. A little irony and skepticism is all it takes. Irony and skepticism, of course, can make critics sound intelligent, which is why they rely on it so much, but it doesn't advance civilization. It takes sincerely determined nut jobs to advance civilization."

Claudia snickers. "You of all people, condemning irony and skepticism?"

"Why? What do you mean?" He looks at her over the rim of his mug.

Sam pockets his hands. "She means, from the guy who brought us the Voice of God app."

"Ah. OK." He puts the mug on the table and wipes his lips.

"Sorry," says Sam. "I guess you shouldn't have fixed the internet."

"That's alright. I guess if I were you I would google me too."

"I didn't have to. Your name's everywhere. They say you're missing, like for two weeks."

"You're hiding out." Claudia's cheeks are flushing. "You don't want to join us at all. You're ashamed to show your face in public."

"Well, kind of, but no. That's not really —"

"Nothing in the stories say anything about running away, Mom."

"No, they're speculating that he was kidnapped. Were you kidnapped, Whit?"

"No ... I mean almost. But —"

"You want to be a farmer, Whit?" She laughs. "Go off the grid? You want to work on Andre's wacko fantasy team, or are you looking for a hideout?"

"I don't know. I mean, maybe. You're right, it started with me just having to cut loose from what I'd gotten myself tangled up in, but now ... I mean there's Kesi ... and I don't know. What I —"

Whit stops and turns with them toward the doorway.

"That sounds like Kesi," Sam says, already moving.

"And Andre. Damn it." Claudia follows her son. "Here we go again."

Kesi can be heard crying out. "Andre, no ... I'm telling you, no. I know this man."

They round the final corner into the vestibule. Andre is framed in the outer doorway, backlit by the afternoon sunlight. He has a shotgun leveled at Kesi who stands blocking Carlton, lying crumpled on the cement floor.

"Jesus, Andre?" says Sam. "Where did that gun come from?"

Whit steps around to Carlton and stoops for a look.

"Crazy son'bitch rifle butted me 'fore my eyes adjusted." Blood spreads down the left side of Carlton's face from a gash above his temple.

Whit bends to examine the wound. "Shit, man, what the hell are you doing here?"

"There's no mystery there, brother," Andre says, spreading his legs into a firmer stance. "You would best clear away. When this pig of the System gets his due, you'll be caught in the spray, brother."

Carlton grabs on to Whit's knee for leverage as he hoists himself upright. "You gonna call me a pig like that, you best go ahead and shoot me, y'old maniac."

Andre's face is all shadow. He nods at Kesi. "Is this the kind of deviant company you keep, sister? No doubt this man has been sent here to destroy our work."

"Don't be a fool, Andre. It's just Carlton." Her hands are extended toward the gun, shaking. "He gave us a ride here, Whit and me. Tell him, Whit."

"Andre, yes ... absolutely. Listen to Kesi."

"Put the gun down, dear," says Claudia. "Let's just talk to the man."

"I say I wanna talk to you damn kooks?" Carlton pushes Whit away. He wrenches his T-shirt off and balls it against his forehead. "That'd make me as crazy as y'all."

Andre cocks one of the barrels and takes a step to the side where he has a clean line of sight on Carlton. "Get up now. There's no way around shooting you. There's nothing else to be done."

"Andre!" Kesi, palms still forward, steps back in front of the rifle. "Would you shoot me too? Am I a pig too, Andre?"

Carlton chuckles. He gets to his knees. "Move aside, Kesi. He ain't gonna do shit."

Kesi throws her head back. "Fuuuuckk."

"Sister, you should heed your friend's advice. I will not release this man. He'll be back with ten more of his kind, and that will be the end of all we have worked for. Move aside, my sister."

Kesi clamps her eyes shut and wraps her arms around her head. Her face contorts. "Fuck you, Andre. Stop calling me sister. I'm not your fucking sister."

Whit takes a step toward her but pulls up when Andre flicks the gun in his direction.

"Don't you remember me?" Her knees loosen and she drops to the floor. "I'm your daughter, you lunatic bastard. I'm Kesi."

Andre yanks the rifle up to eye level. He stands firm but there's a waver in the gun barrel.

Bit by bit, Andre relaxes his shoulders and the gun comes down. "Kesi?"

"Have you forgotten everything?" She covers her face with her hands. "I'm your daughter."

Portia sits alone with Andre for nearly a half hour, calming him with her angelic voice. Finally, she slips the rifle from his grip and hands it to Claudia. The others walk Carlton to the lav to tend to his wound.

"I know. You heal fast." Whit applies a second butterfly bandage to the gouge in Carlton's broad forehead, sneaking glances at Kesi, leaning against one of the sinks.

Carlton nods. "This'll do it."

"You should get an ice pack for the swelling." Whit snaps the first-aid kit shut. "Andre was waiting for you inside the door? How did he know you were coming?"

"Pro'bly he saw me peeking through some windows 'cause I did circum-traverse the building before coming in. There weren't no one present out in the yard, nor a dog."

"Good thing you got there when you did," Sam says to Kesi.

Kesi turns toward the window in the back wall of the building that is darkened by a profusion of mugwort and milkweed.

"And by the way, girl, as messed up as that old man is, I wouldn't of spoke to him that way had I known he was your father. I'd of shown respect, for your sake, though I ain't saying I respect what he's about. And also by the way — which really ain't by the way, it's the damn reason I come back here, which was to warn you — I seen Opie's devotees in the Lexus again."

"Oh, for Chrissake."

"Yup, I take it that's whose sake they think they's doing it for." Carlton turns to scrub his T-shirt, soaking in the sink. "I'd stayed the night at a motel down in Beacon. Had some pretty decent huevos rancheros this morning. Then I head out south on 9W. There they were, making there way up here."

"Who? What devotees?" Sam grabs a bar of soap from the shower and brings it to Carlton.

"Thanks. Yeah, so I figure, if I seen them, they seen me, meaning they know they're getting close to y'all. I double back by another route. They're no doubt still snooping 'round about here somewhere."

"Damn. OK," says Whit. "I guess thanks, though I'm not sure why you care."

"Yeah, don't flatter yourself. Ain't you I'm worried about," nodding sideways at Kesi. "You made your bed, Opie. That don't mean the good people around you deserves to sleep in it."

"Oh, I see, so you think I deserve all this."

"Yup, I do. I don't know the specifics but I see guys like you who's usually standing around looking like a fire hydrant, complaining about getting pissed on. It ain't outright doing the wrong thing, more like not caring enough to put effort into what's right."

"Sorry that I'm a disappointment to you."

"So, hey, Kesi." Sam waits for her to look his way. "When's the last time you saw Andre? I mean, before you came here?"

She stares for a moment. "May 13th, 1985."

"Wow, good memory," says Whit. "Isn't that before you were born?"

"I was a baby."

"Really? You look younger. So, what, your mom told you?"

"Yes, but she didn't have to. It's in the history books."

"What is?"

"Jesus," says Sam.

"What?" Whit watches Kesi turn away again.

"Philadelphia," says Sam. "Whit, you asked about MOVE? That was the day, in Philadelphia. Pretty sure that was the day the cops firebombed MOVE."

"No shit? That damn well explains it, now don't it?" Carlton wrings out his shirt. "That crazy ol' man was in MOVE?"

Whit's glances from face to face. "Am I the only one in the dark here?"

"Crazy ass radicals." Carlton shakes out the shirt with two snaps. "Back-to-earth nut jobs, no offense to them present. But you c'ain't live in a city the way they was living and disrupt a neighborhood and disregard health regulations and expect the authorities to just turn a blind eye."

Kesi hits him with a hard look. "My, aren't we well informed?"

"Saw a special on cable."

"Well, they obviously fed you the same bullshit that was in the newspapers. You've got no idea what really went down. And John Africa, he was a kind, smart man. Yes, he had strong beliefs, but he wasn't a nut."

"He had them people of his all believing that cult mumbo jumbo. Then he gets them armed to the teeth and antagonizing the cops.

Don't sound so smart to me."

"John Africa? Was that Andre's brother?" says Whit.

She looks up at the ceiling.

"They all took the name Africa," Sam says. "They lived together in a house back in the '70s but the city gave them trouble. The cops stormed the house — and one cop got killed. They arrested a bunch of the MOVE guys for murder. Then it was like ten years later in another house when it all totally blew up."

"Your mom tell you about this?" Whit says.

Sam shrugs, then nods.

Kesi turns to Whit. "They lived in that house together — peacefully. It was the cops antagonizing them, not the other way around. John Africa was defending his family. He was fighting oppression. He cared about the destruction of nature he saw in the city and the destruction of his people from dope and from poverty. And dealing with psycho cops, most of them Vietnam vets with PTSD."

"The family'd built this bunker on the roof," says Sam. "The police flew in with a helicopter and freaking firebombed it."

Carlton walks to the shower and hangs his shirt over the curtain bar. "If the cops was vets and they had problems, maybe they shouldn'ta been messed with. Maybe John Africa shouldn't of been harboring guns and putting his so-called Family in that situation. It's all about having no respect for institutions and those that fought for the country."

Kesi steps toward him. "Ah, I see — you're a vet. You're one of those people we should be thanking for keeping us safe. One of the people we should show respect to as they're trying to kill our babies and burn us out."

Carlton crosses his arms and leans against the wall tile. "Yeah, matter fact I been at war — Afghanistan. And I haven't held a gun since and ain't planning to ever again. And I don't excuse what those cops did. Only saying, you mostly got to fault that nut for putting his loved ones in that dangerous situation, all for some anarchist principles."

"They had no choice, Carlton. They were under attack in '85 just like in '78 when Rizzo's storm troopers practically beat one of them to death right on the street. And yes, the six are still in prison and not one cop was punished."

"Kesi?" Whit catches her eye. "Were you and your mom in that house?"

"No, our house was a block away. They evacuated us with the rest of the neighborhood."

"And the MOVE Family in the house — did they get out alright?"

"Jeez, man," says Sam.

"No, everyone did not get out." Her eyes glaze with tears. "Eleven of them died, Whit. Five of them were kids. Five children. Only two people got out."

"And the fire spread," says Sam, after a while. "Like fifty houses went up in flames."

"Sixty-five. It burned two hundred and fifty people out of their homes in the neighborhood — our neighborhood. My mom lost our home that my grandpa left her. The cops and the fire department decided to let the fire go so they could burn the Family out."

Whit rubs his chin with the back of his hand. "So two survivors. Who got out besides Andre?"

"There was a little boy and Ramona Africa." Kesi's voice is low. "Andre? He wasn't in that house. He was with us at my mom's. But she told me that, on that day, he took off."

"Cool. So Andre is like the lost man of MOVE," says Sam. "It's no wonder he's laid low all these years."

"Nah, that ain't right. He ain't no MOVE guy," says Carlton. He looks at Kesi. "They all been accounted for, right Kesi?"

She gives a weak smile. "He thinks he is but it was just him freaking out from everything burning around him. It was the whole Nam nightmare brought back on him. He's a vet too, Carlton. He freaked out and split on us. That's what my mom says. He was never in MOVE. And his name's not Andre. It's Lawrence Tripp."

"And he's been laying low all these years?" says Whit.

"Wow," says Sam. "Poor Andre."

"Well, poor Andre shouldn't have a shotgun," says Carlton, turning for the door. "You think I could get a drink of something, stretch?" he says to Sam.

"Sure, come on." He leads Carlton out.

Whit and Kesi stand in silence.

Whit leans against the sink behind her and strokes her arm. "I'm sorry, Kes. They didn't teach us this stuff where I grew up."

"Yeah, well they wouldn't want people like you to know, now would they?"

"I guess not." His stroking stops. "What do you mean, people like me?"

She settles against him. "I've been looking for two and a half years. I've lived in four places like this. I heard rumors now and again that he'd been here or there, otherwise I would have quit."

"This began after your mother died?"

"How did you know she died?"

"You don't have a cell phone."

"Right."

"So what were you expecting was going to happen when you found Andre?"

"I don't know. I had a lecture worked out in my head. I imagined him apologizing. But then I also thought he'd be this strong, wise ... I don't know."

"Well, hell, why wouldn't you wish for that? I would."

She wipes her nose on her shoulder.

"And, you know, he is strong, Kes. And he's purposeful and pretty damn brilliant. A lot of people wish their dads were like that, me included. Yeah, he's nuts, but it's hard to separate that from the brilliant, and maybe you shouldn't try. What he needs is someone to help him deal with the real world so he can bring some enlightenment to people."

"I don't think that's going to happen. I don't think he can ever come back to the world. It's been so many years and he's just getting worse."

"You're probably right. But, you know, all those years, he didn't have you."

"What makes you think he's going to?"

She sniffs and straightens her back. "You know, you seem to have a pretty good handle on what it takes to be a good person. Why can't you just follow your own rules?"

"I don't know," says Whit. "I'm going to give that some thought."

THREE WEEKS, SIX DAYS AND TWENTY-ONE HOURS AFTER

The Colony, Greenport, New York

Squeej stands hunched over the stool, using the seat as a writing surface to make final edits to his poem. His lips quiver as he reads. He scratches out a line and enters a replacement. He floats one hand above his head, palm wide like a satellite dish.

"Hey, Squee-bo." Stefan rubs at his hair. "We been here quite pretty long time waiting patient. I never see you putting effort such as this into 'today's observations.' How about we get on to it?"

Squeej spots something else. He holds up an index finger with his vibration-monitoring hand and then goes back in with his pen.

Stefan appeals to Claudia with his eyebrows.

Squeej finishes. He pats the air just above the surface of the stool as if settling the poem's capriciousness. He picks up the papers and turns to the group.

Squeej's Story

OK, so Whit, man, you was sayin' you wanted to hear about Ohio.

Sorry, I tried, but it just weren't flowing. I'm thinking, might be 'cause I was so much a part of that Ohio life that I can't pull a story from it — like the thread not seeing the pattern in the cloth, feel me?

We were, yeah, Mennonite and all, being not the Plain Folk but what they call the Moderate kind. And I can see you being all curious about that life, but we weren't all that different from your mall-going, lawn-mowing Ohioans. There was nothing but flat and storyless day-to-day same-old same-old growing up. You had your prayers and your school and your chores and your meals and more prayers. And not so much even rules they'd get on you about so much as what they call the emphasis, you know, on Salt and Light. That's Matthew 5:13, 14 — Sermon on the Mount — salt of the earth, light of the world.

Once I got the cooking itch, though, man, I stepped right out that life like dropping muddy overalls off me, and I was gone without so much as a sniffle. But damn if I don't cry now and again thinking back on those loved ones, because love me they did. And no doubt it's Salt and Light in every drop of my tears. You don't totally shake that upbringing off you or cry that outta you.

But as much as that life had nothin' in the way of stories, life in kick-ass New Yawk City had nothing but. Stories, they come at you like frames in a graphic 'zine, every time you turn a corner, all them chill heroes and villainous, wild ones all buggin' and bitchin' and tusslin' and singin' and crackalackin', all crammed into each panel like post-concert partiers on the D train.

Trini, she first came at me like that, a' anime princess rampaging in, with her stick a-whirl and her teeth bared against them demony ninja hordes. That's how I first seen her.

How that came to be ...? Well, it was like about six, maybe eight months of me working on the prep line for Chef Sanford, and one morning outta nowhere the building across the street blows. It's like freakin' — fa-bloom. Our front windows — the ones I been wiping down like twice weekly, being my record of transgressions — go flying in across the front of house in a gazillion nasty shardlets. We're not open, so no glass stickin' outta customers or nothing. And the crew's all okay but, like, you're not really OK, man, 'cause your head's pumped full of high drama. All us — Oscar, Kaseem, Lana, Jorge — we haul ass it across the street where the building's only by-the-grace-of still standing and there's flames and smoke ballooning out in all aspects.

I see it's Ibrahim, the old Syrian grocer, who got blown out. He's stumbling out of what's left of his shop, black like he crawled out of some mine, and one of his honorable sons is there in front of him, all misaligned on the sidewalk. Ibrahim, his legs go and he hits the ground hard, poor soul. I can see blood pretty bad flowing from one arm. He tries but can't push himself up, him screaming back in at his store something so heart wringin' it's gotta be his wife's name, you know? But before I can make it over to Ibrahim, some big, thick-neck dude's running over from next door and he's on him, yanking him up by the apron. He's shaking that good man Ibrahim all hateful. "You tapped my gas, you dirty..." and calling him all racial stuff.

I get to them first and I lay a hand on big white meaty's shoulder which is all it took to have him smacking me hard enough 'cross my ear to drop me. Sous Chef Oscar gets into it too, but now there's three, four more of meaty's family.

I get back up, but I can't move. I mean I can but I can't, you know, because of the Mennonite way. It's not even a won't, it's like I don't know where the fighting muscles are. And standing there begging for them to stop, again I get the smackdown again and then kicked in my head and my gut and my balls.

Spinning's all I remember and the face right by me of Ibrahim's son, who's not waking up, most his beard singed off and missing most of a' ear.

It was I guess the sound of the sirens and horns brought me back. But also I'm hearing screams like from the meaty boys themselves. I roll myself over and up and look and it's Trini.

So yeah, first time I see Trini, I'm looking up at a righteous warrior, hair spiked and outrageous like it were then, her swinging down with all she's got with a broom handle, coming down thumpa across their shoulders and then cutting back up underside the jaws of them beefy dudes. Then she's pulling me up by the armpit, her stick still winging 'round keeping all them at a distance, standing over old Ibrahim, keeping him safe.

I'd left the Ohio family, no doubt, but the family hadn't left me. I, on that day, showed my example — shining my light of peace — trying at least to work the peaceful way. And no way did it work. And really it was more like the way having its way with me than me working it for any good.

Trini, she was God's warrior for me from first contact. And no, I'm no closer to ever changing over to the violent way, but that's just how it was. Trini had the flame and sword in her like I had the Salt and Light. She was everything I wasn't, but she was good, and we were brother and sister from the start.

Trini at that time was with Margot, having up and split with Ignacio, her old loser boyfriend who'd you'd call abusive 'cept nobody'd think of raising a hand to Trini. He was still pining for Trini and coming 'round with Rosa, him using clueless Rosa like a child to guilt her back and Trini, she wasn't having none of it, and Margot was decent and protective and showed her consideration and love.

And so anyway, after Trini peeled me off the street, we fell in thick as friends. She and Margot needed a living situation and they especially needed a way to duck Ignacio since he'd progressed abuse-wise to tormenting Trini for money he said was owed him. And it so happened I was trying to take over a friend's apartment who couldn't make rent, so we decided to share the place. Trini got a regular shift tending bar down on Ave B, Margot was working counter at a bakery, and so with the hours, we weren't all there at the same time much, but it worked out good enough. And I had every reason to be content.

And what worked out fine too was Ignacio not knowing where Trini'd gone to, so for a couple months, all was chill.

Then we get back to the 'zine action, and not in a good way. One Thursday, which is my off night, I see Instagrams from a friend saying come to the bar where Trini's working for shuffleboard night. So I head down, but little did we know that Ignacio, he too followed that friend and I'm not in the bar more than a few minutes and sure enough he shows up, yanking Rosa in with him.

The place is packed and the bouncer's on him immediate but Ignacio's shoving him off and yelling for his money at Trini, and Rosa is all grisly jumping up at the bouncer's face, and I'm useless as usual in such situations.

Trini's short fuse is lit. I'm trying to calm Rosa down and I look up to see Trini aerial over the bar, trajected at Ignacio. Rosa poor girl's got no idea which of the two to stand by so she's defending them both, snapping at the crowd, which is getting increasingly pissed, picking sides and uploading videos. Cans and glasses and bar snacks is flying, and I hear Rosa whelping. Trini's got Ignacio face down in the glass and sawdust and house pilsner.

We all pull Trini back. Ignacio takes off, leaving a confused-ass Rosa. Trini gets told by her manager to punch out, like permanent.

And so starts a time when, though I still got no right to misery, given my friends and employment, I get all kinda bad thoughts. Maybe it was, like, between poor Ibrahim's tragedy and the Ignatio tussle, things got stirred up inside me. Maybe I felt my family ways coming back at me for penance.

So shortly then after all those feelings come to a head in a truly hellacious night. You'll tell me it was all in my mind — a nightmare, sleeping or walking — but I'm here testifying it was hard cold real. And I'm just gonna rhyme it out for you, my night ride to hell 'cause, I don't know, it's the only way I can deal with the undeal-withable.

Here we go ...

Home from a shift and cravin' my sleep,
Rosa all pathetic whiny for her just-lost master,
Ghosts from Ohio, up on me creep,
Making the slumber I'm seeking the stock of their laughter.
So up I rise, my work-dead legs driven,
Wondering inside what it is I quest after,
A lost missionary, ignoring his mission,
Drifting down Broadway past storefronts with no answers.

In Union Square there, wearing nothing but pants,
With wind whistling chords 'round that statue of Abe,
Was a' African priestess twirling a dance,
Giving off airs of some forgot-about fable.
Told in a fashion words fail to tell,
With motions that'd shake the man from the Mennonite,
Like Herod held in Salome's spell,
I stood 'neath the cold anti-loitering light.

Her freestyle was funky without losing the regal,
Flowin' and poppin' in rhythms amazing,
With bare-breast abandon she scoffed at the legal,
Her feet leaving swipes of macadam a'blazin'.
And on her closed lids, a set of lips was dyed,
Silently, slyly singing to me by winkin',
And on her lips was painted the pupil of an eye,
So with her mouth set upturned, she glared at ol' Lincoln.

Her back screwed 'round in unnatural limbo,
And, like yanked indiscriminate by competing masters,
Her inky appendages twisted akimbo,
In a language with meaning I couldn't gather,

Each pose hitting angles like musical notation,
Spelling out some unknowable truth,
Like 'glyphics from Egypt or characters in Asian,
Or algebra equations from some mystical sooth.

But by and by she made her meaning more plain,
Pulling wrists together as if they'd been bound,
Draggin' her feet like her ankles was chained,
Jerkin' her back like a whip had come down,
Begging for freedom, like a slave to be traded,
Her taunts made clear without a translator,
Her people's captivity, she shrewdly charaded,
A mocking proclamation for the Great Emancipator.

There came on a feeling, there in my daze,
Though all seemed as real as reality gets,
That all about me was staged for my gaze,
That dancer prepping me for what was comin' next.
Then my arms felt drifty and my legs went light,
My vision smeared streaky into vertical stripes,
Alice-ways falling, losing the Square from my sight.
Tumbling through pavement, wiring, and pipes.

Past rebar and sewers, granite and pumice,
Then nothing to see in the darkness insane,
Just a distant rumble approaching all om'nous,
The growing clatter and roar of the Q train.
In that cold and empty sub-earthian car,
Fluorescents blasting my vision to white,
I was holding on dear to the overhead bar,
Of the hurtling Q on its course through the night.

From the next car down — clang — the doors flew open,
And in crawled a freaky ol' soul, so aged,
Her back doubled forward like two-times broken,
Her scalp raw and scabby like scratched at in rage.
She straightened to show me a belly round-swollen,
And toothlessly grinned in a fiendish flirtation.
Her words crackled out like a prophesy spoken,
As that train barreled heedless through Canal Street station.

"I'm pregnant with child to be curs'ed at birth,
Mom-Earth's destroyer, an ungodly eminence,
He'll suckle the last of Her milk to come forth,
Thy own seed," she told me, "thou Father of Pestilence."

The car lights cut out with her speech-ending cackle,
Throwing my bod' into spazanoid cringe,
But just when I thought I'd lose all my spackle,
The train burst out onto the East River bridge.
Spread out below was a view of Manhattan,
And had words been forthcoming, it've rendered me dumb,
'Cause not a light was alit, not a single thing happ'ning,
In that hor'fying preview of the City to come.

Rising up thousands of feet in verticular,
Clogging up every square inch of the Apple,
Was zillions of 'scrapers in every form and particular,
All scratching at heaven like towers o' Babel.
And spanning the river from the Seaport to Brooklyn,
Was freighters and barges, too numerous to number,
Each piled overflowing (let us be forgiven),
With pitiful corpses in eternal slumber.

Down again into the tunnel we rumbled,
The train crying out in screeches and sparks,
Then at Dekalb, the brakes sent me tumbled,
Dropping me tangled and beat in the dark.
The doors sprung open and in came a breeze,
All earthy and wet, like the blow off a rainstorm,
But weird as it was, it put me at ease,
And nearly too late, I dove for the platform.

With eyes near useless and my wherewithal fadin',
I made out the source of the moisturous air,
From somewhere above, it was water cascading,
A brook all a-burbling flowed down from the stairs.
My sight got adjusted, a figure 'came clear,
Posed as holy and straight as a Padre,
Dreads full aflowing, aspect austere,
A bro' I'd later know as our Andre.

I watched as the stream-a-let lapped 'round his feet,
And saw that instead of the concrete beneath us,
The place was thick with this loamy-ass peat,
All living with worms a'churn in the humus,
Like some fast-acting compost but smelling far worser,
The whole nasty business was on itself feeding,
And Andre amused like a medieval sorc'rer,
As sprouts came up springin' like Mom-Earth's new Eden.

Like Almighty'd revved up his Genesis action,
So florals and faunas of various persuasions,
Hit full-blown existence in nary a fraction,
Of the time it took on that original occasion,

Twining round Andre and filling all gaps,
Was everything living, however unprobable,
From kudzu and stinkweed, to lizards and bats,
It was bio all right, but minus the logical.

With all of creation creating in all d'rections,
I barely felt myself riding at all,
On their leaf-ends and tendrils and fleshy projections,
Like mosh pit dancers transporting their idol,
Past Andre I drifted on that nat'ral selection,
Over the turnstiles and up through the stairwell,
Deposited onto Flatbush Avenue Extension,
Dropping me harsh in a nasty-ass fare-thee-well.

Cashless and seeing no cab ride before me,
I strided up onto the Brooklyn Bridge footpath,
The weight of the 'sperience hurting me sorely,
A bod'-thrumming, heart-drumming, brain-bumming
aftermath.
But then like a stove fire, the sun rose upriver,
And betwixt the girders, that orb lit my path,
From shadow and back into glory delivered,
From darkness to daylight, I repeatedly passed.

So devoid of even shreds of thinking power, I somehow make it back home about an hour after dawn. Just as I'm getting in, Margot's heading out and her eyes tell me pretty clear what I look like. I flopped out hard horizontal for a good eighteen hours, waking up with both Margot and Trini leaning over my bed like they was farm hands welcoming back Dorothy.

I spared no details, more probably an exercise in testing its unrealness out on my own ears, and as I tell it, Margot's getting increasingly freaked. She's from Trinidad and of the Orisha faith, not that she'll admit to practicing. And later she's all whisperin' and hissin' at Trini out in the kitchen, but Trini says back on purpose loud enough for me to hear for Margot to stop with the demon-talk bullshit.

And but if it were me raised like Margot in that West African tradition, that's a deep thing, and here I am trying to make rational the old hag on the Q identifying me out as the soon-to-be father of the accursed one and, well, who can blame Margot for getting her freak on, right?

I sit down with Margot again and give her my take, that it was all really a symbolic like revelation meant to remind me of my responsibilities Salt and Light-wise. It was pretty obvious to me I was getting reprimanded for straying from my guidance and losing touch with the Salt and the soil and getting in too tight with wayward folks. But Margot can't see that. And she also can't see how Trini ain't one for ultimatums. And so, by and by, it's Margot packing up her moving boxes, not me.

But here's the part that brings me here to you, because it's not more than a couple days later that Trini, gainfully unemployed, finds a pottery apprenticeship up here in Millerton and, from the potter woman she learns of a working collective looking for new dedicated parties. And when I heard about that — the soil connection and working with what grows out of it and so forth — it was all revealed to me, as real as tasting the Salt on my lips and feeling the sun's Light on my face.

All that falling in place told me too to stop trying to think deep thoughts about that dance of the African priestess and my hell ride on the Q and New Eden rising in Dekalb station. It told me, especially once I'd met Andre, to just accept what transpired as a blessing and trust where my path is.

'Cause, yo, as magical and haunting as it was, it wasn't all that special, my brothers and sisters, if you're open to seeing the specialness in all things. For indeed, all things are in themselves of particular and unique specialness. And seen that way, no doubt, everything you see is a vision, yo. Meaning just seeing any old thing in that particular way, that makes you a visionary.

Sam steps up, twists Squeej by the shoulders, and hugs him from behind around the neck. "You're the visionary, bro."

Kesi is joyful, slapping her knees.

Portia claps with her fingertips. "Props, baby cakes."

"I too will join in adoration of the Squeej," says Stefan, "but at same time, it was a creeped-out thing to be hearing from one's chef, no? In regard to not wanting this kind of vision in someone preparing our meals? Is not a comfortable notion, yes?"

Whit's head is down, both hands raised. "Just wait. Whoa —"

Squeej coughs off Sam's chokehold.

Kesi turns to him. "Hold on. The scientist has a problem with Squeej's premonitions."

Whit looks up at her, blinkless. "Actually, no. I'm suspending disbelief."

"Ditto," says Squeej, knuckling Sam in the ribs to back him off. "Any manner of analysis jus' gonna lead to paralysis."

"Totally. I get that. But the Father of Pestilence thing. You, Squeej ... you are not him."

The group hushes at the emotion in Whit's voice.

He clears his throat. "I am the Father of Pestilence. That witch — she was talking about me and what I would bring on you here."

Portia's small sigh punctuates the silence.

Claudia brushes the hair back from her forehead. "I wouldn't have expected to be saying this," she says. "But I think we may be growing up."

TWO HOURS AND FIFTY MINUTES PRIOR

The Colony, Greenport, New York

Whit steps outside into the evening. To the west, the storage building roof cuts an angled silhouette into a flush of grapefruit sky. He pushes his hands way down into his pockets and stiffens his legs until they shake.

At a blur flashing before him, he ducks, hands trapped in pockets. Rosa lands a few yards past him with a scrabble of claws on loose gravel, a Frisbee clamped in her wide jaws. In a single motion she regains her footing and turns back toward Trini with her prize.

"Damn." Carlton leans back against the Colony flatbed. "Lucky she weren't making her rounds when I came strollin' in here."

"Got that right," says Trini, whipping the Frisbee out again, this time well past Whit. She strips off her work shirt, revealing a skimpy tank top and tight, athletic shoulders. Running down her right arm is flowing script — MADRE AMOROSO — and more ink on the inside of her left — a dagger through a bleeding heart.

"That all bark, no bite thing doesn't apply to this girl," she says.

"You're talking about the dog?" says Whit through clenched teeth.

"Yeah, her too. If something unfamiliar is made of meat and moving, like Carlton here, she figures it's food. What's with you? You cold?"

Rosa makes another aerial grab, but this time falters on the landing. She log-rolls and struggles to find her feet, kicking up dry dirt. The Frisbee never touches the ground.

"No, I actually came out here to catch some cool breeze, and because I've got this annoyance in my legs telling me my anxiety's coming on strong and, by the way, all three of you intimidate the living shit out of me, I just thought you should know."

"Hey Opie, thanks for sharing that and we don't give a shit," says Carlton. "How's that girl doing in there?"

"You mean Kesi? The little girl who saved your redneck neck earlier?"

"Yeah, Kesi who shoulda had her lunatic father in a' institution and me being the one who I recall saved your whiney ass."

Trini plays tug of war with Rosa over the Frisbee. "Seeing Andre must be digging up some deep emotional shit for Kesi. I'm sure we don't know the half of it."

"It'd be nice to get a' actual answer to my question about how she's doing."

Whit turns and leans like an ironing board against the truck beside Carlton. "OK, let's plot Kesi's inner conflict matrix. Say the X axis ranges from 'Dad-totally-screwed-me-up' at zero to 'I'm-not-going-to-let-my-shitty-childhood-define-me' at one hundred. On the Y axis, maybe we start at a base line of 'the-System-totally-screwed-me-up' and run up to 'I-shall-overcome' at the top. In my estimation, her coordinates have gone from about X15-Y25 to X60-Y55 in a single day, after confronting Andre. That was something she obviously needed to do very badly. So, yeah, tough day but productive on the Kesi front — and a lovely front it is."

Carlton looks away and tugs at his earring. "The day you ever talk like a person is the day people might start treatin' you like one."

"Life's complicated and so is explaining it." Whit blinks and jerks his head sideways. He claps in front of his face. "Are these things only attacking me?"

"No-see-ums," says Carlton.

"But I'm touched by your concern." Whit returns his hands to his pockets. "Once again, you double back to help us, presumably out of some misdirected sense of ... I don't know. What do you call it, Carlton? Clearly you're not sympathetic to what we're doing."

Carlton shakes his head at Trini. "You b'lieve this brat? And like you're part of what's doing, Opie? Since when you got a purpose in life?"

Trini smacks the Frisbee against her thigh to knock off the drool, then sends it aloft again. "Hey, you're both still strangers to me. It looks like Kesi, on the other hand, is part of the family so I get why she's here."

"It's just that we can't figure out why Carlton gives a crap, Trini. It's a bit unsettling."

Carlton pushes off the truck and turns to face Whit. "Not that I owe you anything in terms of justifying my behavior, but what I give a crap about is bein' responsible, and that's a state of mind, as opposed to not just looking the other way saying it ain't my damn problem when shit happens right in front of you. That includes aiding people who is obviously alone and on the road needing assistance even if they's too stubborn to know it."

Whit smirks. "Wow. It's like if St. Christopher could talk hillbilly."

Trini laughs. "Shit, man. You get beat up a lot?"

"And yeah," poking Whit's chest, "I give a crap that civilization is fallin' down in chunks around us, which wouldn't happen if people like you spent your precious time being responsible for other people."

"Got it. I'm also getting the feeling you weren't always this responsible. Smells vaguely of penance."

"Yeah, whatever." Carlton steps back and looks toward the windows of the multi-purpose room and the clinks of the table being set for their late dinner.

Trini stoops again and greets Rosa. "So Carlton was saying Andre hasn't seen Kesi since she was a baby?"

Whit crosses his arms and hugs his shoulders in straitjacket position. "Yeah, well, Andre's cozy neighborhood in Philly got invaded by the goon squad — Andre had been back from Nam for some time, but still, when your world erupts into a hellish fireball ... well, cue the psychotic break. After something like that, there was a good chance he couldn't remember he was a father."

"Hey. Girl." Trini calls after Rosa, who has abandoned the Frisbee and is trotting toward the front gate.

"Go right ahead thinking the Philly police was the lawless thugs in that situation, Opie."

Rosa's stress-filled barks come back from beyond the front building. Trini sighs and jogs off after her.

"You speaking from experience, Carlton? In your war situation, were you the lawless thug or the lawless thug police?"

"It's true I seen what happens when marauding thugs become the law. I seen them hackin' limbs off women and children, and I seen us being the only thing between them and genocide."

"Us being who and what army —"

Rosa's barking, further distant, has turned more aggressive. Carlton is in motion.

Whit, legs not fully responsive, lights out as well.

He rounds the building closest to the front gate.

Carlton barrels like a linebacker along the front stretch of chain-link fence. "It's them turds. Hoo — they hain't given up on you yet, Opie."

In the waning daylight, a figure moves straight at Carlton and yet on the opposite side of the chain-links, achieving more vertical motion than forward progress as his belly fat rebounds with each footfall. He runs in a narrow path cleared of undergrowth along the fence line, making for a silver Lexus sedan parked by the entrance drive.

"Holy shit, holy shit," Whit chants to himself, close enough now to see that this is the Vogger who approached Kesi at the rest stop — madras shorts, earbuds, and tropical fruit polo shirt, now two shades darker with perspiration.

Carlton pounds past the man. "Better swim faster than that, Namu. I'm comin' back for you shortly."

Carlton continues at a dead run toward the far corner of the fence line where Rosa has another intruder pinned to the ground. Trini is there working to control her as the man squirms to pull himself back out through a hole cut in the fence.

Whit comes up on the obese Vogger at the fence, whacking at the links with both palms. "You. Stop. God damn it, what the hell are you guys doing here?"

The man's eyes bulge. His arms flail as he musters an effort to put the brakes on close to three hundred pounds of forward-traveling mass. His left knee buckles and he belly flops with enough force to propel him end-over-end onto his back.

Whit, wincing, waits through the silence. A hollow sound breaks from the man's lungs as he sucks for air like a drowning swimmer resurfacing.

He scrambles to reseat his dangling earbuds, chest heaving.

"Yes ... Mr. Reitman is here," he says, eyes on Whit. "I'm with him. What should I...? I mean to say, is it advisable to address Mr. Reitman himself?"

Whit groans. He kicks the fence near the man's head, eliciting a whimper.

"You should make yer way 'round and do that proper, Opie." Carlton approaches, hauling the other intruder by the shirt collar. The slight man skips along on tiptoe to keep from strangling. He too addresses his VoG app.

"Yes, I con ... considered that, b ... but it's what I did do on that pre ... vious occasion was to ..." He lowers his voice to a whisper. "... to run. I ran but can't see d ... doing that at present. And so wha ... what should I next consider?"

"You know, Skippy, that we can hear what you're saying." Carlton gives him a shake. "It might just ruin what's known as your key element of surprise, if that's what you're going for."

"Who's he talking to?" says Trini, holding Rosa back. "Grab his phone, Carlton. Get the number."

"Ha. Tell 'er, Opie. Tell Trini who Arlen here's got on the line?"

Whit twirls and kicks the fence again, spurring the larger half of the duo to speak more desperately into his VoG app.

Carlton laughs. "Namu there, his name's Terry, which I just learned from a brief interrogation with my new pal." He gives Arlen another shake. "Or let's say the warm-up to the interrogation 'cause I intend to spend some time re-practicing some techniques I let get rusty."

Trini isn't laughing. "This some sort of stupid-ass game? I want to know what the hell's going on or you guys can both head straight out the gate and take these clowns with you."

Terry and Arlen clamp their hands over their ears and continue their conversations with new intensity.

Terry: "Yes, do please repeat that last suggestion. Right, well, yes, I know, but I do have a problem with prioritizing and if Mr. Reitman is not receptive, well then ..."

Whit gives Trini a look of exasperation. "It's VoG, Trini. They're talking to God."

Arlen: "W ... well sure, yes, of course I wou ... would very much like to return to the path but ... well I thuh ... think maybe I need to back up and explain."

Carlton releases Arlen. He drops into a squat against the fence.

Arlen: "So ... so yes, there was a path that I could have taken but ..."

Whit turns away.

"You know what a VoG is?" Trini asks Carlton.

Terry: "Yes, yes, my Father. I will try. I know I need to correct this waywardness and try to ..."

Trini's eyebrows shoot up. "Oh shit, that's that Voice of God thing."

Arlen: "And the other path wasn't ... well, it wasn't ri ... righteous, you see, because ... "

Carlton reaches out with a foot and hooks Arlen's feet out from under him so that he collapses fully onto his ass. "Yup, dangerous foolishness is what it is. And your pal here — the hon'rable Mr. Whit Reitman — he's the one's responsible for the whole ungodly catastrophe."

"Oh my God." She turns back to Whit. "You're Reitman? I've heard of you. You're wanted ... or something." Trini's movements get Rosa riled again. She gives her a strong correction with the leash.

Whit rubs his face. "Not wanted. Just in demand."

Terry: "... and I believe that Arlen will forgive me and Miss Katie will forgive me and Senator Jasper will forgive me. Do you think Senator Jas —"

Whit screams and lunges onto the fence, pounding it again with his hands. "Take those goddamn things out of your ears."

Terry cowers, hands curled against his chins.

"Whoa, Opie, hold up. What did he jus' say?"

"He said something about Senator Jasper," says Trini.

Whit hugs his torso and holds fast. Every inch of his body quivers. He falls back against the fence.

"Senator from Georgia," says Carlton.

Arlen and Terry have fallen silent.

"Right," says Trini. "That fundamentalist, post–Tea Party jerk. He's been in the news because of some dirty campaign he's running. The Democrat ... what his name, Warren or Warden or something?"

"Warden," says Carlton. "Jasper's after him 'cause of his gay thing."

"Warden's not gay, man," says Trini. "He has some gay friends. And I guess you think it's okay to attack him even if he is gay?"

"First, no. Second, the thing with Warden is he ain't being truthful about it, which who would expect from low-life politicians anyway, but that's the principle. And three, I ain't sure Jasper'd say any of that stuff. You pro'bly been reading the *New York Times*."

"OK, well you're hopeless."

"I been called worse, like what I should be callin' Opie 'cause he obviously ain't truly forthcome with us about this VoG business. Ain't that right, Opie?"

Whit's breathing quickens. "Oh, shit." He pushes off from the fence and falls back again, rebounding and repeating. "And you ... what, like you're Mr. Genuine? Maybe ... maybe you'd like to tell us what you were doing in combat ... over there in Africa where we aren't even having a war."

"That's a damn sight different 'cause I ain't lying when asked straight questions on the matter. Whereas you had your chance to come clean about things that's probably threatening our safety and hid the truth from Kesi and me, which is close enough to lying to be lying."

Terry rallies enough strength to right himself.

Carlton and Trini are both captivated by Whit, shaking and frantic for breath.

Whit crouches and wraps his arms over his head. He rocks on the balls of his feet. Rosa whines. Trini drops the leash and lets the dog nuzzle up to Whit.

"You look like you're having a panic attack, man," says Trini.

Whit uncoils and hugs the dog, burying his face in her coat.

"No," he says. "It's anxiety ... it's not panic ... I'm not panicking. Do I look like I'm panicking?"

She laughs. "Little bit, yeah."

Whit twists his head toward Carlton. "Getting a kick out of this?"

"This?" He nods at Arlen and Terry. "Sure. You? Seen lots of it — guys way braver than you. You'll live."

"You want a hit of Xanax?" says Trini. "I got some Xanax inside."

Whit jerks to standing, leaving a hand below rubbing Rosa's ear. "Shit yeah."

"OK." She pulls Rosa close again with the leash. "So that just leaves how to dispense with Tweedle and Dum."

Arlen bleats and reaches for an earbud but freezes when Carlton taps the bottom of his shoe and tsks.

"I 'spose calling the police is out of the question, 'cause they'd likely get them out of your hair at least," says Carlton.

Trini and Whit say "yes" and "no" respectively.

"I mean yes, bad idea," says Whit.

Trini nods. She turns toward the buildings with Rosa. "C'mon, Reitman. I'm sure your mercenary friend can take it from here."

"Never been that nor his friend neither. And yeah, you leave 'em to me. We need a little bonding time. They can tell me 'bout their sorry-ass selves and how they managed to track us so good, which is a curiosity of mine being they're both clearly incapable of such things."

TEN MINUTES PRIOR

The Colony, Greenport, New York

Kesi paces half the length of the multipurpose room, eyes on the windows, although nothing is visible in the moonless compound yard outside. Stefan, Trini, and Sam sit in silence around the table. They look up each time Kesi's sandal flaps cease.

"Shit." She spins toward Stefan. "Where are the twins?"

"Shjesus, Kesi, asleep, or should be by this hours."

Kesi resumes her motion.

"Usually Portia, she falls asleep first and then later they do, after they see if they can build a Lego house onto her boobs without they waking her up."

No one laughs.

"Carlton will come back, Kesi," says Trini.

"That's a sure bet." Whit does his best to recline in a folding metal chair by the far wall. His legs are outstretched, ankles crossed. Rosa sits beside him, her jowls across his lap, receiving a scratch behind the ear.

Trini squints toward Whit from across the dim room. "And you're still testy. I usually get more agreeable when I'm on that stuff."

"Makes me brood." Whit closes his eyes.

"You know Carlton had to set up the water boarding," says Sam.

"And get rid of the evidence after. It all takes time."

"Shut up," says Trini. "He'll be back."

Stefan leans forward. "You guys want to hang in my room instead of here? This chairs suck."

Rosa's ears perk up.

Kesi turns back to the windows. A set of high beams sweep past. "That's him."

When Carlton swings the outer door open, the group is there to greet him, clogging the vestibule.

"A more cordial welcoming committee than last time. Where's chef?" He lifts one of two bulging grocery bags. "Asked me for a few things earlier, which I stopped for. Got a couple sixes too."

"Sacked out," says Sam. "He gets up early."

"Ah. OK, I'll just —" He nods toward the kitchen.

They part and fall in behind him.

Kesi gives Sam a look. "What?" he says.

"Oh, and where's the anti-Christ?" Carlton says as he passes into the multipurpose room.

Whit lets out a thin whistle between his teeth.

Rosa trots over to give Carlton's leg a sniff, then circles around Trini before returning to Whit's side.

"Carlton, hold on," says Kesi. "How about filling us in?"

He looks her way as he lays the bags down on the table and removes a six-pack of bottles. He pops one open with a utility knife. "Who wants one? They're cold." He smacks the opener down.

Sam and Trini reach around Carlton. Stefan leans across the table for his.

Whit remains motionless in his chair, head back. Rosa drops to the floor and lays her head onto her folded paws.

"Come on, Carlton." Kesi stands back from the table, arms crossed. "What did you find out from —"

"And where's the ven'rable Mr. Africa?" Carlton says. "He an early riser too?"

Trini lowers her beer from her lips with a sucking sound. "Hopefully asleep, yeah. He's still a bit out of sorts."

"Meaning what?" says Carlton. "Meaning he's still raving?"

"No," says Sam. "Mom just said we should leave them alone. She'll stay in there with him tonight."

"He still got that pump action in there?"

Stefan laughs. "That's right, he does. You want to maybe take it from him?"

Carlton takes a long swig and nods at Stefan. "I can do that, Commissar. Got no problem doin' that."

"You had a bit of problem doing that earlier from what I hear."

Trini backs away toward the hallway door. She looks at Sam, two pinched fingers at her lips. Sam holds up five fingers. She smiles and exits.

"Element of surprise," says Carlton, stifling a belch. "I won't be surprised a second time by anything Mr. Africa tries."

"OK, so I suppose you will subdue Andre?" Stefan slides his bottle across the table from hand to hand. "And then I suppose you will declare marshall law and bring order to these place, huh Sheriff?"

"Well, it does seem that you got a bit of a situation, thanks to your friend Opie."

"What situation?" says Kesi. "Are those guys coming back?"

"It's Opie got this shit storm started by disrespecting people's religious convictions." Carlton leans back in his chair. "Him and his atheist beliefs."

Whit snickers. He sits forward. "Being an atheist actually means you don't believe, big guy. But maybe you're right — let's defer to the people who believe God's talking to them through their iPhones."

"There ya go, indifference to people, like I'd expect from a goddamned atheist."

"Ah fuck, here we go again." Kesi returns to her pacing.

"Wow, you have to appreciate that oxymoron — God damned atheist." Whit leans back and closes his eyes.

Stefan slaps the table. "You know, I've had just about too much. I think maybe we can remind you you are guests in this house — unwelcome guests, yes? So, Carlton, I think Kesi she ask you what went down with those two guys. How about it? Or maybe you prefer just to get the hell out?"

"Sounds good," says Whit. "Leave that beer when you go."

Stefan turns and stabs an index finger at him. "And yes, you can join him, smart ass."

Rosa pushes up to a sitting position and looks around for the now absent Trini. She trots out, claws clicking on the concrete.

Carlton uncrosses his arms and takes his time with another sip of beer, eyes on Stefan.

"Yeah, OK. Well Humpty and Dumber, they say they're workin' for Senator Jasper."

Kesi comes nearer. "And you believe them?"

"Yeah, granted I don't have a tendency to believe people as gullible and spineless as them, but I also got no reason to think they got brains enough to make up what they told me."

"Which is what?" says Kesi.

"That they're operatives, sent on some super-secret assignment to affront your new boyfriend here, is what."

"Confront him with what?"

"That's a bit hard to decipher. I'm thinking Opie's gotta know though."

A sigh from Whit. "Oh, I don't know anymore. You'll need to do the thinking for both of us now, big boy."

Kesi's still looking at Carlton. "You're saying the actual Senator Jasper, who's probably not all that stupid, sent those two clowns on a mission? This makes sense to you?"

Carlton rocks back in his chair. "One of maybe a dozen teams sent out, all going after whatever measly leads they was working with on where Opie'd be, this being all according to the Laurel and Hardy."

"Shjesus," said Stefan. "What they want him so badly about?"

Kesi takes the seat beside Stefan. "These guys tried to kidnap Whit the other night. And today, what ... they made another try?"

"Yeah, well they're obviously not schooled in the fine arts of espionage. And maybe wouldn't have done it if they hadn't got so bungled up with misleading orders comin' from the VoG thing."

The room quiets. Kesi checks out Whit over her shoulder, then looks back at Carlton. "So they didn't tell you what the Senator wants from Whit?"

"Nope. Good chance they didn't know." Carlton finishes his beer and reaches for a second. "But I didn't take it that far, figurin' Opie here knows and we'd just ask him. I mean, ain't that simpler?"

All heads turn to Whit.

He scratches his nose and pulls himself upright. "You're not going to believe me anyway."

"You're probably right, but nevertheless," says Kesi.

"Yeah ... so ... the big man is getting warm. He wasn't able to squeeze the truth out of those two because, like most servile acolytes, they've been kept blissfully in the dark. I doubt they know why Jasper wants me. Somebody want to pass me a beer?"

"No," says Kesi. "Which is why? Why does he want you?"

He lets out a breath and rubs at his scalp. "Jasper's slick enough to see how susceptible Voggers are to suggestions. But I didn't design the app to offer real advice. I didn't want it actually accomplishing anything. That was the whole point, if there was a point, which there wasn't. Anyway, Jasper wants me to change that ... for his own express purposes."

"Ha. No shit," says Stefan. "You mean he wants VoG to feed his people his instructions?"

"Bingo. And not just these volunteer clowns. As it happens,

Jasper's Southern fundamentalist Christian constituency overlaps quite a bit with the VoG demographic."

"No," says Kesi. "Jasper wants the app to tell people to vote for him?"

"Actually, he wants God to tell them, but yes."

"Good lord," says Stefan.

Kesi's features soften. "And that's what this is all about? They sent out these guys to grab you up so Jasper could persuade you to work for his campaign?"

Whit looks at her for a moment, then shrugs. "Basically."

Carlton flutters his lips. "Yeah, come on, Opie, tell her the rest. 'Cause that doesn't explain why you turned tail out of New York."

Whit's fingers tap on his knee. "Can we just leave this alone? What does it matter? It's not like they —"

"I'll save ya the trouble," says Carlton. "I know admitting you been lyin' is painful."

"Hey, I didn't lie, it's just that —"

"From what I figure, Jasper hired a' actual pro to work some gentle persuasion on your Mr. Reitman, Kesi. He must of scared the bejesus out of ya, right Opie? And so you packed a few T-shirts and took off. Am I warm, as you might say?"

Whit looks nauseated. He crosses his arms.

Kesi turns her chair to face him. "Is that what happened, Whit? Did they rough you up or something?"

He puffs out a breath. "No, they didn't have a chance. Like he said, I took off."

"Just like that? You dropped everything in your life and ran?"

"Look, it started all lovey-dovey. Jasper's chief aid called first with an offer. Then he called again, then Jasper himself, making vague allusions about supporting his campaign, blah, blah, God Bless America, your nation needs you and, heck, we'll pay you four million dollars. I turned the pompous dick down flat and, well, said some stuff that was probably unwise about giving my friend at *New York* magazine a ring. About a week later, a couple of creeps paid me a visit. And, yes, they were persuasive, mainly because it looked like they were the kind of guys who enjoy their jobs a little too much."

"Sweet shjesus," says Stefan.

Kesi's mouth is open. "You turned down four million dollars?"

Whit stares at her for a second. "Sorry, I know I'm not living up to your low expectations. But I wrote the app to mess with people, not to mess them up. There's a difference. And considering how the VoG joke turned all perverse on me, I wasn't about to make things a hundred times worse by helping that asshole build his power base."

Kesi watches him while he wipes his nose.

"There's one other thing, I guess," he says.

"What?'

"My girlfriend. I was worried about my girlfriend, Jesse. Her name's Jesse."

"Oh." Kesi's look is steady. "You haven't mentioned a girlfriend."

"Right. After the second visit at work from Cappy and Mr. Leonard — totally not cool — I don't see them for a few days, so I'm congratulating myself on toughing it out. After work, I meet Jesse at our neighborhood place. She's waiting at the bar. There they are, occupying the stools next to hers. Mr. Leonard gives me this grin that was all I needed to see.

"I knew I had to get Jesse clear of the whole thing and then clear out myself. When I told Jesse the story, she wasn't about to let our hollow relationship stand in her way."

"So she moved out?" says Kesi.

"Boston. She has an old roommate there."

"And you think, genius, they cain't find her there at least as easy as they found you here?" says Carlton. "You ran thinking you're keeping her safe and your other friends safe? The way to keep them safe is to man up and settle the thing."

"Maybe you're right. I don't know. I did kind of freak out. And there was about a week or so of drinking in there that interrupted my logical flow."

They sit for a while.

Rosa barks in the distance.

"What's with the beast?" he says. "And for that matter, what happened to Trini n' Boy Toy?"

"Likely she is letting Rosa out before sleep," says Stefan.

"That's a lot of money," Kesi says.

Whit leans back. He drags his palms down his face and drops them on his lap. "That's not something I ever cared much about."

"What did you care about?" she says.

He shakes his head. "Finding something to care about."

They look toward the windows as Rosa gallops by, all snapping barks.

Carlton and Stefan stand.

Carlton turns to him. "You know how to use that gun of Andre's?"

Stefan nods. "Yes. OK. I will try."

"If he don't give it up, bring him with it."

The two take off for the hallway door, but Carlton pulls up short and turns back. He grabs two full bottles out of the bag, and then makes his exit at full tilt.

Whit and Kesi are on their feet.

"I'll see if I can help Stefan," Kesi says.

Whit nods, frozen for a moment, then follows after Carlton.

Banging through the exit door at a run, Whit makes it a few yards into the muggy blackness before slowing to a stop. The door makes its long closing squeal behind him. Then, in a burst, from the front of the property, comes Rosa's snarling and the clanging of something striking a metal fence post.

Whit takes off toward the noise, a hand outstretched in the darkness. A blue-white light pops on ahead originating beyond the frontmost building. Two rapid cracks of gunfire echo through the yard.

Rosa whelps. Another shot sounds out.

Whit stumbles, catches himself, and rounds the corner of the building, only to be blinded by the headlights glaring through the front fence about twenty yards ahead. The sulfurous odor of gunpowder reaches him.

Three figures, separated by some yards, are in motion between him and the lights.

Trini shrieks. Three more quick shots blast out. Whit stops, nearly toppling forward.

A pitiful wail rises up out of the white light. Whit raises his hand to shield the glare.

Sam drops to his knees beside Trini's body.

Mr. Leonard stands about ten yards beyond them by the perimeter fence, his fall of silver hair is radiant in the headlights. Handgun raised, he rounds Rosa's body on his way toward Trini.

"No. No!" Sam falls on top of her.

Mr. Leonard shakes his hair back and extends his gun.

"Stop!" Whit waves his arms. "Over here. I'm here."

Mr. Leonard's head cocks toward Whit, but his pistol remains steady.

A small projectile passes through the air in front of the headlights. It makes contact with a thunk and then smashes on the hard ground. Mr. Leonard staggers, arms awhirl. A large shadow interrupts the projected light, and Carlton is on him.

With a backswing, Carlton undercuts Mr. Leonard with his second beer bottle and then hammers it down on the man's wrist. The gun flips free and scrapes across the gravel.

Carlton drops his shoulders and, in a sudden move, inverts Mr. Leonard and pounds him down on his upper back.

Sam sits and pulls Trini onto his lap. He raises her hand to his face.

The two men are entwined and rolling. Carlton manages to throw a leg wide and kick the gun in Whit's direction. It skids to within a few yards of him.

Sam calls out. "I need a phone! Please. Call an ambulance. Please."

Whit makes his move toward the gun, but his head snaps back. His scream is cut short.

Cappy is behind him, one boot heel planted, one knee in the small of Whit's back for leverage. Nearly all of his weight drags on a cord wound just above Whit's Adam's apple. He increases the pressure until Whit's knees lose strength. He takes control of the cord with his left hand, reaches forward with his right, and grabs Whit's belt loop.

Whit wheezes, his chest contorting with the effort. He throws an arm back but fails to make contact. He swings the opposite way. His movement is checked with a jerk on the cord.

"Nasty way to break man's neck, Mr. Reitman. Maybe you want me stop? You want me stop?"

Whit stamps the ground with both feet, shoving his back into Cappy's chest, then relents.

Cappy eases up. "Okay, but you try fuck with me like that, I cut you. I maim you, Mr. Reitman."

Cappy releases his hold on Whit's pants.

Whit sucks in air and falls into the noose. He dances his way back up, propped against his assailant. Cappy pins Whit's right ear against his head with the flat of a knife blade.

Sam calls out. "You! Do you have a phone? Call someone. Please."

"Okay? You get me, now, Mr. Reitman?" says Cappy in a whisper. "Senator Jasper would no like it if I maim you but we just say is unfort'nate accident, right, Mr. Reitman? Accident happen, right?"

Whit raises his trembling hands. He forces out coughs. "Ge' ... get her help."

"Shut up," says Cappy, edging the knife into Whit's ear.

From the shadowed ground, Mr. Leonard lows like a cow and chuckles.

"Get on with," Cappy calls out. "You wasting my time, a'hole. I know you be fucking up now. Get on with, damn it, you sick a'hole."

Carlton lets out a cowboy whoop, then another. The animal sounds from Mr. Leonard grow frantic and high pitched.

Cappy grabs Whit by his shirt collar and yanks him forward toward the gate. "Damn that damn sick a'hole. We get into car, now, Mr. Reitman. Go, you." He pockets the knife and pulls a chrome pistol from the small of his back.

"Please," calls Sam. "You have to help."

Mr. Leonard makes long, gurgling whimpers.

He screeches.

From the front building, a cold floodlight pops on. Sam, illuminated, staggers toward Cappy and Whit, palms shining red. "She's bleeding a lot, Whit," he says.

"Back off," says Cappy, thrusting the gun toward him. "Too late for her. Back off or I shoot you in fucking face."

Carlton is sitting on Mr. Leonard, the lanky man belly down on the asphalt. His hair is back tight against his scalp, gathered at the base of his skull in Carlton's fist, face displayed like bagged prey.

"Kid, run inside." Carlton's voice is hoarse. "Run, now. Make the call. Run."

Mr. Leonard's teeth are bared in a manic smile.

Sam weeps. He turns back toward Whit. "I can't do anything. I can't. Goddamn you."

Whit closes his eyes.

Carlton calls out. "Damnit, kid, listen. Go!"

Sam trips into a run toward the buildings, the crunches of his footfalls receding.

Cappy resumes dragging Whit to his left to bypass Carlton on his way to the car.

Carlton whistles. "Bruce Lee finally got ya, huh, Opie? He that unsightly New York creep you was talking about?"

"Shut up." Cappy stops. "Bruce Lee, he Chinese, you a'hole. I Cambodian. Not Chinese."

"Yeah, like there's a difference. And, Opie, who's this salamander specimen I got here? Eerie damn piece of work, this one."

Cappy whacks the pistol against Whit's temple, then swings it toward Carlton. "Fuck you. You know what good you, better let Mr. Leonard up and do it fast 'cause I maim your friend here. I blow three his fingers off, then I shoot you in face."

"Oh, it ain't like Opie and me are friends or nothing, Brucie. And, hell, even for my friends, I don't put myself out all that much."

Mr. Leonard lets out a new kind of wail as Carlton twists his hair another turn.

"As for shooting me," Carlton says, "I been shot before. Bigger gauge too. It didn't stop me from rippin' the throat outta the guy done it. Would only take a heartbeat, me snapping Mr. Lizard's neck and coming for you."

The gun goes off.

Carlton flings back like a bronco rider.

"Stop. No!" Kesi calls out from the yard far behind them.

Whit throws an arm back around Cappy's waist and bolts to his left, taking Cappy down with him. He finds Cappy's hand on the cord and wrenches at the thumb.

There's a deafening rifle blast. Cappy flattens Whit to the ground.

Whit's cheek smashes against the gravel, eyes facing the buildings. Andre, bare chested, dreads flopping, trots in from ten yards out, his pump action leveled at the waist.

"One and only warning shot, sir," shouts Andre. "I'll ask you only once to remove yourself from the property."

"Andre, wait!" Kesi is at his heels.

Stutter-stepping to a halt, Andre pivots toward Mr. Leonard who has freed himself and is charging forward. He pumps the rifle, jerks it to eye level, and fires.

Kesi screams at the sight of Mr. Leonard, airborne and spinning back.

Carlton is curled on the ground, hugging his gut. With the other hand, he jabs a finger toward Cappy and Whit.

Cappy jumps up to a crouch, taking aim at Andre. Kesi, a yard behind her father, reaches for his shoulder.

Whit rolls over, digs his heels in, and springs backward, smashing his skull into Cappy's teeth.

Kesi falls short of Andre. "No, don't!"

Cappy's pistol fires first, deafening all to the sound of Andre discharging the last of his rounds.

FOUR WEEKS AND TWENTY-ONE HOURS AFTER

The Colony, Greenport, New York

"Hold up, bruh. Not sure where we at."

Sam lowers his notebook. Portia's lost face matches Squeej's.

"Come now, Squeej," says Stefan. "Just can we let the man tell his story?"

"Previously, on *As the World Turns* ... to shit." Whit's voice is steeped in evening meds. He's stretched out flat, thumbs twiddling on his chest.

Kesi, within an arm's length of him, sits with Andre's legal pad in her lap. Her fingers run in circles, tracing the indentations of the coffee mug rings.

"Oh, right, right." Squeej sits cross-legged, hands gripping his ankles, rocking left to right. "Andre was about ready to tell his story in the story. Is that Andre-Andre's story? I mean, did you write the Andre story, like, in the story? Or is this one of the ones Andre wrote?"

Sam squints. "Do you mean did the me-guy in the story write Andre's story for him?"

"Nah, meant you-you."

"It's Andre's story that he left. It's in there." He nods at Kesi's lap.

"Cool, cool." Still rocking. "Go on, dude. Proceed."

Claudia watches Kesi. "Did you read Andre's MOVE story, hon?"

She nods a few times before answering. "And I'm a little freaked by it."

Then Whit says, "I'm heading out tomorrow."

Kesi looks at him, then down at the pad.

Claudia waits through the lack of response, then wiggles her fingers at Sam.

"You don't have to go," says Portia, the sweetness all but gone from her voice.

Whit's twiddling slows. "Yeah, it's ok, but I do have to. Go on, Sam. Tell it, man."

Sam's Story, Cont'd.

Alright.

So it's about an hour and a half since we got to the Colony. We're waiting it out in the Hydro Lab within earshot of the multipurpose room where the telling is underway. Carlton's making small talk to keep Father Andre loose, but every time an outburst of catcalls reaches us from down the hall, it dumbs him down too.

Time comes when we're not hearing much in the way of crowd noise and Suzie comes in to say we're on deck. Before Father Andre has a chance to huff for air, Trini and Carlton grab their sticks and him by the elbows and follow Suzie down the hall into the kitchen, which has got all sundry people hanging about. There are the usual oddsmakers looking for Tellers they can add to their payroll, but one look at Carlton and they're scratching the back of their ears and moseying into corners.

We can hear now coming from the big room just beyond that there's a Teller at work, and she's either scary as all bejesus or in other ways scary damn effective, given the awe-level. I see a not-yet-seen-by-me wistfulness come over Trini. She lets go her grip on Father Andre and pushes in between onlookers clogging the doorway opening into the hall. I nudge up next to her, feeling drawn myself.

The young Teller stands tall on the platform before the unlit crowd. Her back is arched, palms upraised, willow limbs under-stroked by footlight candle-glow. There's a pureness to her voice that's like you're not so much hearing but feeling sweet music passing through you, like breezes through branches. She's about as Asian as a blonde gets, with high cheekbones and eyes that smile into a squint. And she's pale, though more inked than not, made graphically obvious because she's wearing nothing north or south of her thong.

Carlton too steps up, snatching a liberally pierced neighbor back by the choke chain and shoving his head through the doorway for a gawk. Noting Trini's rapt attention, he whispers something in her ear — from the tone of it ill-refined — earning himself a sharp elbow in the plexus. He laughs through the gut-wrench and steps back.

Then Trini, eyes still pinned to the Teller, reaches behind as if her hand has a will of its own and grabs on between my legs as natural as if she's found my hand, keeping hold there too, like she's in need of some kind of assurance and, me, kind of impressed but otherwise spellbound as she.

As best as I can make out, having come in late, the tale in progress circles 'round the ruler of a coast kingdom who's been hexed by a mal-o-violent seductress. And then there's a thread about an ogre-machinist laboring to build a Clock of Lost Souls. But the plot hardly matters. The Teller sings out in such colors that no doubt her directions to the nearest chemical pool would sweep the audience towards weepy. And at her disposal is a nubile bod and the instincts to punctuate her lines with a rotational wrist here, a rockable hip there, and breasts bobbing with such control it's like there's another sub-plot being carried out thereby.

The story comes to climax, there are some final words that

echo like chimes through the old factory room, and she's done. The audience expels a common sigh, like air hissing out from a punctured dream. They sit mum for the longest of short seconds before a gut-originated, "Yeah, baby!" resounds from the back, setting off all manner of appreciation noise.

Somewhere in there, I've got Trini on me like a climbing vine, pelvis grinding a figure eight and her teeth against mine. She's got her stick behind me, using it like a lever to shove my ass forward. She opens with a hunger, and I'm deeply involved with a tongue that, believe me, is whole and fully operational.

The Teller flits off stage, light as a fawn. The onlookers in the doorway fall back like scattered by a breeze, excepting Trini and me stand our ground. We trade looks with the Teller and I see Trini closing her eyes like trying to lock in the image.

"You're up, Fatha'," says Suzie. "And I'd say you got your work cut out for ya after that."

The old man is staring down at the tremble in his old hand. When he fails to move, Suzie asks, "Can I get you somethin'? Maybe cool tea for your throat?"

Father Andre looks up. "Why that would be most welcome. Thank you, sister."

Suzie slaps her knee. "Ho, my God. That's freakin' rich." She turns and leaves, laughing still.

Carlton throws Trini a get-yer-shit-together look. She dismounts like nothing happened, and they take Father Andre again by the arms.

The crowd noise co-merges into rhythmic clapping and stomping. It's all intended to draw the Teller back, but she's not hanging 'round for encores.

"Now Father, remember," says Carlton, holding back in the doorway, "they're looking for a diversion, not a mess of preaching about the great coming. Carnal fantasy and gore, that's all it takes. And no truth, damnit. No truth, or so help me..."

They're chanting now on top of it all — "Teller, Teller, Teller" — and banging on cans, plastic buckets, and other hollow things.

I slip past them into the room, figuring maybe I'll lead the way for Father Andre. No sooner am I in the space but I hear "Get 'em!" and "Yeehaa!" coming at me, followed sure enough by some of the smaller of the aforementioned percussion instruments.

I spin back and see Father Andre oddly aglow and smiling at Carlton in a way that would seem devious, were that a possibility in the old man.

"I've realized that truth, brother, is secondary," he's saying.

Carlton, pulling his head back at that — and me to safety by the collar — says, "I don't follow."

"There's only the vision — the terrible, infantile colossus. Truth will follow the vision, my brother."

And with that, Father Andre steps out of Trini's grip. He moves at full stride into the hall and across the floor toward the dais, shoulders up wide and commanding. He shakes his dreads back behind him and lets go with a shout that builds as it rolls up to the beams. "Brothers, sisters, thank you. You ... tonight ... have come ... to bear .... witness!"

As I reenter the hall, I can see a half dozen standing with various items in hand, cocked and aimed at Father Andre, but down go the arms, one by one, as the unruly chanting peters out.

"That's him!" someone screams, "but he's bigger than what's they say."

And then someone else, birthing the legend that never was, shouts, "It's the glory makin' him big. Look to the glory!"

Mumbly expectation rises from the crowd and shouts back and forth over who first saw Father Andre and when — all lies. People are also shouting for me to get down in front, so I crouch and pull back against the wall, watching Father Andre climb the stairs to the dais. Trini's there a second later squatted down beside me, holding her stick upright like a battalion's colors. She's there close and I'm just recognizing the clove and sassafras smell of her, and it's got my head swimming back to our previous closeness.

I put my lips to her ear. "You're going to talk to me now, aren't you, Trini? A couple words — that's all it'll take to make up for what you took from me just then."

She looks at me, and I can see she's considering. But the crowd noise drops off again and there's Father Andre, tall and mighty, his mismatched palms held out wide.

People generally settle down in their seats, those that have them, but I see one lumpy guy stand up in front — he's stunted from the waist down so it's an abbreviated process — leaning forward with a squint to check out Father Andre's hands. He gurgles up a laugh and turns to see if anyone else is noticing, but just then Father Andre starts.

"In all creation!"

He lets it echo and fall.

"Think on the word, brothers and sisters. Creation. Creation ongoing. Everything, the whole glorious universe, is still coming into being. It will always come into being. And in all creation, nothing endures. Those were the words of Ovid, the Roman. But in the same breath, he tells us that nothing ends."

Father Andre swings his index finger across the crowd. "You probably believe you've seen death, isn't that right, friends?"

He waits. The puzzlement is thick. Some grumble, and then from here and there, "Yuh, better fuckin' b'lieve" and "Death, hell yeah. Seen it, delivered it."

"No, good brothers and sisters," Father Andre says, "there is no death. That's just ebb in the tidal flow of creation. Waves, my friends. Ovid says, As wave is driven by wave. And each, pursued, pursues the wave ahead, so time flies on and follows, flies and follows. Always, for ever new.

"No death, friends. No birth! No children. Because even as babes, we are as ancient as we are fresh to the world."

"He's right!" shouts some egret-looking crone a few rows back.

"Right, ha," someone else comes back with. "Only right about him is the turn he took at the exit for batshit loco."

Father Andre pauses for the desired hush and then begins.

Father Andre's Story

A child, brothers and sisters, at a time when there were children.

The child stood one afternoon in the musty, unlit front room of a row home. She wore two pairs of PJs and tattered socks, her sweater a threadbare, oversized hand-me-down. From outside, came the chatter of children and the rattling of roller skates. She strained for a view through the gaps in a boarded-up window. The day was cold and bright. All she could see was part of the stoop of the home across the way. A patrol car passed by.

Sitting on a lopsided stool across the small room was one of her adult brothers, engaged in mending boots for the child. He protected his hand with an old baseball mitt as he sewed with a crude iron needle, working it through the boot leather with rusty pliers.

"When I'm done with these," he said to the child, "you can go back on out to play."

"They cheated," she said.

From the floor over their heads, they heard muffled footsteps and the scraping of furniture. Her little nose wrinkled. She huffed, sending out a cloud of breath into the chill air.

She asked Brother Lawrence to watch while she huffed again near the window. The sunlight cut through her breath. "Look at the tiny stars," she said and pointed to the dust mites lit up in the beams.

"That's hope, Sister Kesi," he told her. "There's hope everywhere in Mom Earth's world if you know how to look for it."

But little Kesi's smile faded when she heard one of the kids roll by again. She turned from the window and sat against the baseboard.

He looked her way again and crossed his eyes.

She pushed out her lower lip.

"So tell me, how did they cheat?" he said.

"They used technology." She stamped her foot.

"Oh, now I know you're telling a story," he said. "Those are good family members, just like you, sister."

She stamped her foot again and slid farther down the wall until only her head was propped against it.

Again, they heard the sound of movement from upstairs, and then a tremendous thud shook the floorboards.

She asked Brother Lawrence what the adults were doing up above.

He put the boots down and headed for the stairs. "Clearing the bedroom for His arrival," he said.

Kesi started to ask another question, but someone rapped at the window behind her. She scuttled on all fours to grab a quilt, then back to her spot under the window and curled with it, ignoring the taunts from her Family-siblings out on the stoop.

Someone in the audience whistles a sharp one from a dark corner. "This all we gettin', old Teller? Little girl troubles? She ain't even old enough for the good kinda girl troubles."

"I'm gonna come back there and fix it so you got no reason to be in'erested in girls no more," says an egret-looking crone. "Been a while since I seen a innocent child." Her voice, cracks at that.

Father Andre nods at her and continues.

And so, my sisters and brothers, the winter sun was down by the time little Kesi woke. She found a gnarly carrot to eat in the kitchen and a piece of turnip.

Drowsy, she headed up the dark stairs. The second floor landing was so cluttered with furniture she had to crawl beneath an end table to pass through. From underneath, she could see in through the bedroom door. Her adult brothers and sisters were covering the floor with an assortment of blankets, mattress pads, and pillows.

On the third floor, she crawled from bed to bed over the children to find her spot between Sister Audra and Brother Gilford. She slipped into sleep to the deep, comforting sound of her adult brothers and sisters chatting in the bedroom below.

Well into the night, Kesi was stirred by her Brother Mavis crying in his sleep. She made her way across to where he was curled on the floor and rubbed his back.

Kesi felt an odd vibration running through the floorboards. She laid her ear down and picked up low moans and hums.

The sounds became more pronounced as she descended to the second floor landing. On her belly, she wound her way through the furniture legs to the doorway of the cleared bedroom. Not much light found its way through the boarded windows to illuminate the scene, but as her eyes adjusted, she made out bodies in motion spanning the floor. After a time, she could match the adults before her with the overlapping sounds of satisfaction.

Father Andre here closes his eyes, collecting himself to go on. The abbreviated patron near the front is up again on his feet. "Shit, man. Some details. Wanna hear who's doin' what-which to who-how."

His immediate neighbor gives him enough of a shove to topple most guys, but with the low center of gravity and such, he holds his stance.

"It's immaterial, brother," Father Andre says, and resumes.

Little Kesi was among the first children up in the morning. The second floor landing had been cleared and three of the adults were taking stock of the scant food stores in the kitchen. Sister Angelique helped Kesi put together a bowl of dried oats, flax seed, water, and buttermilk. She winked at Kesi as she added a short drizzle of honey.

Kesi sat on Sister Angelique's lap. "I saw you last night," Kesi said to her. "I saw you and the other adults making love."

Sister Angelique worked to untangle Kesi's hair as the girl ate. "It looked that way, maybe, little sister," she said, "but something else was happening."

"But you were making babies?" Kesi asked.

"Yes. One," Sister Angelique said.

Kesi joined the children outside that afternoon. They unraveled the yarn from a discarded sweater and were stringing a web across the small patch of front yard when yelling reached them from down the block. Four of the adults were running home carrying boxes of produce. They ordered the children upstairs. Kesi and Brother Gilford screamed as the adults tore through the yarn pattern on their way to the porch door.

Up on the roof, the children busied themselves with a similar game, stretching string from the spikes that protruded from the parapet wall, around the tarpaper-covered outlook cabin and across to the rear wall.

From below, they heard Brother Lawrence and Sister Angelique trading accusations with the cops who leaned against their cruisers on the far side of the street.

"That food was discarded by the System," Sister Angelique told them. "The System is wasteful and corrupt. And you're nothing but its corrupt agents looking for excuses to undermine our Family."

"When we see you people running through the streets with firearms, we've got no choice but to investigate," said the cops.

"A fabrication!" said Brother Lawrence. "You saw nothing of the kind. Leave us to live our lives as we choose. What you see before you are people living a good life. Learn by our example."

That evening, Brother Lawrence gathered the children and

explained that they would not be able to play outside. "They are trying to intimidate us, little brothers and sisters, and we won't let that happen," he said. "We'll stay inside for now, but they will tire of their lies because, in their souls, they're like us. Their hearts will be true to them and they'll soon tire of their bullying."

The adults spent the next day scavenging materials for use in further securing windows and doors. Despite the seriousness of their actions, they sang as they worked. Brother William told the children that it was all preparation for the arrival of Orisha.

"Who is Orisha?" young Mavis asked.

"Someone wonderful," he said. "He's from Africa, like us."

"Does he know Mom Earth?" said Brother Mavis.

"Oh, certainly. Mom Earth is his child as we are her children."

The barricading of the house continued into the next day, drawing more police. The adults waited until dark, then sneaked out through the rear basement window to forage for food and water. Some stood guard on the stoop and on the roof, shouldering planks fashioned into the shape of rifles.

Kesi and the children at first invented new games in imitation of the adults', but after a few days, with the meals infrequent, they became irritable. The adults did their best to distract them with stories and music, but before long, they began to snap back at the children.

After a week of isolation, even the bickering and complaints waned. The adults dozed away their days in the blanketed room. The children avoided them, giving in to the solace of sleep as well.

One dismal afternoon, the house as dark as night, Kesi sat upstairs listening to the icy rain crackle against the side of the house. She heard a moan rise from downstairs, at first blending with the cries of the wind. Kesi was reminded of that earlier night, but there was no pleasure in what she heard this time. And as the hours passed into evening, the collective wail was broken by sharp cries of pain.

The younger children were tearful. Kesi huddled with Mavis and

Audra in the darkest corner of the bedroom. From outside, she heard the neighbors voicing their concern, and soon additional police cars arrived, their lights cutting red and blue slashes across the ceiling.

Brother Guilford went to the window. "I don't get it," he said. "Those cops came up the walk but they turned back."

"They're scared like us," said Kesi. "Probably even more scared than us."

Eventually, although the moaning continued, the hunger-weakened children fell off to sleep. Then there was a scream from downstairs, and then more came, so horrific the children imagined the adults being torn bodily apart.

A few rows in front of Father Andre, the dwarfish guy's up again. "Now we're talkin'! That's like what I do to 'em, my women, right there."

This time, the dwarf gets smacked good by the guy who went at him before plus two women a row behind. "OK. Shit, man," he says rolling into a ball on his seat.

My friends, truly it was a night of horror for the children. They stood at the head of the stairs and called down in panic, but the adults' screams went on for hours.

At last, the noise ended. The children heard nothing but their own sniffling. In time, emptied by exhaustion, they drifted back to sleep.

The next morning was a brighter one. Sister Angelique, looking worn, came up to see the children. She held out her hands to lead them downstairs.

Kesi's view of the adult's second floor room was blocked at first by Brother Guilford and the older children crowding the doorway. She could see one of the men hanging a blanket over a window to further block the light. And yet the bedroom was aglow from somewhere within.

They stepped into the room. On a coffee table draped with the Family's best quilt was an infant. The newborn sat upright. He was as black as polished onyx but somehow emanated an amber light. Kesi was unable to look away.

The audience grumbles. An obese woman, hair woven in a mask over her face, stands and calls to Father Andre. "Sweet Lord, it's an accursed thing."

The egrit-crone suggests a route back to the zoo for the woman. There's a spirited exchange, but the two get shouted down before the issue of who's ugliest is settled.

Father Andre raises his hands.

Accursed, yes, that you might well assume, but there was indeed a wondrous light coming from the infant. The adults of the Family, far from intimidated, were laughing and embracing their children. Lawrence alone kept his composure. He told the children that the baby's name was Orisha, the Creator.

The Family stood entranced as the child's radiance intensified. "I am and yet I am not," the strange child said. "I am Ifa, the Messenger. In time, I will have things to share with you."

Ifa's eyes were not yet open but they bulged and slid beneath the lids as if he was finding each of them as he spoke. The adults sighed with delight, but Kesi noticed that Brother Lawrence looked disturbed.

At Ifa's request, the Family retreated downstairs to bathe and neaten the house. Brother William discovered sacks of groceries on the stoop, left by the neighbors.

The Family presented the food to Ifa. The infant laid his hands on the offering but told them to take it back. All that day and through the night, the Family sat in the room, replenishing themselves and listening to the magical child recite creation legends.

"To me, all the histories are known," Ifa began. "I will tell you of the days of the Descent."

Ifa told the Family of the outcast god, Orisha, accompanied by his sibling Odudúwa, the one who stole from heaven the gifts Orisha was prescribed to give to men; how the two were forced to travel arid lands to the brink of the dark chaos, roaring aloud with untamed waters, and there, with only desert or the perilous sea as choices, how Orisha set into motion the scattering of islands; how ramparts sprung forth from the waters; how the new island shores were assaulted by the turbulent sea and how, in time, the waters resolved into placid lagoons; and how Orisha there founded a city for unborn men, those dumb spirits hungering for life.

"Orísha, the Creator, yearned, and called
To him the longing shades from other glooms;
He threw their images into the wombs
Of Night, Olókun and Olóssa, and all
The wives of the great Gods bore babes with eyes
Of those born blind — unknowing of their want —
And limbs to feel the heartless wind which blew
From outer nowhere to the murk beyond."

When Ifa was done, Brother William stood to speak. "You say, we must suffer on Earth," he said. "Why, Messenger, would the great Creator, Orisha, put us here to suffer?"

"Orisha yearned for men to live and to provide for him the riches he desired, as the wealthy exploit their slaves," was Ifa's answer.

In the dawn hour, Ifa dismissed the Family. As Kesi rose, she noticed that Ifa appeared to have grown. While maintaining the plumpness and proportions of a newborn, he seemed twice the size, and his eyes had opened.

Downstairs, she found Brother Lawrence. She asked why he had left the room early in the night.

"Trust your feelings, little sister. Don't believe Ifa if what he says doesn't seem right." Brother Lawrence said this in all earnestness and yet looked as if he didn't quite understand his own thoughts.

"But Ifa's full of magic," Kesi said.

"One day, Sister Kesi, you will have children. You will know your child as no one else can. Ifa is magical, but he sprung from us, and a parent knows when a child is a false child."

For the next few days, the Family's mood see-sawed. Ifa inspired adoration and great joy, and yet the Family faced escalating confrontations with police and city bureaucrats. With Ifa in their presence, the adults were more protective of their home than ever, behavior the agents of the System interpreted as revolutionary activity.

The tension in the house set off rare arguments among the adults. One evening, Kesi followed the sound of a quarrel to the roof. Five of the adults were present. Brother Lawrence seemed greatly agitated. He believed that Ifa was some sort of demon, come to take advantage of their open, abiding nature.

"You're talking foolishness," said Sister Angelique. "The Creator would never send a Messenger to deceive us."

"Even the Creator can fall prey to demons," said Brother Lawrence. "The gods are fallible creatures, same as us. Look how Mom Earth has been ravaged and exploited."

Late in the afternoon of the fifth day after Ifa's arrival, there was yet another tense exchange between the Family and the cops. The adults stood their ground on the front porch. Then, without warning, gunfire broke out from the street. The adults withdrew and rushed to blockade the entrances. Sister Angelique took the children to their third floor room. Other adults climbed to the roof and shouted in outrage but were answered again by shots from the police.

Once things quieted, Kesi and the Family gathered again in the second floor bedroom. Brother Lawrence sat in a corner, his head down. Kesi joined him and held his hand.

Ifa had grown so that, from his seated position, he looked down on the adults. His skin had become scaly and chalky gray. And the emanations, once warm and welcoming, were now crackling with unnerving intensity.

Kesi saw that branches had begun to grow from Ifa's stomach, twisted and dry like dead brambles. As Ifa spoke, Kesi crawled around behind and saw that a second mouth had formed on the back of the creature's hairless head. She could see the lips move, as if he was whispering prompts to himself.

At this point in Father Andre's story, I have to tell you, I'm fairly engrossed, but I feel Trini tensing her back against me and I see that the crowd is now mostly out of their seats and emitting agitation noises. Carlton is leaning in to us like he's waiting for a go signal from Trini, his staff looking about ready to splinter in his grip.

I'm thinking I never got an audience in nearly this state and I'm wondering, were it me, if I'd stoke things hotter or cool it down. It's the kind of choice great Tellers know how to make. As for Father Andre, he's doing one thing the great ones do, anyway — feeding off the emotion in the room, even if that's mostly irascibility.

Ifa, my good brothers and sisters, at that time spoke again of the ancient gods, but this time he drew a line of inheritance to the Family. He spoke of the Family's mission to reclaim the Earth; of resistance in the face of the System's temptations and spiritual corruptions. He spoke of the need for revolution.

The adults were troubled. Brother William assured Ifa of their devotion but explained with tentative words that they had run out of food and that it had become impossible to escape at night for foraging.

"Sit with me here for a full day," said Ifa. "After a day of fasting, I will provide with food. And from then on."

Brother Lawrence stood, shaking his head. "Tell us how? You talk now of miracles, Ifa," he said. "Where will this food come from?"

"Why do you call me Ifa? My name is Amazimu." The creature smiled, revealing spiky rows of teeth.

"Abomination! Abomination!" the hair-mask lady is shouting, and it's got the front couple of rows bouncing up and down, pounding the floor and, in a few cases, each other.

Trini's up and off toward the dais. Carlton takes a step forward but checks himself, slapping one hand on my shoulder to keep me in place, as if I'm contemplating a move.

As Trini runs in, she gives her stick a high snappy twirl and brings it down across the back skull of one trollish miscreant preparing to launch a jug at Father Andre. She drives the stick's butt end into the guts of another and in a low sweeping action rakes three or four sets of shins before taking up guard position in front of the Teller.

Father Andre's arms are raised, eyes clamped shut to the distractions.

Brother Lawrence, my friends, stood before his Family and appealed to their reason. "Do you hear?" he asked them. "Ifa has changed his name."

"But you are mistaken," said the creature. "I have been Amazimu all along."

"You told us you were the Messenger," said Brother Lawrence. "Tell us now what news you bring. We have suffered. Our children go without food. We have defied the System. Tell us now."

"A message, yes, Lawrence," said Amazimu. "There will be food and there will be knowledge. Sit with me now and I will provide food that will enrich your soul like music played by the gods. Sit and fast with me."

The adults of the Family were shaken but, after more discussion, they defied Brother Lawrence and settled in for their stay.

Kesi left the room with Brother Lawrence. "They are devoting themselves to a demon," he told her. He had no words of consolation but offered his arms for comfort.

Outside, the police occupation continued, and yet the System's forces seemed oddly patient, as if there was a bigger plan afoot.

The fasting stretched on beyond the first day. In the late evening of the second, Kesi, woozy from hunger, wandered about the rooms downstairs, taken by the quiet. Even the street sounds had dissipated. By the foot of the stairs, she could make out a scratching sound coming from the second floor room, like dry leaves dragging along a sidewalk.

Brother Lawrence carried her upstairs. With difficulty, he pushed the door ajar. They could see that the room was filled to the walls with Amazimu's tangled branches. Brother Lawrence put his shoulder to the door and forced it wide, cracking off the thorny growth that barred his way.

Amazimu had grown in body as well. Still seated, his broad head was bowed, shoulders hunched against the ceiling. He now threw forth an acid-blue light. Brother Lawrence, cringing from the glare, snapped off more limbs so he could enter. The Family stood lifelessly against the four walls, pinned back by the branches.

Brother Lawrence whimpered at the sight of it. He pushed in toward the nearest of the Family, Sister Angelique, but as he broke off the brittle limbs, others took their place. He retreated to the hallway. They heard a roar beating down from overhead. He found Kesi a hiding spot beneath a chair and headed to the roof.

As if timed to their discovery inside, a helicopter was diving in towards the building. Fighting the chopping air, Brother Lawrence worked his way to the front parapet and called out to the neighbors for help. With that cue, the police flooded him with spotlights and commenced shooting.

He dropped to his belly, and pulled himself to the roof hatch, the helicopter winds buffeting him from above. And then the explosion hit the roof, throwing Brother Lawrence down the stairs.

Crumbled on the third floor, he waited out the rush of hot air that poured down the stairwell. Then he heard Kesi scream with a shrillness that pierced him like a needle.

Kesi was gone from her spot on the second-floor landing. Brother Lawrence reentered the bedroom. Amazimu's dry limbs were alive with blue emissions. Kesi's screams continued. Through the radiance, Brother Lawrence could make out the child being taken into an orifice nearly dividing Amazimu from groin to breastplate.

Brother Lawrence charged the creature and plunged his hand deep into the abdominal opening where he managed to get hold of Kesi's waistband. With a desperate effort, he pulled her free.

I'm not sure if Father Andre means for that to be his final line, but the audience has had enough, all growls, bared teeth, and bulging eyes.

"The Family perished in the blue flames!" screams the lion-faced lady, like they were her own.

"No, no, it was a living fire," says Father Andre, who's got a beatific kind of smile going.

"The child!" calls out the egrit-crone. "Is the child saved?"

"Indeed," says Father Andre, "in a glorious fire of rebirth. The Family is lost to us, but they live on in Mom Earth. She will return them to us. And she will open a path to our renewal as well."

"He lies!" Half-Height is up on his chair again, turned to the audience. "Look at his abominational fuckin' hand. It's the fuckin' hand of a biocoder. It went into a biocode vat or some shit."

Everybody gasps into a damn scary hush.

Father Andre steps to the front of the dais. "No, brothers and sisters, witness the truth," he says, raising his unblemished hand roofward, "for I am that same Brother Lawrence and this is the hand that plunged into the belly of the demon Amazimu and retrieved Mom Earth's blessed daughter!"

Carlton raises his stick high. "OK, I think that's gonna about do it," he says and, chest first, powers into the now just about totally lost-it assholes in the front, compressing a good number toward Father Andre. But fast as the rabble arrive at the dais, they turn tail, grasping various body parts, which I can only guess is Trini's doing since I'm hunched down following in behind Carlton.

When we reach the dais, Carlton breaks left, domino'ing a few down so as to get swinging room for his stick.

There's Trini within feet of me. She's reaching up, trying to get a grip on Father Andre's pant's leg.

Carlton's got his stick fully engaged, doing the work of five guys, but it's not enough. From the other three sides, I'm getting clawed and pounded, notably in the kidney-rib vicinity, making enunciation a tough go.

I latch on to Trini's shoulder and try to pull her toward the exit. She shoves me off. I go at her around the waist, getting me in return her stick somehow across my teeth. She spins from me, whipping the thing wide and downing about a half dozen rioters and me in the process with another good crack across the temple.

By the time I roll myself over, Trini's back to pulling at Father Andre. And somewhere between then and when I get boot-stomped into an hour-long oblivion, I hear Trini say to me, "Nobody stops me. Don't you ever." And yeah, that could have been a later-recalled figment of my unconsciousness, but it sure sounded like her voice, the one I'd never heard before.

When Sam pats his thigh and looks up, all eyes in the multi-purpose room are on Kesi, doubled forward, Andre's legal pad clutched to her chest.

Whit sits up. He wiggles over and rubs her arched back. "Mom Earth's blessed daughter, would you like a Kleenex?" He kisses the back of her neck.

Kesi uses Whit's T-shirt tail to wipe her nose. "Andre — he saved me from the fire."

"Well, no," says Sam. "Like you said, you guys weren't in the fire."

Kesi straightens. She uses her palms to wipe back tears. "No, I know. He thinks he saved me. Or he wanted to think he saved me. What a crazy bastard."

Portia sighs. "Sammy, look sweetheart, do you want to talk to us about why you've written Trini into your story?"

Sam throws his head to the side to clear his bangs. "No."

Squeej perks up like he's going to say something, but then doesn't.

"I thought if I wrote about her I wouldn't need to talk about it." Sam taps his thigh.

There's a long silence.

"And so what in the hell. Whit, you are leaving?" says Stefan. "Suddenly you have now an exit strategy? Back to New York?"

Whit slides his hands down from Kesi's back. "I called the hospital. Carlton checked himself out this morning."

"No way," says Squeej.

"Yes, well he heals fast and all that shit," says Whit. "Anyway, I thought I'd head down there and give him a hand until he's back on his feet."

Kesi laughs. "You're not serious."

"You talk about new-formed orifices," says Stefan. "Carlton will surely make one for you, man."

"Yeah, yeah, all that. And then, also, I figure I'd look for Andre."

Claudia laughs to herself. "Wow."

"And fuck you all. This is not about me finding inspiration to change my life."

"Oh, no way we was thinkin' that," says Squeej. "You're seriously still an asshole."

"Yes. Thanks for understanding." Whit reaches long to give him a high-five.

Kesi nods. "OK, well, Carlton and Andre — I need to see them too." She turns to look at Whit.

"Yeah? That may improve my chances of survival considerably. Thank you."

The others look at each other.

"But hey," says Kesi. "I'll come back."

Squeej scoots over and puts an arm around her shoulder. "Cool, cool. Do you think there's any way we can clear Andre's legal shit so he can come back too?"

"Sure," says Whit. "I've got funds I need to do something worthwhile with. We'll get him the best justice money can buy."

Sam shakes his head. "No way Andre will go near anything like that. But maybe if we can find him, we can at least check up on him from time to time."

"Worth a try," says Kesi.

Sam stands and stretches. "But I guess ... well, Whit can come back, assuming he does some actual work around here. With Andre gone, I'll need help figuring out this engineering stuff."

"True," says Squeej, "what with the solar converters and wind turbines and all."

Whit is staring. "You're really okay with that, Sam?" he says.

"I figure if you split for good, what you did will eat at me. And I'm not willing to let you do that to me forever. So, yeah."

"Basically, you want me here so you can make me suffer."

"Pretty much on a daily basis."

"OK." Whit nods. "Deal."

NINETY MINUTES AFTER

The Colony, Greenport, New York

The alternating EMT lights beat out across the yard, casting Kesi's shadow in pulsating multiples left and right before her as she makes her way to the gap in the back fence. Once in the fields, she strikes out along the tree line on the east side. In the darkness, she pushes herself into a jog, the tall grass whisking at her shins and catching in the straps of her sandals.

Andre's grumbling rolls back to her from ahead — "national prisoners" and "debasement" and, again, "institutional debasement."

She calls to him without success, her voice weary. A few yards more and he comes into view, his Army surplus duffle bouncing on his back.

Andre carries the bag easily, his pace purposeful and unhurried, like a postman making his rounds.

Kesi catches up and matches his stride. Her breath shudders. She reaches out to his shoulder to steady herself but withdraws her hand before making contact.

Andre walks on, eyes forward. "The struggle, Sister — the struggle continues. We mustn't become complacent."

"Andre, listen —"

They come to a short stand of woods delineating the outer border of the Colony's fields. Ahead is a path through a stand of trees and the county road beyond. She grabs the sleeve of his jacket and coaxes him to a stop.

"I didn't come to tag along, Andre. I have to get back."

He nods and looks up as the branches overhead catch a breeze.

Kesi raises her chin to the air and pulls her collar out. "I've got to get back, but I wanted to say goodbye, you know?"

He pats her hand, still clutching his sleeve. She lets go.

Andre looks at her. "Do you like ginger ale?"

Kesi whimpers and, hearing herself, covers her face with her hands to cry.

"Your mother could not get through a day without ginger ale. I was forever running out to fetch her ginger ale."

Kesi is smiling when she pulls her hands away. "Don't bring home lemon-lime."

Andre laughs hoarsely. "Hell, no. Get your head handed to you."

She shakes her head for a time, wiping her eyes and nose. "We couldn't live in that house they gave us, Andre."

"Of course not." He nods. "Those shoddy row homes they tacked up after the conflagration. They got those cardboard excuses up in a hurry. I hear the roofs leaked buckets full with the first rain."

"Mom, she said they just wanted the outsides to look good enough for the newspapers 'til the shit storm blew over. She wouldn't move us in."

"No stoops on those homes, that was the final disgrace. A front porch or a stoop is your home opening its arms to your neighbors. After a trauma like that, people need their stoops and their porches. But the City-System, it knew how to kill the revolution with that simple omission."

A siren whoops out from the yard and then another a moment later, approaching from far off.

"Andre, I have to go back."

He lifts the duffle off his shoulder to adjust its position.

"In the days ahead, Sister, keep the people talking. Construct the narrative. If there's no story, there will be no common understanding and no peace."

"I'll try."

"Revolution." He smiles and lays his palm on the side of her neck. "Revolution is your father." He takes a breath and looks at the field beyond her. "And the earth will be your mother."

She pulls his hand down and squeezes.

"I'll find you again, Andre. We'll have lots of time to talk."

He returns the squeeze. "There's no need. There's no need."

Andre lets go and turns down the wooded path.

He is visible for a moment longer but Kesi doesn't linger. She spins and kicks into a run back to the compound.

About the author:

Rick Moss is the author of two novels. His first, *Ebocloud*, is a literary thriller about a cataclysmic social media movement. His editorials have appeared in *USA Today* and he is a regular contributor to *Forbes*.

Most of the author's career has been devoted to design — print, video, multimedia and web. He is a principle and co-founder of the online business forum, RetailWire.com, where he oversees and writes editorial and marketing content for such clients as IBM, SAP, Oracle and Microsoft.

Rick Moss lives in Brooklyn with his wife, Catherine.

Acknowledgments:

Thank you, Bruce Kluger.

Thank you, members of the New York City Writers Critique Group.

From among my sources of inspiration, I would like to cite:

MOVE: Sites of Trauma, Johanna Saleh Dickson – 2002, Princeton Architectural Press

Self Sufficient City: Envisioning the habitat of the future – 2010, Institute for Advanced Architecture of Catalonia

Dear Reader:

I'm so grateful that you took the time to read *Tellers*. Writing this novel brought me great joy and I hope a bit of that rubbed off on you.

If you have a few minutes to spare, I would truly appreciate a short review on *Tellers'* Amazon page or perhaps on Goodreads or your favorite book lover's site. Reviews from readers like you make a tremendous difference in exposing books to more folks.

I would also love to hear your thoughts on *Tellers*. Which of the stories within the book was your favorite? Which character did you most identify with? Please visit tellersnovel.com and use the form on the Contact page to send me a note. I promise to respond.

Thanks and best wishes,

Rick Moss

Website: tellersnovel.com
Twitter: twitter.com/rickmoss
Instagram: instagram.com/ricksmoss/